Lanterns Over Matanzas: The Semiquincentennial Crossing

Terri Propst

Library of Congress Control Number: 2026907411

ISBN: 979-8-9936572-3-3

LANTERNS OVER MATANZAS

DEDICATION

For the keepers of history—
those who preserve the stories of Florida's shores,
so the light of the past continues to guide the future.

LANTERNS OVER MATANZAS

TABLE OF CONTENTS

PROLOGUE

St. Augustine, Florida
Winter 2026

The cloth fell away, and Frederick Douglass faced the plaza again.

For a moment, the crowd went quiet, as if the bronze figure had drawn the breath from the square itself. Then applause rose beneath the pale winter sky.

Cameras flashed. Tourists leaned over barricades. State officials shifted closer together for photographs.

The governor stepped forward and lifted his voice above the wind rolling in from Matanzas Bay.

"Today we honor a man whose words helped shape the conscience of this nation," he said, gesturing toward the statue. "As we prepare for America's two hundred and fiftieth year, we remember the voices that demanded liberty be more than a promise."

The monument was part of Florida's America250 initiative—new memorials, restored landmarks, and historical programs meant to frame the state as foundational to the American story.

And now Frederick Douglass stood at its center.

More than a century earlier, Douglass himself had spoken in this city, challenging Floridians to reconcile their celebrations with their contradictions. His voice had once echoed through rooms that preferred silence.

Now his likeness stood in bronze in the Plaza de la Constitución, layered among Spanish foundations, British transitions, and American banners.

History, carefully arranged.

The governor finished speaking. Applause swelled again as the crowd surged forward to photograph the statue.

Eliza remained near the edge of the plaza.

She studied the placement more than the ceremony.

St. Augustine had always been a city of layers. Spanish stone beneath American brick. Colonial maps beneath modern sidewalks. Every generation choosing what pieces of the past to display—and what to leave buried.

The statue gleamed in the afternoon light.

Frederick Douglass, cast in bronze, staring forward as if still waiting for the country to catch up with him.

Eliza folded her arms.

Douglass had never been comfortable.

He had been necessary.

By dusk, the plaza emptied.

The crowds drifted back toward St. George Street. Horse hooves echoed against brick. Lantern tours gathered at street corners.

The city exhaled into evening.

Eliza returned to the statue alone.

The winter sun had dropped low enough to throw long shadows across the square. In the fading light, Douglass's face looked different—sharper, almost severe.

Less ceremonial.

More watchful.

She read the inscription again.

Orator. Abolitionist. Statesman.

A man who demanded that America reconcile its ideals with its actions.

The bronze caught the last gold of the sun.

Douglass had once stood here in flesh and voice, unsettling rooms built to preserve comfort. He had insisted that celebration without justice was hollow.

Above her, the American flag cracked once in the wind.

Eliza remembered the governor's speech from earlier that afternoon—legacy, liberty, education—words polished for ceremony.

But Douglass had never spoken in polished comfort.

He had spoken with urgency.

With disruption.

She stepped closer to the pedestal.

“Statues are easy,” she said quietly.

Bronze required funding. Dedications required planning. But truth required courage.

A streetlamp flickered to life beside the statue, bathing Douglass in amber light.

In that glow, he did not look triumphant.

He looked unyielding.

Eliza rested her hand briefly against the cold stone base.

History did not survive because it was comfortable.

It survived because someone refused silence.

She turned toward the seawall, where the scent of salt drifted in with the evening wind.

Night settled over Matanzas Bay.

The water moved slowly in the dark, brushing the seawall with quiet persistence.

Eliza stood at the edge of the bay and thought again of Frederick Douglass.

Not the statue.

The insistence.

He had understood that names mattered.

Not symbolic names. Real ones.

The enslaved had been renamed. Cataloged. Stripped of lineage. Douglass had reclaimed his name as an act of defiance.

Eliza whispered another name into the wind.

“Apochi.”

The syllables felt fragile and immense all at once.

For centuries, men like him had been reduced to footnotes—*native*, *convert*, *labor*, *casualty*. Their names dissolved into the margins of records written by others.

Douglass had demanded that America confront what it preferred to overlook.

Eliza had crossed centuries not to change the past—

—but to prevent its erasure.

The statue in the plaza honored a man who fought to have truth recorded.

Apochi had fought only to endure.

Yet both had resisted disappearance.

Eliza closed her eyes and listened to the tide moving below.

When she returned from 1565, she would bring back more than memories.

She would bring record.

Documentation.

Names.

Below her, the tide brushed against the seawall again.

Some names were cast in bronze.

Others were nearly swallowed by sand.

Both required someone willing to speak them.

Eliza opened her eyes and looked across the dark water.

Tomorrow, she would step into a century where history had barely begun to write itself.

The past did not ask to be rescued.

It asked to be remembered.

And remembering, she now understood, was an act of moral courage.

Tomorrow, she would step into the year 1565.

And history was not ready for her to remember it.

Chapter 1: The Lanterns Rise

Eliza POV — 2026, St. Augustine waterfront

The first time the lanterns appeared over Matanzas Bay, they shimmered like ghosts rising from salt and memory. The air smelled of brine and tar from the replica caravels docked for the upcoming 250-year celebration—fresh paint barely masking the ancient scent of pitch and rope. Fireworks scaffolding framed the skyline, waiting for July, waiting to commemorate a nation two and a half centuries old. Dr. Eliza Rowan stood alone along the seawall, the Atlantic wind tugging at her hair, her pulse louder than the tide against the coquina walls of the Castillo. She had engineered the crossing to honor the Semiquincentennial—to let modern America feel the fragile breath of its beginnings by stepping into the living soil of 1565. The coordinates were exact. The mathematics precise. They were meant to witness, not interfere.

But beneath the hum of generators and distant traffic, another sound began to bleed through the night. Spanish voices—urgent, breathless—carried across centuries. The crack of musket fire split the dark. Cannon smoke rolled thick and bitter over the marshlands, and the scent of gunpowder burned sharp enough to sting her eyes. Pedro Menéndez's fleet carving its foothold into a wild coast. Survival before freedom. Blood at Matanzas Inlet long before fireworks would ever bloom over this water. The lanterns lifted higher, their glow shifting from warm gold to something deeper—almost warning. Eliza's breath caught as the wind turned hot against her skin. This was no pageant of history. No safe observatory of the past. And as the temporal fold opened—silent, invisible—one impossible thought struck her with sudden, terrifying clarity: what if history did not want to be remembered? What if someone in 1565 was about to see her step through the light?

The lanterns did not rise all at once.

They appeared slowly over Matanzas Bay, one at a time, as if the water itself were remembering how to hold light.

Along the seawall, families gathered with folding chairs and paper flags. Children leaned over railings. Vendors called out for lemonade and kettle corn. Banners announcing America's Two Hundred and Fiftieth Anniversary snapped in the coastal wind.

The air smelled of salt, sunscreen, and anticipation.

Dr. Eliza Rowan stood apart from the crowd, one hand resting lightly against the coquina wall of the Castillo. The stone was cool beneath her palm, porous and patient—formed from crushed shell and time. She liked to think of it as sedimented memory. Every layer compressed, never erased.

Above her, fireworks scaffolding floated in place, waiting for night to claim the sky.

But the true spectacle was not overhead.

It was beneath.

Hidden below the old fortifications, the Lantern Array hummed in harmonic alignment. Quantum resonance braided with geographic permanence. A machine designed not to rewrite history—but to witness it.

St. Augustine had been chosen for a reason.

Continuously inhabited, layered by empire and faith and rebellion. Spanish stone. British flag. American fortification. Civil rights marchers crossing the same streets centuries later.

A nation did not begin cleanly in 1776.

It accumulated.

She had argued that once. Publicly. And been dismantled for it.

"Florida is not peripheral to American history," she had said at a conference hall far from the salt air. "It is the preface."

Polite laughter. Measured rebuttals. A senior historian describing her thesis as 'regional romanticism.'

She had not flinched. But she had remembered who remained silent.

Tonight was not revenge. Tonight was proof. Not for the academy. For the record.

Behind her, the access door to the lower chamber opened with a soft hydraulic sigh.

"Eliza."

Gabe's voice carried upward from the stairwell.

She did not turn immediately. Instead, she watched as another lantern shimmered into existence over the water—faint at first, then brightening to steady gold. It hovered above the inlet where tides once ran red with conflict long before fireworks would ever bloom.

"Stability holding?" she asked.

"For now," he replied, coming to stand beside her.

He followed her gaze across the bay.

"You always look at the inlet," he said.

"That's where the story begins."

He studied her profile.

"No," he said quietly. "That's where we choose to begin it."

The distinction hung between them.

The wind lifted her hair.

Below their feet, the Array shifted into final alignment. Solar position. Lunar pull. Coastal magnetics. The Semiquincentennial date amplified harmonic resonance beyond their most optimistic projections.

"Window opens in thirty seconds," Gabe said.

She exhaled slowly.

"We're observers," he reminded her.

"Yes."

"No interference."

"Yes."

He hesitated.

"And if something feels different?"

She looked at him then.

"History doesn't belong to us," she said. "We belong to it."

A flicker passed across his expression—admiration edged with something more vulnerable.

He nodded once.

"Signal tether is locked," he said. "I'll be right here."

The lanterns over the bay brightened in unison now, their reflections trembling across dark water like living constellations.

The crowd behind them cheered, assuming the display had begun early. They had no idea.

Eliza stepped toward the stairwell.

For a moment, she pressed her palm fully against the coquina stone.

Stone built from shell. Shell built from life. Life layered upon life.

We build with memory.

The thought came unbidden.

Then she descended.

Belowground, the chamber glowed gold.

The Array pulsed in concentric rings, light folding inward on itself like tidewater reversing direction.

Gabe stood at the console, eyes steady, hands sure.

"You don't have to prove anything," he said quietly.

She met his gaze.

"I'm not proving," she replied. "I'm remembering."

The harmonic field expanded. Air thickened—light bent.

And as the first true lantern rose above Matanzas Bay, Dr. Eliza Rowan stepped forward—not to change what had been written, but to witness what had been layered beneath.

Above, fireworks would soon celebrate 250 years.

Below, she was about to walk into the first breath of a story that had never stood alone.

Chapter 2: The Conference

Flashback — Boston, academic conference, pre-novel

Boston had smelled like polished wood and old certainty.

The conference hall was paneled in dark oak, the kind meant to imply permanence. Portraits of long-dead historians lined the walls, their oil-painted gazes tilted toward a future they had not imagined sharing.

Eliza adjusted the microphone and let the room settle.

"Florida," she began, steady and clear, "is not peripheral to American history. It is the preface."

A ripple moved through the audience—not disagreement yet, but alertness. The polite sharpening of attention reserved for claims that threaten hierarchy.

She continued.

"St. Augustine has been continuously inhabited since 1565. Spanish, Timucua, British, American. It is not a sidebar to 1776. It is a living archive of survival, empire, faith, conflict, and adaptation. If we begin our national narrative in Philadelphia, we mistake declaration for origin."

Slides shifted behind her: maps layered over centuries—shorelines redrawn. Flags replaced. Names changed.

She did not rush.

"America did not begin cleanly in revolution," she said. "It accumulated. It layered. The foundations of governance, conflict, religious identity, and cultural negotiation were tested long before independence was declared."

From the third row, Gabriel Navarro watched her without blinking. He had read the paper three times. Had corrected a citation at two in the morning and sent it without commentary. Had told himself that intellectual rigor was the purest form of support.

Now he saw something else. She wasn't presenting data. She was staking ground.

A hand lifted near the front of the hall before she had fully concluded.

Dr. William Cartwright. Harvard. Colonial American Studies.

He did not wait for invitation.

"Dr. Rowan," he began, voice warm in the way expensive wool is warm—soft, structured, difficult to challenge without seeming impolite. "Your argument is compelling. But surely you concede that revolutionary ideology, not colonial endurance, marks the true beginning of American identity."

Murmurs of agreement.

Eliza folded her hands lightly on the podium.

"Identity is never singular," she replied. "It is constructed through continuity and rupture. Florida embodies both."

Cartwright smiled.

"Yes, but Florida in 1565 was Spanish. Catholic. Monarchical. Hardly proto-American."

A few quiet chuckles. Gabe's jaw tightened.

Eliza did not react to the laughter.

"Precisely," she said. "America inherits from what it resists and what it absorbs. To ignore Florida's layered sovereignty is to misunderstand the complexity of the nation that emerges."

Cartwright tilted his head, considering her as one might consider a graduate student who has read ambitiously.

"An interesting reframing," he said. "Though I wonder whether we risk regional romanticism when elevating peripheral territories to foundational status."

There it was.

Peripheral.

The word landed softly and cut deeply.

Eliza felt the shift in the room. The subtle recalibration of attention. The quiet relief of those who preferred their origin stories tidy.

She held Cartwright's gaze.

"With respect," she said evenly, "St. Augustine predates

Jamestown by forty-two years. It predates Plymouth by fifty-five. If chronology and continuity matter in historical analysis, then Florida is not peripheral. It is prior."

The room stilled.

Cartwright's smile thinned, almost imperceptibly.

"Chronology alone does not confer ideological primacy," he replied.

"No," Eliza agreed. "But it does demand acknowledgment."

Silence. Measured. Controlled. Professional.

Cartwright glanced toward the moderator. "I appreciate your enthusiasm for your region, Dr. Rowan," he said finally. "But the Revolutionary framework remains the accepted genesis of American identity."

Accepted. Not proven. Accepted.

The moderator thanked them both and moved the session forward. Applause followed—polite, restrained, diffuse.

Eliza stepped down from the podium with her spine straight. She did not look at Gabe immediately.

He rose halfway from his seat, then stopped. A calculation flickered across his face—the cost of public disagreement, the risk of attaching his emerging reputation to a thesis that had just been labeled romantic.

He told himself she didn't need defense. He told himself neutrality was professionalism.

By the time he reached her in the corridor, the room had emptied.

"You were strong," he said.

She studied him. "I was correct."

"Yes."

"And?"

He hesitated. He could still walk back in. Still challenge the framing. Still say that chronology and continuity mattered.

Instead, he chose caution dressed as pragmatism.

"It's a difficult room," he said. "You knew that."

Her eyes did not harden. They cooled.

"Rooms are only difficult," she replied quietly, "when no one is willing to move the furniture."

The sentence settled between them.

He opened his mouth. Closed it.

Down the corridor, Cartwright's laugh echoed faintly.

Eliza adjusted the strap of her bag and walked toward the exit without looking back.

Gabe remained where he stood, staring at the dark wood paneling, aware that something had shifted—not in the academy, not in the discipline—

In them.

He had watched her defend the coastline of an idea. And he had stayed seated.

Interlude: The Furniture

Gabe POV — Cambridge, three months after Boston

Three months after Boston, Gabriel Navarro woke at 2:13 a.m. with the tide in his head.

He did not live near water. His apartment in Cambridge faced brick, streetlight, and a narrow strip of indifferent sky. But that night he heard surf where there was none—steady, patient, impossible to ignore.

He sat upright in bed and reached for his laptop.

The problem with Eliza's thesis had never been data. It had been framing.

He opened the resonance modeling software he used for coastal magnetic studies—an unrelated project funded by a department that preferred safe applications. He entered coordinates without allowing himself to think too hard about why.

Latitude. Longitude. St. Augustine.

He ran the first simulation as an act of stubbornness. If the numbers failed cleanly, he could finally set the argument aside.

The screen filled with harmonic output. Stable. Too stable.

He adjusted for sediment density. Human occupancy duration. Architectural continuity. He layered in variables no one had asked him to measure—ceremony sites, fortification stone, shoreline shift.

The waveform intensified.

Geographic continuity amplified temporal resonance in a way he had never seen.

He leaned back slowly.

"It accumulates," he muttered to the empty room.

That had been her word. Accumulation.

He ran the model again, stripping out Philadelphia. Jamestown. Plymouth. None of them held the same sustained harmonic pattern. Not because they were unimportant. Because they were episodic.

St. Augustine was continuous.

The realization did not feel like triumph. It felt like an indictment.

He saw the oak-paneled room again. The portraits. Cartwright's warm dismissal. His own folded hands.

Rooms are only difficult when no one is willing to move the furniture.

He closed his eyes briefly.

Then he did what he should have done in Boston. He moved.

At 3:47 a.m., he drafted the first schematic for what would become the Lantern Array. Not a machine to prove her right. A machine to test the premise properly.

If time imprinted itself differently in places of uninterrupted habitation... If geography could hold layered memory... Then history was not a straight line. It was sediment.

By sunrise, he had a working theoretical framework.

He did not send it to her immediately. He stared at the file name for a long moment before typing: Lantern_Prototype_01.

He attached it to an email without explanation.

Subject line: You were onto something.

He did not apologize. Not yet. He hit send.

Outside his window, the sky lightened over a city that believed its origins were tidy.

Somewhere far south, tidewater pressed patiently against coquina stone.

And for the first time since Boston, Gabriel Navarro chose not to stay seated.

Chapter 3: The Fracture Begins

Gabriel Navarro POV
Control Chamber Beneath the Castillo de San Marcos
St. Augustine, 2026

Gabriel Navarro had always trusted numbers more than people.

Numbers did not hesitate. They did not flinch under scrutiny or abandon you in conference halls full of polite academic executioners. They aligned, or they didn't. They resonated, or they collapsed.

The Lantern Array had resonated.

Until now.

The control chamber beneath the Castillo de San Marcos hummed softly, its vibration threading through stone quarried centuries before either of them had been born. Coquina held memory, Eliza liked to say. Porous, layered, patient.

Tonight, it held something else—instability.

Gabe stood before the curved monitor array, hands braced against the console as gold harmonic waves rippled across the primary display.

At the center pulsed Eliza's bio-signature.

Steady.

But thinning.

Like a star receding into fog.

"Come on," he muttered. "Stay anchored."

Aboveground, the city prepared for spectacle. Fireworks barges floated in position over Matanzas Bay. Banners announcing the Semiquincentennial snapped in the coastal wind.

Down here, destiny was misbehaving.

The Lantern Array had been calibrated for geographic resonance, not chronological aggression. It established harmonic entanglement with fixed coordinates—latitude, longitude, sediment density, and historical continuity.

St. Augustine had been perfect.

Continuously inhabited.

Layered like a palimpsest.

If any place on Earth could hold a stable temporal echo, it was this city.

The waveform spiked.

A sharp deviation fractured across the screen.

"Eliza…"

Her signal dipped.

The chamber lights flickered.

An auxiliary monitor chimed—a system Gabe had never programmed to speak.

ARCHIVAL DATABASE RECONCILING

He frowned.

"Reconciling what?"

Historical metadata began scrolling.

Parish registry.

Burial record.

Then—

A new annotation appeared.

And vanished.

Gabe's pulse thudded in his ears.

That wasn't possible.

The Array did not alter history. It created harmonic overlap—molecular phase displacement without mass insertion.

She wasn't supposed to be physically there.

The primary waveform destabilized again.

Widening.

Distorting.

She wasn't just observing.

She was interacting.

Gabe forced himself to breathe slowly. Panic would not help. Equations would.

He recalculated phase stability, fingers moving across the glass interface.

If her cohesion had increased past density thresholds, the Array might have allowed partial materialization. The Semiquincentennial alignment—the lunar pull combined with solar resonance over coastal magnetics—had strengthened the bridge beyond projections.

He had warned her about that.

No.

He had questioned it.

She had believed in it.

Believed enough for both of them.

A memory flickered through him.

Boston. Three years earlier.

An oak-paneled conference hall.

Eliza is at the podium.

"Florida is not peripheral to American history," she had said calmly. "It is the preface."

The room had shifted.

A senior historian dismantling her thesis with surgical condescension.

Gabe is sitting in the third row.

Silent.

Calculating risk.

Choosing caution.

The shame of it burned now.

Her waveform thinned further.

"Eliza, if you touched something—"

An alarm pulsed once.

Not catastrophic.

Not yet.

He pulled up municipal live feeds.

Aboveground, tourists strolled along the bayfront unaware that time itself was fraying beneath their sandals. Fireworks scaffolding rose against the darkening sky.

In four days, the nation would celebrate 250 years of independence.

If the Array destabilized fully, there might be no stable record to celebrate.

The archival monitor flashed again.

A parish ledger entry from September 1565 shifted by a single line.

A name appeared.

Indigenous.

Half-formed in faded ink.

It hadn't been there before.

Gabe stared.

"What did you do?" he whispered.

Not an accusation.

Awe.

She had argued history was not static—that it breathed, resisted, and adapted.

He had insisted the math would constrain it.

Now the math was bending.

He initiated a partial retrieval protocol.

Then stopped.

Forcing reentry during harmonic expansion could shear her molecular cohesion.

Best case: catastrophic injury.

Worst case: temporal displacement without an anchor.

He clenched his jaw.

"Think."

The Array required dual biometric authorization for full collapse or reinforcement. They had built that safeguard together after too many late-night debates about hubris.

She was out there.

And he could not reach her.

Instead, he narrowed the stabilization grid, creating a defensive containment field.

If she moved, the system would follow.

Tracking not geography—but emotional spike patterns encoded in her neural telemetry.

A feature he had added quietly.

Redundancy, he had told the oversight committee.

But it had been devotion.

Her signal flared suddenly.

Bright.

Violent.

The display is filled with cascading resonance data.

For one impossible second, Gabe smelled salt and smoke in the air of the chamber.

Gunpowder.

The waveform steadied.

But differently.

She wasn't lost.

She was somewhere specific.

And history was responding.

Gabe leaned closer.

"Okay," he murmured.

“You were right.”

Aboveground, a test firework launched prematurely over Matanzas Bay, bursting into gold against the twilight.

Below, the Lantern Array glowed brighter than it had ever been designed to glow.

And Gabriel Navarro understood with sudden, terrible clarity—

They had not built a machine to visit history.

They had built a door.

And Eliza Rowan had stepped through it.

He straightened slowly.

Resolve hardening.

“If you can hear me,” he said softly, though he knew she could not,

“Don’t try to be careful.”

His fingers hovered over the console.

“Be brave.”

The waveform held.

For now.

Chapter 4: Arrival

Eliza POV — 1565, Florida marshland

She arrived in pieces, molecular and meaningless, a half-mapped nerve ending sloshing with memory and panic. The crossing delivered her not onto solid ground but into the drowned light of a Florida marsh, September 1565, where the air itself pressed down like wet burlap on a wound.

It was the smell that reached her first: not the briny memory of St. Augustine in winter, but the full rot of unfiltered life—salt and mud, blood and tannin, the chemistry of things left out to fester—water pressed up from every root, every clutch of crushed grass. The humidity was carnivorous. It hunted through her shirt, her hair, the shallow cavities behind her knees and elbows, pooling there until she was slick as an unscaled fish.

Eliza staggered into the world with the grace of a drowning woman. Her boots, chosen for archival neatness rather than survival, pulled from the mud with a sound like a lung unclogging. The shock of cold made her gasp, but the air was so dense with suspended moisture that inhaling felt like swallowing a cupful of live shrimp.

She bent double and retched—pure adrenaline, nothing to expel—and only then did the rest of her arrive. Sight, afterimage, meaning. Above her, the sky was a low fever, sun pounding through cloud so thick it looked like it had been hammered into tin. On every side, the marsh grass stood taller than a man, tipped with seeds that flashed bronze where the light found them. Channels of black water cut ragged through the mud, moving not in currents but in pulses, like blood returning to a heart.

Her body had not reassembled correctly. Every cell sizzled with a latency she couldn't shake, as if her bones lagged behind her flesh by a half-second. She ran her hands up her own arms, feeling for seams, but found only heat rash and a constellation of mosquito bites already rising pink against her skin.

She tasted copper, salt, and something old. Her heartbeat did not so much pulse as pound, loud as a drumbeat in her ears.

For a moment, she was blind with the newness of it—overstimulated, out of air, drowning in the organic. Her mind grabbed at sensory anchors: sweat, yes, but also the crude, sharp stink of gunpowder. Mud, but beneath that, the marsh's own sweet rot. She blinked, rubbed grit from her eyes, and tried to stand up straight.

That was when she saw them.

Across a wide channel, Spanish soldiers moved in a staccato line, their armor incongruously bright in the killing heat. Iron breastplates flashed in the sun as the men splashed forward, musket barrels and pikes bristling over their shoulders. The air around them shimmered with gunpowder smoke, drifting low across the grass, curling around them like the ghost of fire not yet spent.

Eliza watched, fascinated and afraid. They advanced not as a unit, but as men each fighting his own private war with the marsh—some cursing, some gasping, a few turning to scan for threats in the reeds. The officer led from the front, sword drawn and pointed at a patch of sky that had never heard of him. Voices carried: Spanish, barked, and rapid. She recognized a handful of words—avanzar, cuidado, por Dios—but mostly she heard the rawness of purpose.

She took inventory. Hands: shaking but intact. Feet: half-submerged, but both accounted for. Clothing: every stitch already soaked through, the polyester blend now a mistake for which she had no words.

She tried to catalog her position—both geographically and temporally. East of the city, likely. The marshlands before the fortifications had been raised. The summer storm season was ending, but the ground never dried fully. She remembered this from the records: a floodplain that refused to be tamed, stubborn as the people who had called it home before the conquistadors ever raised a cross.

She tried to breathe. There was no place for breath here; the air had already been claimed.

A sound erupted behind her—a chorus of mosquitoes, a cloud so thick it seemed sentient. They landed in waves across her neck, her hands, her hairline. She slapped them away, left smears of her own blood along her arm, and tasted the iron for a second time.

She felt her own body turning on her. Heatstroke coming, or shock, or simple terror. But she would not allow herself to collapse. Not here, not with the experiment just begun.

She gripped the cypress knee beside her, fingers digging into its rough bark, grounding herself in the tactile. She focused on the pain. Catalogued it.

Then she heard a different sound—one that did not belong to

the ecology or the invading army.

A human voice, low and unhurried, coming from the marsh behind her. Not Spanish. Not English.

She turned, slowly, unwilling to trust her own vestibular system. The world slipped sideways, then righted itself.

Someone watched her from across a drift of reeds, partially obscured but unmistakably present. The silhouette was still—no armor, no boots, only the outline of a man in native dress, watching with an attention so focused it seemed to pin her to the spot.

She froze, unsure whether to call out, to run, to fold herself back into the marsh and try to re-enter the century as less of a violation.

Instead, she did what she had always done best.

She observed.

The man did not move. She saw the ripple of bare arms, the flash of ochre across his skin, a cord of shells at his throat. His eyes never left her. He did not seem surprised to find her here; only curious as to what kind of animal she was.

She realized that her own arms—pale, exposed, marked by mosquito and sun—must look as strange to him as his did to her. She thought of the centuries that separated them, and how close the distance felt now.

She did not speak. She nodded once, carefully, and waited for him to do the same.

The Spanish line crept forward, musket muzzles bobbing, and with each step, the past solidified around her.

Eliza steadied herself. She tasted the salt, catalogued the heat, and willed her nerves to settle.

She had not come to change the past. She had come to bear witness.

Now the past was looking right back.

The moment between sight and certainty stretched so long that Eliza thought the world itself might give out.

She could feel the stranger's gaze pressed into her, unwavering and almost physical. He stood half-shrouded behind a woven lattice of cattail stems, the lower half of his body masked by water so dark it looked like an ink spill. A sun-browned arm steadied him against the trunk of a cypress; the other held loosely at his side. The posture was ambiguous—defensive, not yet hostile. He was taller than she'd anticipated, the cords of his shoulders outlined by clay pigment and the faint glint of wet skin. At his throat, the shell cord caught the afternoon light and refracted it onto the inside of his jaw, a pale scythe of color.

She ran a silent roll call of every historical description, every forensic sketch, every artifact slide she had ever studied. Nothing matched the gravity of the living man. She tried to remember whether the Timucua of this coastal branch were known for patience or for preemptive violence. The sources contradicted each other. The truth, as always, had been lost somewhere between the lines.

Eliza did not move, though the urge to bolt surged in every tendon. Her boots had sunk another inch into the marsh floor, and she felt the suction holding her in place—a literal anchor, the past refusing to let go.

Across the water, the man's eyes did not blink. She expected them to be brown, but from here they flashed almost gold in the slant of the sun. He saw her, not as an apparition or threat, but as a phenomenon to be understood. The recognition was mutual: the observer observed.

A solitary egret picked through the channel between them, oblivious to the collision of centuries in progress. Its feet drew ripples in the film of oil and algae, and Eliza tracked its path as a way to stabilize her own pulse.

She wondered if her own appearance seemed as impossible to him as his did to her. She wore nothing like the garb of the colonists or the mission Indians that would arrive decades later—no linen cap, no skirt, not even the missionary black. Just field pants, a battered shirt, and the laminated compass pendant that now pressed, uncomfortably, into her breastbone.

She let her hands drop slowly to her sides, palms open, signaling nothing to conceal. Her right wrist, already stippled with mosquito blood, trembled slightly in the open air.

Apochi (she did not yet know his name, but he would always be Apochi now) mirrored the movement. He stepped fully into view, letting the reeds part. The careful choreography of a man who had survived by reading predators, weather, and every subtle tilt of the world around him.

They watched each other as the marshland breathed—a windless respiration, hot and damp and absolute. She could feel the tide pushing against the land, a pulse that had never ceased. In that moment, the distinction between witness and participant vanished; they were both at the mercy of the landscape, both improvising survivals.

She thought: I am the least probable thing he has ever seen. And also, he is the most improbable proof of everything I have ever risked.

He did not flinch. Did not call out. Instead, he cocked his head just slightly, as if to see whether she would break pattern and reveal a more familiar shape.

The moment splintered by increments. From the left, a crackle of musket fire, distant but decisive. The Spanish phalanx had reached the next channel, and their movement set birds skyward in a white, frantic cloud. She and Apochi turned, in near-unison, to track the disturbance.

When she looked back, he was closer—half the distance, now standing on the same muddy bar that propped her up. His feet, naked and sure, gripped the slick terrain like second nature. He carried nothing but a length of palmetto spear, not pointed at her, not at rest. Suspended.

Eliza swallowed and tried to speak. The only sound that emerged was the involuntary wetness of her own breath. He waited, as if he had expected nothing more.

The silence between them was not empty. It was the packed hush of mutual calculation, the overlap of two realities briefly admitting both could be true.

She thought of every page she had read, every record that ended with 'unknown,' everybody in the margins of history marked by nothing but conjecture and loss. She thought of all the ways one world could be real and still vanish from the record.

The world flickered—the damp, the heat, the relentless hunger of the present moment. Then, as if by script, he spoke first.

Not English. Not Spanish. A ripple of sound that twisted the familiar syllables of Spanish into something more liquid, less certain. He repeated it, softer, the second time.

She had prepared for this, or thought she had—her phone's language pack loaded with reconstructed dialect, but the phone was dead weight at her hip, and the moment had no patience for algorithmic crutches.

She repeated the word back to him, best as she could, and he smiled—a small, private smile, not for her benefit but for his own confirmation. A field test passed.

He gestured at her boots, then at her arms. In a single, economical motion, he pantomimed her struggle to move and the swamp's refusal to let go. It was absurd, but also the first joke in human history, and she felt it as such.

She grinned despite herself, and in that instant, something unclenched in her chest. The fear did not go away, but it found a place to sit.

Another musket volley, closer this time. The two of them jerked to attention, the truce recalibrated by the sound of approaching danger.

He pointed at the Spanish, then at the sky, then made a gesture as if shading his eyes from a painful light. It took her a moment, but she realized he was asking if she was with the men in metal, or if she was something else—a third thing, neither native nor invader.

She held up three fingers. He laughed, openly, and pointed at her again, nodding.

They moved together, awkward but aligned, deeper into the reeds, putting the tangle of grass and root between themselves and the oncoming soldiers. He led, and she followed, boots finally coming loose with a sucking pop.

Her whole lower leg was caked in silt and blood, but it felt almost ceremonial now—a mark of initiation.

He said another word. "Mato." She did not know its meaning, but the rhythm was soft, inclusive. She repeated it more quietly, and this time he did not correct her.

The marsh had its own pulse, and she could feel her body syncing to it. Every splash, every footfall, every shiver of adrenaline. Even the ache in her jaw had subsided, replaced by the deep, low drum of survival.

He stopped them at a higher patch, a rise where the grass turned to bramble and the water fell away, leaving only a thick, moist loam underfoot. He faced her squarely now, studying her with the kind of interest she had only ever seen in the eyes of the truly curious.

"Name?" he asked, the first English word spoken with the flat, analytic tone of someone who has heard it in practice but not in context.

"Eliza," she said, pulse hitching. "Eliza Rowan."

He nodded, once. "Apochi."

They stood that way, balanced on the edge of something neither could name.

Behind them, the world's oldest city was being born in blood and fire. Between them, a third history had just blinked into existence.

The past did not want to be remembered. But for now, it had no choice but to see itself.

Eliza lifted her foot. The marsh took it as an invitation and tried to steal her boot outright; she yanked free with a wet, sucking noise that echoed embarrassingly across the water. The sudden shift in balance almost sent her toppling, but she managed to plant her other heel on a hummock of earth and locked her knees.

Everything in her body felt loose and misthreaded. She willed herself to look steady—shoulders up, chin out, face blank. The way men at academic conferences always looked when pretending they belonged in rooms they'd inherited.

She wanted to say something—to affirm her presence, to assert some narrative control. But her throat rebelled; it felt constricted, caked with salt and damp, the taste of every inhaled mosquito wing sharpening her gag reflex. The words jammed in her jaw, and all that emerged was a short, animal cough.

Apochi tracked the movement. His eyes never left her hands, but when she coughed, he showed his teeth in the ghost of a smile. Not amusement, but recognition—he understood what it was to fight the body and lose.

He shifted his grip on the spear. Not a threat, just a rebalancing. Up close, she saw it was fire-hardened at the tip, the wood smoothed by endless handling, its haft wrapped in river-tough cordage. She wondered how many things in this world were engineered so perfectly for their purpose, then realized she was cataloguing again—retreating into the analytic because the present was too sharp to touch bare.

A patch of open water now separated them. She thought about what this would look like from above: two improbable points, each equally vulnerable, balanced on the thinnest strip of dry ground.

The Spanish voices grew clearer—commands, then a low, rhythmic chanting as they urged each other through the flooded ground. The men themselves were still out of sight, but the percussion of their march shuddered across the wetland. At intervals came a metallic clatter, as if the soldiers' very bodies were at odds with the softness of this world.

Apochi held up his left hand, palm forward. It was the most universal gesture possible, and she obeyed, standing motionless.

He pivoted his body toward the noise, angled himself to half-hide behind a birch, and signaled her down with two deliberate sweeps of the hand.

Eliza bent at the knees, pressed herself as low as she could go, and wedged into the trough between cypress roots. The ground here was cool and alive, crawling with beetles and things that moved in a straight line only until they found something to circle. The sensation of tiny feet traversing her ankles brought her back to the present: she was here, corporeal, and—if her calculations were true—undocumented, unfindable, unless she did something monumentally stupid.

For several minutes, nothing happened. A single dragonfly hovered in the heat shimmer, wings vibrating faster than her pulse.

The first of the soldiers emerged into view. She counted nine. They wore battered helmets and partial breastplates, armor more ceremonial than effective in the humidity. Their leader, mustached and younger than she'd imagined, barked an order and pointed toward a thicket to their right. Two broke off and scouted, blades drawn.

Apochi did not move, but his breathing changed. She recognized the readiness—how the body prepared to run even as the mind demanded stillness.

One of the Spanish paused to drink from a canteen, leaned his back against a tree, and spat onto the ground. The act was so ordinary, so human, that it startled her.

Then the group moved on, splashing deeper into the marsh, their sounds receding into the hiss of insects and the deep, sustained basso of unseen frogs.

When the noise was gone, Apochi stood up, shook off the tension, and looked directly at her. This time his face was different—

less the inscrutable observer, more the wary neighbor whose property line had just been trespassed.

She tried to speak again.

"I'm not—" The sentence stuck.

She pointed vaguely in the direction the soldiers had gone. "Not them," she managed, her voice a coarse rasp.

He nodded once. Whether he understood the words or just the intent, she couldn't tell. But he seemed satisfied.

He beckoned her forward with the spear tip, then turned and vanished between two trunks so close together she doubted she could fit. She scrambled to follow, ignoring the squelch of her own steps, the agony of thigh muscles that had spent the last decade in climate-controlled comfort.

The land rose. Each step took them further from open water, higher into a swath of saw palmetto and wild fern. The shade here was dense, the air thick with something sweet but not floral—maybe the slow rot of fallen fruit. The sound of the Spanish was gone, replaced by the background roar of living things: birds, frogs, the friction of unseen mammals burrowing through leaf litter.

They stopped at the edge of a tiny clearing, a natural blind with sightlines in every direction. Apochi leaned the spear against a tree and squatted, gesturing for her to do the same.

She sank to the ground, suddenly exhausted. Her hands were shaking less now. Her mind was a balloon stretched to bursting, every thought crammed with three possible explanations for every sensation.

He watched her. She could feel the scrutiny, a soft pressure—not predatory, but scientific, as if he was taking the measure of her oddities.

She glanced at her own hands, the translucent skin marked by a dozen bites and one deep scratch that had somehow avoided her notice. She pressed the wound closed, then looked up and realized he was offering her a handful of torn moss. She took it, using the rough green pads to stanch the bleeding.

They sat in silence for a long time. Neither attempted to explain. The air between them was thick with questions, but for now, observation was enough.

She studied the man across from her: the geometry of his posture, the efficient way he moved, the patience in his face. She wanted to ask how many Spanish he'd seen, how long he'd lived here, and whether he had ever watched the ocean as a thing older than any army or fort.

Instead, she said: "Eliza." Not her last name, not her title, just the single word.

He considered, as if weighing the value of names, then replied: "Apochi." He tapped his chest, then pointed at her with the same solemnity.

"Eliza," he repeated.

The syllables landed differently in his mouth—rounded, soft, as if he was storing the sound for future use.

He pointed at her compass necklace. "What?"

She unclipped it, held it out. It was heavy for its size; a vintage silver disk engraved with letters that meant nothing to him. He turned it over in his palm, then pressed the north-pointed arrow and watched it spin.

"Why?" he asked.

She considered the question. She could not answer in any

way that would make sense. Why here? Why now? Why her, instead of a trained specialist in paleo-linguistics or military survival?

She gestured toward the sky, to the invisible city that would one day be built here. “To see,” she said, and hoped it was enough.

He seemed to accept it. He handed the compass back, and she noticed how gently he placed it in her palm—no suspicion, just an acknowledgment that the object belonged to her and not to this world.

A breeze found its way into the hollow. It smelled of rain. The light shifted, and for the first time, Eliza noticed the ring of old burn marks in the clearing—evidence of dozens of fires, none recent. A site of old gatherings, memory pressed into the earth.

Apochi drew a line in the dirt with a stick, then another crossing it. He pointed at the intersecting place, then at the east, where the Spanish had gone, then at her.

A map. She was at a crossing. The message was almost comically direct.

He looked at her, and she knew—absolutely, in that moment—that he saw her not as a ghost or an omen, but as a possible ally, or at least a witness whose truth might outlast any monument or story the invaders could muster.

She smiled, the first real smile since crossing. “We build with memory,” she said aloud, not expecting him to understand, but wanting the sound in the air.

He repeated the phrase, syllable by syllable, as if taste-testing the intent behind it. Memory. Memori.

They sat together until dusk stretched the shadows, and the insects changed their rhythm.

When they finally stood, it was not as hunter and hunted, or even as subject and observer. It was as if two bodies, unmoored from their certainties, were facing the unknown together.

She followed him into the darkness, and for the first time, the future did not feel like something borrowed, but something she could invent.

Above them, unseen, the lanterns waited.

Chapter 5: The Man Between Tides

Eliza POV — 1565, Florida marshland

She comes to in thick air, every surface slick with it—the entire world built of water and decay. Her face is pressed to something that is not quite earth, not quite plant: a mat of reeds warped by salt and the pressure of too many tides. There is a smell, immediate and unignorable. Brine, tannin, blood. Something rich with the memory of rot and memory's refusal to let go.

A cough rattles her chest. It is a childish, desperate noise, and she despises it. Eliza tries to rise, but her limbs have been demoted in the hierarchy of needs—they no longer serve, only ache. Each movement feels like the dream of running in place as disaster closes in. She lifts her head; her vision fractures into wet glass, heat, and humidity refracting every edge.

Something hums at the border of her consciousness. Not a

machine, not a warning, but the realization that she is both here and impossibly unmoored—her internal clock vibrating at two contradictory frequencies. For a moment, she thinks she can feel the Lantern Array itself, the memory of quantum harmonics still prickling at the base of her skull. But the present, in all its biological certainty, asserts itself through pain.

Her hands find mud. The mud finds her back. She pushes upright and immediately regrets it—an ache hammers through her jaw and up into her temple, electric and punitive. Her teeth have been grinding, though she cannot recall the moment she lost the luxury of unclenched sleep. Her mouth is sour with copper and something older.

The air is not a medium here. It is an organism, and it presses into every exposed surface, colonizing skin and scalp and even the inside of the nostrils. Eliza tries to breathe shallow, to minimize the invasion, but the air insists. It tastes of ocean but not the clean, bright kind—this is the flavor of estuary, of history's sewage backflow. The taste is so intense that it creates a phantom pressure at the roof of her mouth.

She is aware, with embarrassing clarity, that she is being watched.

The observer is near but not close. He has the patience of someone raised to believe that death comes most often to those who rush to meet it. She cannot look at him yet—her neck is not ready for such ambitions—but she catalogues what she can with peripheral vision and academic instinct. There is a presence in the pattern of the ground; a shadow that moves but not like a soldier, not like anything European. She tries to recall every forensic slide, every lecture on the Timucua, but the data in her mind is jumbled, reordered by need and pain.

A cloud of mosquitoes, a microclimate unto itself, seethes at the edges of her vision. They do not hesitate, do not discriminate. They land, feast, and die, driven by an algorithm older than language.

She runs through a mental checklist:

- Arms: present, bruised, scraped.

- Legs: responsive, untrustworthy.

- Clothing: soaked, smeared with algal greens and oxidized blood.

- Instruments: unknown. She can't remember whether she arrived with her kit or if it was shredded into archival tape by the crossing.

Finally, she turns her head and meets the gaze of her watcher.

He squats with perfect equilibrium on a cypress root; the kind of balance found only in those who have never been given chairs. His skin is sun-burned in layers; clay-red streaks run diagonally across his chest, blending with sweat into a kind of impromptu armor. He wears, loosely, a drape of woven fiber and a cord of shells that does not attempt to conceal the structure beneath. His face is sharp, as if the cheekbones and jaw have been planed down for aerodynamics.

His eyes are black, or seem to be, until a passing sunbeam fires them amber and gold. She is reminded, stupidly, of the first time she saw a wolf in an enclosure—how the animal's gaze was not wild, but undomesticated.

Apochi, she thinks, and the name is not a guess but a conviction. It has not been spoken in her presence, but she recognizes him by the weight he gives to the act of seeing.

He holds a shell, deep and iridescent, its interior stained with a liquid that is probably water but could be any number of things that kill the uninitiated. He does not move. She recognizes in the set of his mouth that he is waiting to see what sort of animal she will become: prey, threat, or the sort that dies of its own confusion before he must intervene.

"Water," he says at last, in Spanish thickened by another tongue but precise in its consonants.

The word detonates a memory—her dissertation defense, the first time she lost her train of thought and covered with "water, water, everywhere," and then immediately regretted the cliché. She wants to laugh, but the effort would cost too much.

Instead, she nods once, wary, and reaches for the shell. Her hand is shaking. Not dramatically, not enough to telegraph an immediate medical crisis, but enough that it betrays her. She hates that.

He sees, and for a second, his lips twist with something like humor. She catalogues the movement: a man who has seen much, who is capable of irony, but who is not amused by the world's laziness.

The shell is heavier than expected. The water inside is warm, carrying the taste of river and a faint, familiar bitterness—like an old bottle, not quite clean, not quite remembered. She drinks. The water does not kill her. It stabilizes the horizon of her vision, gives her the illusion of competence.

He stands, shifting his weight in a way that doesn't disrupt the surface of the marsh at all. She envies the precision of it. He speaks again, the Spanish more certain this time.

"You are not Spanish."

"No," she says. Her voice is a bandaged thing, barely audible.

“Not French.” He cocks his head. The movement is not human in the sense of academia or city streets. It is an animal, and she is aware of the urge to respond in kind, to present her teeth, to show that she too can operate in the grammar of survival.

“Not French,” she confirms.

He studies her hands, her arms. “You wear strange skins.”

Eliza looks down. Her field shirt is indistinguishable now from the color of the mud. Her pants are torn at the left knee, the blood dried rust-brown, and the fabric already going to threads at the seam. The compass necklace is gone, or at least she cannot find it at her throat. A small, ridiculous grief blooms in her. She tries not to show it.

Another boom rolls over the inlet—Cannon fire. The sound travels not as a report but as a pressure wave, rattling the marsh and sending birds skyward in a silent explosion of white.

She jerks involuntarily. He notices, and this time the humor in his face is not a smile, but the acknowledgment of shared misery.

“You fear thunder,” he observes.

She wants to say: I fear what comes after. But she does not.

“Who are you?” she asks, not as a challenge, but because the script must eventually be followed.

He considers this as if the question is larger than the answer could ever be. “A man who knows this land,” he says, then, “and who is alive because he does not rush to meet the unknown.”

She wonders if it’s a proverb or a warning.

They exist in mutual calculation for a long moment. The mosquitoes have found her face again, but she ignores them. The ache in her jaw has faded to a tolerable level. She catalogues the man's posture, the scars—one visible on his left forearm, the kind that happens in childhood and never heals symmetrically. His hands are scored with old and new rope burns. She wonders how many knots he's tied in his life; how many times he's slipped a cord around the neck of an animal or a person or a memory he can't let go.

"My name is Eliza," she offers, and this time her voice almost works.

He repeats it, slowly, as if tasting the phonemes for sharpness: "Eh-lee-sah." The sound makes sense in his mouth, in this heat.

She wants to ask: Are you real? Or is this a trick of quantum afterimage, some backwash of the Lantern Array, a hallucination built from the detritus of five centuries' worth of memory? Instead, she says: "Thank you for the water."

He nods once, a gesture that is not gratitude but recognition.

Then, abruptly, he crouches again—closer now, within arm's reach. She tenses, but he does not touch her. Instead, he places the shell at her feet and says, "It is dangerous to stay here."

He looks toward the horizon, where another plume of smoke is rising, this time blacker and sharper than the others.

"Your people come," he says, but she hears the plural. The possessive is uncertain.

"They are not my people," she says. It feels like a confession, but also like the first truth she's told today.

He regards her as if to say: That is the only answer he respects.

The air shifts. A wind picks up from the inlet, freshening the salt smell and breaking the humidity's hold for a few seconds. The relief is almost erotic in its intensity.

He stands again, this time offering his hand—not to lift her, but to steady her if she chooses to try.

Eliza hesitates. Then, for the first time since landing, she accepts.

His grip is dry, firm, unornamented by the hesitations of her own time.

He helps her to her feet, and the world does not end.

But it does, for the first time, feel like a place she could exist in.

They stand in the liminal space between water and land, neither party willing to name it safe. The wind has shifted, and so have the terms of encounter. She is upright, but only just—her balance achieved through sheer force of documentation. If she looks past Apochi, past the fevered curtain of marsh grass, she can see a smear of smoke against the horizon. The boom of cannon is less distant now, the intervals tightening.

Apochi studies her with open calculation. He is unembarrassed by the intensity of his observation. For a moment, Eliza has the sense that he is reading the sinews of her body for their intentions—like one might read clouds before a storm or the subtle tremble in a wounded bird.

He asks, in deliberate Spanish: “Are you a scout for the men in metal?”

She shakes her head. The action saps her, and she braces with both feet, unwilling to let him see how close she is to sitting down again. “I have no side,” she says, the words shaped by months of language drills but delivered with the accent of someone who has only ever spoken from the perimeter.

"You say that as if it is virtue," he replies, not moving. "But men without sides are usually dead in the end."

The words aren't cruel; they're field notes.

She takes a careful breath and pushes the conversation into territory she hopes will make sense. "I am here to observe. Not to join."

He lifts his chin a millimeter, as if he's heard this story before. "You walk alone. Yet you are not Timucua, not French, not Spanish. Your skin does not belong here. Your voice—" he tastes the next word, "—is not grown here. Who sent you?"

She considers the truth: A man in a windowless lab built on the foundation of old brick, a city that believes itself a copy of older, truer places, a pulse of theory and guilt. None of these are answers that will survive sunlight.

"No one sent me," she says, and this time the words are not rehearsed.

His eyes do not waver. "Then why do you come through fire, through water?"

She almost laughs, a dry bark of sound. "Accident."

He allows the word to settle, then says, "Most accidents do not dress themselves in questions." He squints, as if seeing her anew. "You look at this place as if it has already ended."

She absorbs that. It is not a misunderstanding; it is, in fact, the most precise description of her interior state since she woke. She files it away, but not before it hits her in the unarmored place she hides from even herself.

“I study places like this,” she admits. “I come to know how they end, and how they don’t.”

“Does it help?” He cocks his head, the motion again more animal than human.

“I don’t know yet.”

Apochi nods, a slow, considered movement. “You carry storms in your eyes,” he says, and it is not a compliment or an accusation. “Like someone who has already seen the flood, but stands in the dry.”

The words resonate. She cannot decide whether to be grateful or angry.

He crouches again, but this time not to offer water. He lifts a handful of black marsh mud and lets it run through his fingers, slow as time. “The ground here remembers everything,” he says, voice barely above the drone of insects. “People leave, come back. Blood soaks in, dries, washes away. It is never clean, not really.”

Eliza feels the grit of the marsh on her own palms, a physical anchor that steadies her as the sky pulses with another round of cannon fire. This one is close enough that a brief, wind-borne rattle of musketry follows the boom.

She flinches, a reflex she cannot control.

He watches, filing the reaction away. “Thunder,” he says. “You fear it.”

She shakes her head, but not in denial. “Not the thunder. The people who bring it.”

For the first time, his mouth softens at the edges, a smile not for her but for himself. “You are not so different.”

He wipes his hand on a stand of reed and gestures toward the east, where the land rises by slow degrees out of the swamp into the pine hammock. “My people go inland now. Away from the metal men, the thunder.”

She follows his gesture. The way is narrow, barely a path at all, but there are signs of recent passage: trampled grass, the pressed print of bare feet, the splintered stem of a palmetto that has been used as a walking stick or a weapon.

Apochi points to a different direction, toward the smoke and the persistent echo of gunpowder. “That way is death today. Maybe tomorrow.”

She weighs her options. The world narrows to two lines: one into the teeth of history, the other into its memory. Both paths terrify her.

“You must choose,” he says, standing. “To follow, or to vanish into the story that is not yours.”

She hesitates. Not because she doubts the danger, but because she is unsure if she has the right to survive on someone else’s terms. The academic part of her brain wants to ask about customs, about violence, about whether it is acceptable to walk behind or beside. The survivor in her has already made the decision.

She reaches out, and his hand meets hers halfway.

Their fingers interlock, and the contact is more than pragmatic—it is a declaration, not of trust, but of shared risk.

The ground is uneven, the mat of reeds slick and unreliable. She steps forward, and he steadies her, a subtle pressure guiding her weight onto solid footing.

Behind them, the next round of cannon fire breaks the silence, and the decision is made real.

They move together, away from the thunder, into the memory of land that remembers everything.

Chapter 6: The Spanish Foothold

Eliza POV — 1565

At dawn, the bay breathes smoke and new history.

Eliza stands on a muddy spit of marsh, her calves burning from hours spent braced in the tidal muck. She can barely feel her toes. The mosquitoes have long since mapped every millimeter of exposed skin. Around her, a braided mat of broken grass and driftwood floats atop the water, littered with half-rotted reeds and the white husks of dead crabs. The air is so heavy with humidity that her shirt clings to her back like a second skin, cold in the morning, then instantly too warm, the fabric holding every molecule of water it can steal from the sky.

She tastes salt. The decay of last year's fish harvest—the coppery tang of her own sweat.

Across Matanzas Bay, the Spanish fleet is coming in.

The first ships cut through the tide with the implacable slowness of predatory fish. Their hulls are black and barnacled; their sails ragged from Atlantic weather. Above each prow, the red-and-gold banner of Castile and Aragon unfurls in a sequence of timed gestures—one, two, three, each revealed by the shore wind as if by deliberate choreography.

The men on board are not yet visible, but the commotion is: lines thrown and lashed, barrels rolled into position, the echo of shouted orders carrying easily over the flat water. From this distance, the fleet could be mistaken for a small merchant convoy, except for the purposeful way they arrange themselves—galleons first, then caravels, forming a phalanx as the harbor narrows.

To Eliza, the approach looks less like a landing than like a ritual sacrifice.

The ground at her feet shifts. She almost loses her footing; a sudden pressure wave passes through the marsh as something large—maybe a ray or a gator—burrows beneath her vantage point, displacing water with patient violence. She steadies herself on a battered length of cypress, already snapped by an earlier hurricane, and scribbles the detail into her notebook. Her handwriting is worse than usual, the ink beading on the damp page.

She documents anyway. Her hand knows the rhythm: time, tide, observation. Her brain tries to keep pace, shoving memories into sequence, desperate to record every deviation between lived and recorded history.

She tastes blood. A new bite erupts behind her ear. The itch is nearly blinding.

Above the marsh, the sky brightens by increments. There is no sunrise here—just the slow clarification of everything that might want to kill you. She counts at least three hundred birds overhead, none of which appear in any Audubon database. She hears the shrill, almost electronic cry of a limpkin echoing from the far side of the bay.

The fleet draws closer. She can make out the forms now: Men in iron breastplates, catching sunlight even this early—a forest of pikes. Two men stand at the prow of the lead galleon—one hunched, shirtless, with the scars of a hundred beatings across his back; the other tall and rigid, his helmet fixed with a white feather that wags in the wind like a challenge. She recognizes the feathered helmet from a hundred woodcuts and museum dioramas: Pedro Menéndez de Avilés, Admiral and soon-to-be Governor, the man who will name this place St. Augustine and, in the same breath, make it a city of the dead.

The men on the decks do not speak. There is no need; the language of their approach is sufficient. They come in the service of the Church, the King, and their own exhaustion.

Behind Eliza, a wind rustles the sawgrass. The scent of fresh sweat and something medicinal—willow, maybe—slides across the back of her tongue. She feels rather than hears the approach of Apochi, who has tracked her from the moment she stumbled away from his kin's encampment.

She does not turn to look, not yet. The sense of being observed is constant now, not paranoia but the baseline state of the world.

From the left, another presence: the French.

She scans the distant edge of the mangrove, squinting against the glare. There, half-hidden by palm and shadow, a clutch of men in blue wool and battered linen. The telltale white cross of the Huguenot stitched on their sleeves, crude and unblessed. They do not move as the Spanish ships near, but their stillness is predatory. One of them, a boy with hair so pale it is almost translucent, raises a battered telescope to his eye. He scans the bay, then lowers it. Their captain—a man with the sharp nose and pinched lips of a Paris not yet starved of options—leans over and whispers something.

Eliza logs the French presence. She feels the tickle of historical irony: a standoff, two European worlds about to crash into the unyielding continent. She records it in her notes, writes: Not a collision, but an overlapping. Memory layered atop memory.

The Spanish ships finally reach the shallows. The flagship grounds itself on a sandbar and lists slightly; the other vessels drop anchor or beach themselves in series. There is a precise choreography to the landing. Each galleon disgorges a stream of men—soldiers first, then work crews, then the clerics in black, the last group carrying nothing but books and the implements of mass.

Eliza studies the priests. Their black cassocks hang oddly, sweat-soaked and sunstruck in a climate that does not forgive black cloth. One of them, the tallest, stumbles in the mud and is caught by a fellow. She watches him cross himself, the gesture so familiar it feels like a signal from a different lifetime.

The first man off the lead ship wades directly into chest-high water. His boots are instantly lost to the mud. He moves with the doomed purpose of someone whose choices have all been made elsewhere, by other men. A second man follows, this one carrying a banner—white silk, embroidered with a papal seal. The cloth snaps in the wind, then collapses, waterlogged, around the man's shoulder. They stagger, almost comically, toward the firm ground at the edge of the mangrove, where they plant the banner and kneel.

Behind them, a row of soldiers forms a perimeter. Muskets are held low, but the intent is clear.

Menéndez appears last, perfectly timed for maximum visibility. His armor is an ostentatious mesh of gold-inlaid plates, a suit made less for battle than for imposing belief. He steps into the water without hesitation, but with every step, his boots fill, and he sinks a little deeper, until his knees are nearly invisible. He does not break stride. The men around him clear a path, hauling themselves onto the marsh bank by raw strength. He stands alone at the water's edge, looking not at the land but straight up at the sky.

He raises a hand, and the priests begin to sing. The Latin washes over the marsh: thin, reedy at first, then building as other voices join. The wind batters the sound, lost in the noise of the birds and the sea, but the intent is obvious. This is consecration by conquest.

Apochi edges closer. He says nothing, but the quality of the silence changes—tenser, charged. Eliza feels the chill of his gaze along her shoulder. She wants to tell him that she is only here to witness, not to intervene. But the word for witness does not exist in his language. The closest word is for "those who survive and remember."

She scans the French line again. No movement, but the eyes of every man are locked on the Spanish ritual. She wonders if any of the French are praying. Or if, in this moment, their only faith is in the capacity to endure the next hour.

The Spanish finish their prayer. The tallest priest opens a battered Bible, lifts it toward the sun, and recites something that Eliza cannot hear, but which history has preserved: "To bring light where darkness dwells." She writes the phrase down, even as she tastes its poison.

Menéndez speaks next, his voice carrying above the others—loud, sharp, almost performative. Eliza recognizes the cadence of a man trained in command. The speech is not for his own men, but for everyone watching: the French, the indigenous, the future historians who will try to make sense of what comes next.

He declares this place La Florida, possession of the crown and the Church, a city to be named for the day of its landing.

Augustine.

There is a moment of stillness, as if the marsh itself absorbs the words and pauses to decide whether to accept the intrusion.

Eliza's notebook is now heavy with damp. Her wrist cramps from the effort of writing, but she refuses to stop. The world will be built from these details, not from the stone and blood that the conquerors think will last.

The French captain shifts, and for a heartbeat, she wonders if he will order an assault. He does not. Instead, he raises a hand in a gesture so ambiguous it could mean nothing or everything. His men stay in place.

Apochi finally speaks, so softly that she almost misses it.

"They have come to drown themselves," he says, voice flat. "All of them."

Eliza considers the line; decides it is not a metaphor.

On the Spanish side, the work crews are already hauling crates ashore. They unpack iron spikes and shovels and begin to grid out a perimeter for a fortification. There is no hesitation, no adjustment for the fact that the ground is barely ground—just the promise of it. Within minutes, the first soldier collapses from heat or exhaustion. He is dragged to the shade, slapped awake. No one helps him remove his armor.

Menéndez remains at the edge, alone for a long moment, staring up at the unmarked sky. Eliza wonders whether he sees anything there—a sign, a portent, a God who answers back. Or perhaps he is simply remembering Spain, the cool churches, and the crowded alleys of home. She wishes, for an instant, to know what he believes he is doing. Then she remembers her place, the imperative not to interfere.

The ritual resumes: the priests move to the makeshift altar, bless it with seawater, and lay out a wooden cross. The cross is small, rough-hewn, unfinished. It looks ridiculous against the marsh and the men's grand claims. But the act is not for show. It is for the record.

Eliza writes: They do not build with memory. They build with ritual. And with ritual comes the myth of permanence.

A gull swoops low, tries to grab a strip of salted meat from an open crate. It is batted away with the butt of a musket. The impact is so forceful that the gull crumples, dead or stunned. It floats on its back for a moment before righting itself, then paddles away, leaking a trail of blood into the clear water.

Apochi stares at the dead bird. He does not blink.

The French do not move. Instead, one of the men—tall, gaunt, already sunburned—scratches a mark onto the trunk of a palm tree. Eliza cannot see the mark, but she records the act anyway. Even the smallest resistance is a kind of memory.

The Spanish begin assembling the first wall. They drive iron spikes into the mud, lash them together with rope, and the roots of mangrove pulled from the shore—the entire structure wobbles, as if aware of its own impermanence. The soldiers curse as they work; some make jokes, others spit, and a few slog through the mud with the inertia of men who know no other trade.

On the opposite bank, the French break formation. They retreat into the shadows, evaporating as quietly as they appeared.

Eliza feels the tension drain from the marsh. The worst is not over, but it is at least deferred.

She closes her notebook, sealing the wet pages together. Her hand is trembling again, not from exhaustion but from the cold clarity of what she has just witnessed.

This is not the beginning of a nation. It is the beginning of a siege.

Apochi is already moving away. He does not wait for her to follow.

As she steps off the muddy spit, her boots nearly pulled off by suction, she turns once more to the Spanish. Menéndez is no longer alone. A cluster of soldiers stands around him, listening intently as he maps out the coming weeks. They do not see her. Not yet.

Eliza makes her way through the marsh, the stink of salt and rot more familiar now than the antiseptic air of home. She wipes a new layer of blood from her arm and feels the burn of the bites as the mark of her own belonging.

At the edge of the mangrove, she pauses. She looks back.

The papal banner, sodden with seawater, barely lifts in the wind.

History, she thinks, will record this as a triumph. It will ignore the dead gull, the fever already kindling in the lungs of a dozen men, the way the fort walls sag with each new tide. It will forget the moment when three worlds saw each other and, for an instant, knew the contest was already lost.

But memory is sediment. It collects, and hardens, and endures.

Eliza ducks into the shelter of the trees. The last light of dawn washes the bay in gold. The ships, beached and battered, cast long shadows over the water.

The air is thick with the hum of things that refuse to die.

By noon, the marsh is a crucible.

The Catholic priests emerge first; their black robes already streaked with sweat and creek mud. They set up a makeshift altar on a leveled raft of oyster shell, unpacking their missals and sacraments as if the only thing required to sanctify hell is the right Latin. The cross they carry is raw timber, its surface gouged by what looks like animal teeth. They drape it with a linen cloth, now instantly translucent in the humidity.

Menéndez stands at the center, helmet off, his hair a dark helmet of its own. He does not kneel, nor does he join the prayers. Instead, he watches the horizon, the red line of sunrise now long dissolved, replaced by a white violence of sky that promises storms by afternoon. Around him, the officers form a wedge—adjutants, petty nobles, even a few mercenaries who only last week had been looting their own quartermaster. They mutter, elbow, and spit. Even the most pious among them keep one eye on the bush beyond the waterline, as if waiting for the first evidence of an enemy.

The priests intone: "Benedic, Domine, hanc urbem nostram." The words melt in the heat.

Eliza catalogs the gestures. She's seen the ritual in books, in reconstructed paintings, but never in situ, never on the raw, bleeding margin of a world that refuses to behave. She notes how the priests' voices crack, how the sweat darkens their scapulars, how the men in the first row cross themselves not out of faith but reflexive dread. The holy water, drawn from the bay itself, is more salt than fresh. When it is flung onto the first coquina blocks, the brine leaves a faint trace of white crust behind, like the afterbirth of a failed chemistry.

The ceremony is over in seven minutes. The priests vanish

into a tent already erected on the least flooded ground, leaving Menéndez to stride forward and call the first roll.

The soldiers move. There is no deliberation, no hesitation; they are driven as much by the orders as by the fact that standing still invites death by dehydration or arrow. The perimeter forms instantly: pikes at the ready, arquebuses angled for maximum coverage, helmets low. The rest of the crew—ship's carpenters, masons, conscripted laborers from the jails of Cádiz and Havana—begin the work of turning swamp into wall.

The first haul is a fiasco. The coquina, still wet from the quarry, crumbles under its own weight. The men curse, but their curses are small compared to the shouts of the overseers, who drive them forward with lengths of driftwood. Eliza watches as the blocks are manhandled into place: a line of six men, all barefoot, forced to carry each piece on their backs because the only available wheelbarrow broke in transit.

One worker slips and is crushed beneath a corner of the stone. The impact is audible, a wet, dull thud, followed by a single shriek. The man does not die immediately. The soldiers drag him to the shade and ignore the sound.

Blood soaks into the porous coquina, the effect more visible than on any clean European flagstone. The stone seems to drink the blood, seeding it with pink threads.

Eliza finds herself cataloguing the taste of the air—salt, yes, but now edged with iron and the acid of fear. The soundscape has shifted, too: above the clatter of tools, there is the omnipresent drone of insects, louder than any church organ. The mosquito swarms are so thick that men swat at them even while carrying loads, slapping at their own necks in a doomed attempt to slow the feeding.

Menéndez does not participate in the labor, but he walks the line, shouting corrections. He switches between Castilian and the rougher port dialect of his conscripts, modulating his tone from kingly to vulgar with ease. At intervals, he stops to speak to the priests, who bless each major addition to the structure with a sign of the cross and a muttered incantation. The pace is brutal—by the time the first wall is up, three more men have collapsed, one vomiting blood from what Eliza guesses is heatstroke.

She writes it all down, or tries to. The ink runs in the humidity, and her handwriting is reduced to a series of desperate, short strokes. She can barely keep up with the number of names spoken and erased—some men are called only by their function, "Navarrete" for a region or "the Moor" for a man who does not speak Spanish at all.

The gunpowder element arrives by midafternoon. The soldiers set up two small cannons, neither of which looks like it belongs in this century. They fire them twice, aiming into the mangrove to "discourage" any approach from the marsh. The wet air muffles the shots, but the impact is spectacular—fronds and birds exploding skyward in a chaos of green and white.

Apochi watches the process from a low vantage point, half-submerged at the edge of the bay. He blends in so completely that Eliza almost misses him; only the flicker of his hair, wet against his shoulders, gives him away.

She wants to tell him that the Spanish are building with fear, that every act of aggression is a prayer for someone back home to notice their effort. She wants to explain that the stones will outlast the men, that the children of the future always inherit the violence of the present. She wants, in some impossible way, to apologize.

Instead, she writes the scene as neutrally as she can. She catalogues the ratio of labor to muscle, the arc of sunlight on the armor, the way the soldiers' hands tremble slightly after each shot of gunpowder. She tries to remain an observer.

But then the strike happens.

A boy, no more than sixteen, staggers under a load of mangrove poles. He slips in the mud, the poles tumble, and two land on the bare foot of the overseer. The overseer's face hardens; he brings his baton down on the boy's shoulder, once, twice, three times. The sound is both louder and softer than Eliza expects—a percussion followed by a muffled sob. The boy does not cry out. He simply resumes his work, head bowed, face hidden. The overseer follows him for a few paces, swinging the baton in short, measured arcs, not for punishment now but for punctuation.

Eliza's pen stops moving.

The moment is not unique, not even notable by the standards of the day. But it breaks her: not the violence, but the ordinariness of it. The efficiency.

She grips her compass so hard the edges dig into her palm. She wants to intervene, to speak, but the words choke in her throat. Even if she could, it would mean nothing.

Above, a flock of ibis wheel in lazy circles, their cries almost mocking.

She looks at the coquina wall. It is already stained by more than one kind of blood. She wonders how many layers of suffering it will take before the stone is considered sacred, or merely beautiful.

By evening, the first wall stands six feet high. The marsh is a slurry of shattered shell, discarded tools, and human waste. The laborers are allowed a single ladle of river water, no food until sunset. Some men laugh; others retreat into sullen silence. A few whisper in prayer, but Eliza cannot tell which god they invoke.

The priests emerge again, faces red and shining, to bless the completed section. They use more holy water, flicking it onto the stone with a sprig of rosemary. The overseer who struck the boy kneels for the blessing, head bowed, lips moving in rapid, silent invocation.

Eliza writes: They build with stone, and with steel, but mostly with bone.

Her notes are smeared and nearly illegible.

In the shadows, Apochi moves away. She senses his disappointment, or maybe it's her own.

The sun sets without ceremony. The only sound is the long, tired exhale of men who have nothing left to give.

Eliza closes her notebook and lets her hand drop into the muck. The water is warm and alive. It crawls up her wrist, then her forearm, erasing the sting of the day.

A single fire is lit on the Spanish side, its smoke drifting low across the marsh. The mosquitoes, undeterred, press closer. She breathes in the smoke, the sweat, the lingering ache of what she has witnessed.

This is how it begins, she writes, but cannot finish the thought.

She watches the fire burn down to embers, the wall looming against the dusk.

There will be no monument to this moment—only the coquina, hungry for another layer of memory.

Night falls without warning, as if the sun gave up.

Eliza stays longer than she should in the shadowed margin where marsh meets pine. It's quieter here, the ground firmer, the air laced with the sullen spice of cedar and mud. She watches the last of the Spanish day shift—their bodies huddled around crude fires, their faces painted orange by the glow, their armor stacked in careful rows. Stakes and fresh-dug ditches mark the perimeter, but the only thing keeping the dark at bay is the fear that something worse lives within it.

In the deeper water, something moves.

A series of small canoes, barely more than hollowed trunks, slip along the channels between islands of grass. Eliza sees them first as shadows, then as shapes: Timucua families, the men poling at the stern, women and children crouched low, all of them wrapped in bundles of woven mats, pelts, and river reeds. The children are so still, it's as if they are sleeping; the adults do not speak.

They move with the tide, not against it. They vanish into the reeds with no splash, no wake, only the memory of having existed at all.

Apochi is not among them. She suspects he is always nearby but chooses not to be seen. Perhaps he knows she is watching. Perhaps it matters.

Eliza writes: The Spanish build with stone and gunpowder. The Timucua build with forgetting.

But even as she records the line, she knows it isn't right. What the Timucua do isn't forgetting. It's refusal: they will not let their history be pinned to the walls of a fort, or a ledger, or the testimony of an enemy. They move their memory forward by carrying it whole, undivided, private, and intact. The world will never recognize their story unless someone is willing to see it written in the spaces between—between the stones, between the lines, between the cycles of loss and persistence.

On the Spanish side, the pace of construction accelerates into a desperate pace. Men work by torchlight, hauling more blocks, lashing down thatch, digging in the black muck until their nails turn blue and their hands crack open. The air fills with the sound of coughing, with curses, with the low, hollow chant of the overseers trying to keep their men alive by sheer will.

A child's scream cuts through the night.

It comes from the laborers' quarter, near the fire, and it is so sharp that for a moment, even the soldiers stop. The boy—she can't tell if it's the same one as before, or a different one, or maybe just someone smaller than the rest—has fallen into a pit, or been pushed. His arm is twisted wrong, bone already ghosting white through the skin. The overseer is on him in a second, trying to pull him out, but only succeeds in tearing the boy's sleeve and deepening the wound.

The priests come to administer confession. They don't try to help.

Eliza watches, feeling the first tremors of fever behind her eyes. It is not an unfamiliar sensation, but here it is sharper—magnified by the knowledge that the violence of this place will ripple through centuries, that every wound inflicted now will echo forward, no matter how many stones are stacked or prayers recited.

She presses her fingers to her temples, then to the compass at her throat. The metal is cold and reassuring, an anchor to the world she left, to the idea that documentation is a form of rescue.

But even rescue, she is beginning to realize, is a myth.

She closes her notebook. She no longer wants to write. She wants to see.

Far down the channel, the last of the Timucua canoes merges with the darkness—no one on the Spanish side notices. The focus is entirely on the wall, on the fire, on keeping the bones inside the body until morning.

Apochi appears beside her, silent as the moon.

He kneels in the grass, close enough that she can see the thin white lines of old scars along his forearms. He smells of river, of fire, of something wild but clean. He looks at her with a question, not in words, but in the way his eyes search her face, her hands, the tremor in her shoulders.

She shakes her head once, unsure what he is asking. Unsure what she could answer.

He reaches for her hand. She lets him take it. His grip is warm, the skin rough, alive with the same pulse as the river behind them.

They watch together as the wall grows higher, as the torches gutter and are relit, as the prayers of the priests mix with the howling of the mosquitoes and the cries of men already half-dead from the effort of building something that will surely fail.

Eliza feels the sediment of memory settling in her bones. It is heavier than she expected, impossible to shake.

Apochi lets go of her hand, stands, and walks back into the marsh. She remains, alone with the noise and the stench and the certainty that nothing she writes will ever capture the full violence of this night.

She looks at the wall. She looks at the empty water.

Somewhere in the future, she thinks, they will call this history.

She wonders, not for the first time, if that is the right word.

The night is total now, the only illumination the embers of the Spanish fire, the phosphorescence of insects, the slow burn of blood memory.

Eliza does not sleep. She cannot.

She writes only a single word before dawn.

“Endure.”

Chapter 7: Ripple

Gabe POV — 2026

The control chamber beneath the Castillo de San Marcos is a contradiction—stone quarried by hand, circuits arranged by algorithm. Amber pinpoints from the Array's sensor grid ripple along the ancient coquina, drawing quivering constellations across walls that predate every diagram in Gabe Navarro's field notebook. Here, history is not recited; it is inhaled, metabolized, then pressed into digital service.

Gabe hunches in the glow of the monitors, four in a row, each cycling through their own flavor of crisis. His left thumb works in circles over a stress callus at the joint of his index finger; the hand is poised a millimeter above the glass interface that governs the Lantern Array's calibration. Each movement is cautious, incremental; he does not trust the system to forgive a missed decimal.

The air in the chamber vibrates at a frequency only obsessive people and hard drives can detect—part ozone, part kinetic anxiety. It seeps through the fabric of Gabe's shirt, already damp at the collar and cuffs. Sweat beads at his temples, pooling just enough to sting when he blinks.

The primary screen demands attention: a side-by-side comparison, with a Civil Rights commemoration plaque on the left—"established in 1964, site of first integrated lunch counter"—and on the right, the same plaque, but "established" has vanished, replaced by "formalized in 1964." The word shimmies into existence as he watches, no transition, no rationale—a micro-eraser at work.

He toggles to the next window: a municipal database entry. British Florida, Treaty of Paris. The date "June 1763" flickers, then corrects itself to "July 1763." He double-checks the revision log. The change is time-stamped two seconds ago, tagged with a marker: [origin uncertain].

He tries to breathe evenly. His lungs respond with a judder, then snap back into rhythm. This is why he kept the voice recorder propped beneath his monitor, even though the chamber's audio suite had been upgraded last year.

He depresses the button, voice low and clipped. "Timeline drift detected. Micro-alterations appearing in municipal, state, and archival records. Monitoring stability index." The words hang in the air, a litany for the machines and for himself.

He should be documenting every blip. But his eyes cannot leave the third screen: Eliza's 2018 thesis, the digital version, the one that had upended her career before the ink even dried. The PDF is set to read-only; at least it's supposed to be. Yet, in the margin of Chapter 1, the phrase she had fought to preserve—Florida is not peripheral to American history. It is the preface—stutters for a moment, then resolves to: Florida is not peripheral to American history. It is the footnote.

A pressure builds behind Gabe's eyes, sharp as static. He flexes his hand, accidentally hitting the Array's recalibration field by a micron. A low chime pings, not quite a warning, but a reminder that even non-actions have consequences now.

He toggles to the harmonic stabilization module. The gold waveform is behaving like a patient with arrhythmia—stable for six, seven seconds, then a pulse, then a gap, then three quick flutters in a row. He logs the anomaly, voice barely more than a whisper: "Harmonic sync deviating from projection. Not catastrophic. Yet."

He glances at the wall clock—3:14 a.m.

Aboveground, the city is dark, or as dark as it gets, with streetlamps and security lights casting salt-white shadows on the old bayfront. The rehearsal fireworks are scheduled for tomorrow, but tonight the only detonations are here, in the subtle shattering of what was supposed to be a closed-loop experiment.

He thinks about calling Eliza—protocol says he should—, but he knows she is somewhere deeper in the records now, deep enough that a recall could destabilize more than just her neural telemetry. Besides, if she's tracking the change, she'll be at the site of impact, not in the chamber with a hand on the panic switch.

He massages the base of his skull, fighting a wave of vertigo. It's nothing, just a familiar aftershock from too many hours in the chamber. The lights on the ceiling swim in and out of focus, refraction lines forming a web across his vision. He logs the sensation, knowing someone on the review committee will eventually ask: "Vestibular dissonance increasing. May correlate to micro-alteration density."

The last window on the console, the one he tries not to check every five minutes, is the live feed from the archival servers. The metadata for the "First Thanksgiving in America" has just been updated. The date is right, but now it carries a parenthetical—"subject to dispute."

He grinds the heel of his hand into his eye socket. There is a mechanical satisfaction in the discomfort. It means he's still here, still anchored, while everything around him edits itself into something more convenient, more palatable, more gone.

He reopens the thesis file. Watches the phrase "It is the footnote" blink at him in blue. He highlights it, unsure what he means to do. He types, slowly, as if the machine might take offense at the revision.

He replaces "footnote" with "preface." The cursor blinks, but the correction holds.

For now.

He logs the change in the experiment's running journal. "Intervention on non-canonical record. Hypothesis: Self-correction possible at minor node, but risk of timeline rejection."

He sits back, the stone cold against his spine. He tries not to think about the compounding effect, how each small erasure invites another, how the sediment of history can be scraped away with nothing but intent and an empty line in the ledger.

He drinks from the water bottle on the console. The water is warm and slightly metallic, but he does not taste it.

A final sweep of the monitors. The Civil Rights plaque remains "formalized." The British Florida entry does not revert. But Eliza's thesis holds steady, her voice clawing back from footnote to preface.

He closes his eyes. The hum of the Array fills the chamber, not soothing, but definite. As long as the machines work, as long as the code can log a contradiction, the world is not yet lost.

He logs out of the console, but leaves the displays active. He sets the recorder to continuous mode. There is no going dark now.

He leans forward, forehead almost touching the screen.

"Hold steady, Eliza," he says.

He is not sure if she can hear. But the words feel necessary, a defiance whispered into a room that has never asked for permission.

He waits; fingers splayed against the glass.

He will not blink first.

The Array's containment field is no longer a tranquil pond. It's the surface of an unstable sun, oscillating at frequencies Gabe has never modeled, let alone survived.

He reads the spike before the alarm sounds—Eliza's bio-signature on the graph doesn't just rise; it splits, forming a jagged double-helix that climbs until the screen runs out of color-coding. He drags the mouse to zoom out, desperate to get context, but the dual signatures only widen, red and gold spiraling together.

A second signature. Not derivative, not shadow. Independent.

He brings up the neural telemetry overlay. Eliza's is familiar: the rapid, analytic cycles, the hard resets after emotional overload. But next to hers, the newcomer is baseline, slow, built for a world that does not run on urgency. If Eliza's brainwave is a lightning strike, the other is a tide.

He feels his own pulse quicken, the old arrhythmia kicking in. "No, no, no, no," he mutters, though he is not sure what he wants to prevent.

The console responds with a new warning: Timeline stability: 84%. Risk threshold exceeded.

He toggles the retrieval protocol, thumb hovering over the soft trigger. The whole chamber shudders at the possibility—a single command, and the Array will collapse the harmonic, forcibly recalling Eliza at the molecular level. Safe for the timeline, ruinous for the subject. "Not yet," he whispers, but the option gnaws at him.

The anomaly worsens. The historical record is fracturing. He sees a cascade of micro-alterations: in a Civil Rights oral history, a woman's maiden name reverts to the Spanish spelling; in the lighthouse construction records, a French engineer appears for the first time in three hundred years; in the personnel files from the Castillo’s 1937 restoration, a workman's next-of-kin switches from 'unknown' to a Timucua name.

Each shift is minor—a drop in the ocean—but the pattern is accelerating. He logs it, hands flying over the interface. "Compound drift. Timeline correction attempts are increasing in frequency. Subject is…"

He stops. He cannot bring himself to say "lost." So, he says: "Subject is diverging."

The Array's central column begins to hum in earnest, the light building from gold to blue-white, threatening to shatter the calm of the stone chamber. Gabe's hands shake as he recalibrates the feed, praying the hardware can hold. He can almost hear Eliza’s voice in his head: “It accumulates.” That was her phrase, the one he’d laughed at until the math proved it out.

He thinks about what happens if he pulls her now, half-merged, with two pulses beating in the same body. The best-case scenario is an unscheduled return and a hospital bed. Worst-case is she is neither here nor there, neither witness nor memory. Erased not by war or fire or erasure, but by his own lack of courage.

The alarm builds to a relentless, stuttering whine, loud enough to rattle the glass in the console. Gabe flicks off the external speaker, needing the silence.

Aboveground, the city is motionless, but here—beneath the fortress, beneath the weight of centuries—something is deciding whether to accept or reject the story Eliza is trying to write into the world.

He brings up the emergency override screen. His finger rests on the icon. He could do it. He could fix this, save the experiment, and preserve the fragile consensus the committee demands.

But then he sees it—a line from the session log, old but unforgotten, from the Boston conference years ago. "Rooms are only difficult when no one is willing to move the furniture."

He closes his eyes. For a moment, he is back in the oak-paneled hall, Cartwright's voice crisp and bloodless, Eliza's back ramrod straight at the podium. He remembers the heat in her face, not embarrassment, but a refusal to abandon the field. He remembers doing nothing, letting the room's inertia smother the argument.

He opens his eyes. His finger hovers over the recall command, then withdraws. He does not touch it.

"Not this time," he says.

He pivots, pulling up the harmonic resonance settings, and expands the field tolerance. The system howls in protest, but the new parameters settle, absorbing both signatures, Eliza's and the other, until they are two waves locked in resonance, neither one cancelling the other.

The Array's light flickers, then steadies. The chamber exudes a deep, vibratory calm, as if the coquina itself approves.

He logs the intervention: "Dual bio-signature stabilized.

Timeline drift contained. Subject co-adaptive with local vector."

He sits back, every muscle shivering from the crash of adrenaline, and looks at the stone wall nearest him. The light from the Array projects a shifting tapestry across the surface, centuries overlaying each other—Timucua red ochre, Spanish luster, British indigo, the whitewash of American restoration. The wall absorbs all, indifferent to revision, patient as a tide.

He rests his palm on the old stone. It is warm now, vibrating with quantum feedback, alive in a way he cannot explain.

He does not speak. He lets the moment settle, the stability index creeping back toward 90%, the screens calming to a gentle oscillation.

He will not force her back. He will not erase what she has found.

He logs the decision in the official record: "No forced recall. Subject permitted to pursue full narrative resolution."

He stands, stretching muscles that forgot they were attached to a body, and circles the console. The walls hold steady. The light holds steady. Eliza's dual signature holds steady.

This time, the room is his to move.

He glances up at the stone vault overhead, half-expecting it to collapse under the weight of the moment. But the ancient coquina is patient. It has weathered worse.

He places both hands on the console, grounding himself in the hum and heat of the present.

In the world above, the night is still. Here, history is being rewritten not by decree, but by the risk of letting something unfamiliar—something as wild and alive as tidewater—exist beside what was always there.

He watches the Array cycle, the pulse of Eliza's presence strong and insistent, buoyed now by the second signature.

He does not blink.

He will bear witness.

Night falls over St. Augustine in the only way it knows how—by degrees, each darker than the last but always leaving just enough light to suggest the city's refusal ever truly to sleep.

From his seat beneath the Castillo, Gabe Navarro listens to the tide of celebration above. The town is an echo chamber: plastic flags crackle in the dusk, the distant hum of generators for the waterfront concert, the practiced megaphone of a police sergeant rerouting Fourth-of-July traffic a block from the seawall. Each sound filters through centuries of stone, softened, as if the world above were the ghost and not the other way around.

He rotates through the monitors, slower now, savoring the absence of red. The Array's dashboard is smooth as glass: harmonic sync at 97%, timeline drift negligible, micro-alterations plateaued and mapped for audit in the morning. He logs it in the record, voice more relaxed than at any point since the project's launch.

"Subject maintaining temporal position despite persistent anomalies," he says, letting the recorder catch his unfiltered cadence. "Recommend continued observation rather than forced retrieval. System stable. End log."

He lets the silence grow, this time not a threat but a comfort.

The air in the chamber is cooler now. The stone has shed the day's heat, leaving a faint chill that lingers just above the floor. It's a familiar sensation, the kind he associates with autumn fieldwork, with childhood trips to the basilica, with the moments after a crisis has crested and begun to recede.

He stands, stretching arms and back, the joints crackling with their own private memory. He walks a slow circuit of the room, hands trailing along the coquina wall, feeling the subtle pockmarks, the fingerprints of a million mollusks now merged into sedimentary permanence.

The Array's energy is low and sustained—a soft, vibratory hum that suffuses the whole chamber. Gabe places his palm flat against the wall. The contact is grounded. The stone, once quarried by unwilling hands, is now a custodian for the story no one else will remember. He closes his eyes and leans into it, the vibration climbing through his wrist and into his ribs.

"Hold steady, Eliza," he says, this time not a plea but an instruction to the universe. The words reverberate, caught by the Array's acoustic pickup and looped faintly back into his ear. A closed circle. A promise.

He lingers there, the old stone and the new technology entwined, before returning to the console. The monitors have shifted to passive mode. Nothing in the system expects further action tonight. The calendar in the bottom right corner glows with tomorrow's date, the Fourth, the day when all the city's history will be called up for display, condensed and re-broadcast as spectacle.

He could go home. He could close the Array for the night and trust the safeguards and protocols.

He does not.

He pulls the second chair beside the console, turns it to face the wall, and sits. For a long time, he watches the shimmer of residual energy move across the stone, mapping the patterns of resonance, wondering which part of the world above will feel the echo first.

In his mind, he drifts to the marshes, to the sound of gunfire muffled by humidity, to the way the past always finds a way to survive the future. He thinks of Eliza, out there on the edge of the unremembered, and feels not fear but respect.

He wonders, briefly, what the stone will say of him, centuries from now. Whether his fingerprints will last, or if the sediment will fill in the space and smooth it over, history's old trick for absorbing every error, every hope, every impossible ambition.

He speaks into the empty room: "We build with memory."

He does not need to hear an answer.

He leans back, lets the night deepen, and waits for whatever comes next.

The stone holds steady.

The Array holds steady.

Above them, the city prepares for dawn.

Chapter 8: Village Firelight

Eliza POV — 1565

The sun has not yet burned off the night's humidity, so the marsh is wrapped in the damp that seeps past skin and memory. Eliza follows Apochi, picking a path where his feet have pressed the grass into submission. His stride never hesitates—where she steps with calculation, always searching for the next dry hummock or tangle of roots that might betray her balance, he moves with a certainty that feels less like memory and more like muscle.

Each time she stumbles—splashing muddy water onto her pant leg, catching her ankle in the hidden teeth of submerged sawgrass—she expects a comment. Apochi does not look back. He keeps his eyes on the horizon, letting the early light stripe his shoulders, and only slows if her lag threatens to separate them. When this happens, he stops so gently that she nearly walks into him, then resumes without signaling.

She is, by her own accounting, deeply out of her element. Field work, in her world, meant note-taking in climate-controlled reading rooms and walking neat rows between grave markers for a local preservation society. This is the opposite. The marsh is alive and carnivorous; mosquitoes form clouds so thick they move like weather, and every surface glistens with the reproductive intent of unknown species.

She catalogues everything. The way the black mud beneath the waterline oozes up between her toes instantly chills her skin. The resinous bite of wild rosemary as she brushes past a thicket. The shriek of a bird she cannot name, punctuating the silence every few minutes like the echo of a long-dead alarm. Her notebook is gone—left somewhere near the Spanish encampment the day before, pages too sodden to salvage—but the urge to document remains, now turned inward, desperate to find analogy or structure.

In the absence of data, her mind defaults to metaphor. The world is a thesis she has yet to formulate.

After what feels like a full hour of trudging, they reach higher ground. The transition is subtle; the water recedes from their path, yielding a sandier, more stable substrate. Palmetto and scrub pine cluster in loose ranks. Here, the sun finally cuts through, gilding the edge of every leaf and warming her from the shins up.

Apochi stops at the edge of a low ridge and gestures, not grandly but as if introducing a relative at a wake.

Below them, the village.

Eliza is prepared for a rough camp—a few lean-tos, a circle of old fire pits. What she sees instead is order so natural it would not register as deliberate if she weren't trained to look for it.

Palm thatch roofs, conical and perfectly symmetric, are arranged in a nested spiral. Each home—she counts at least fifteen—set at a polite interval from its neighbor, none aligned to a compass point, but all turned slightly as if to share in the limited shade. At the center, a wide communal hearth, embanked by low, curved benches woven from cane and palmetto strips. Smoke rises in a thin, consistent column, disciplined by the absence of wind.

She sees children first. Not because they are the loudest—here, even play is conducted in a quiet that respects the ambient soundscape—but because their motion is the least predictable. Two girls chase each other around a line of drying nets, their feet bare, hair bound in topknots with what look like woven grass bands. A smaller boy, ribs like piano keys, dangles from the lowest branch of a live oak. He watches her with flat, analytical interest, then swings down and vanishes into a hut's dark entrance.

The adults are at work, but the tasks are nothing like the "traditional lifeways" she's seen in dioramas. Women squat in pairs, shredding palmetto leaves with bone scrapers, their hands moving at speed, the resulting strips coiled into mats at their feet. Two men kneel over a pile of shellfish, prying them open with stone chisels and sorting the meat into bowls made from smoothed gourd halves. An old woman, silver hair tied in a knot at her crown, tends a shallow fire with one hand and a baby with the other. The baby, only slightly more expressive than a frog, stares at Eliza and then erupts into wet, gurgling laughter.

Fishing nets hang on lines strung between tree trunks, beads of water clinging to the hemp like morning dew. Past the huts, a neat patchwork of maize grows in raised beds, the stalks higher than her head, leaves slick with insect life.

The whole scene is suffused with the smell of woodsmoke, wet grain, and a baseline musk of humanity that reminds her, suddenly and uncomfortably, of her own childhood in the outskirts of

Jacksonville—her father's garage in summer, when every tool and inch of concrete held the ghost of old sweat.

Apochi watches her take it in. He says nothing for a long time. She realizes he is giving her the chance to adjust her expectations, to revise her mental image to accommodate the reality.

He leads her down the embankment, never needing to announce himself to the villagers. They know he is coming; several nod or call a greeting in a language that is neither Spanish nor any of the Timucua samples she's heard reconstructed. It is liquid, all consonant blends, and sudden softening at the end of words.

She tries to keep her focus, but the pace of input is overwhelming. Everything is data. The uneven wear on a woman's kneecap, the pattern of pigment on a child's face, the way every tool seems worn but not worn out, suggesting a cycle of constant repair.

At the edge of the central hearth, Apochi stops. He nods to a cluster of men working a log into planks with obsidian blades, and they return the gesture with unforced respect. She is aware that her own presence draws more curiosity than alarm; the adults appraise her with the quick, efficient attention of people who have seen every kind of disaster arrive on their shore, and yet still bother to register the details.

Apochi speaks in his native tongue. It is shorter than she expected. One of the women—barefoot, hair streaked with mud from some earlier chore—answers with a longer passage, then gestures at a shaded mat by the hearth.

He turns to Eliza and says, in his precise, careful Spanish: "They wish you to sit. You are not to stand over the fire."

She nods, too grateful for the chance to rest to consider the etiquette.

The mat is rough but dry, woven thick enough to keep the heat of the ground at bay. She lowers herself onto it, trying to keep her knees together, then realizes that everyone around the hearth sits in whatever posture they prefer, dignity unchallenged by comfort.

Apochi sits beside her, but not so close as to suggest ownership or protection. He surveys the village like a man counting his own breath—slow, measured, entirely present.

A woman approaches. She is older, eyes set deep in her face, and she carries a bowl of something that steams gently. Without a word, she sets it between Apochi and Eliza. Apochi inclines his head.

"For you," he says.

She peers into the bowl. The contents are ambiguous—milky, flecked with greens, and suspended in a gelatinous broth. She dips a finger and tastes. The flavor is so alive it shocks her: bright, almost citrus, then a slow bloom of umami she cannot place.

"It is fish," Apochi says, sensing her confusion. "But not the kind you know."

She wants to ask which kind, wants to make a note, but the warmth of the food and the exhaustion in her limbs collapse her curiosity into gratitude.

She looks up. The woman who brought the bowl watches her with an expression almost like a test. When Eliza goes back for a second taste, the woman's face relaxes. A verdict has been rendered.

Apochi's gaze follows hers. "If you do not eat, they will think you are a spirit. Or ill."

"Or rude," Eliza says, and the word sounds strange in her mouth, as if the concept itself is an artifact.

He shrugs. "Spirits are often rude."

She nearly laughs, but stifles it, not sure if humor is currency here.

The meal changes something. Within minutes, the suspicion around her edges softens; the children creep closer, one bold enough to poke at the tread on her boot. She flexes it, sending a small cloud of dried mud into the air, and the child recoils, then giggles.

"Why are you here?" a girl asks, Spanish awkward and deliberate.

Eliza hesitates. She wants to say "to observe," but that feels both predatory and impossible to translate. She says, "To learn," instead.

The girl considers. "From who?"

Eliza glances at Apochi, who is now busy stripping bark from a length of river cane. "From everyone," she says, and the girl looks satisfied.

As the village resumes its routines, Eliza notes the absence of hierarchy. Some older women seem to command respect, but no one shouts or issues commands. Tasks flow into one another with a logic that is not visible but undeniably present.

Apochi breaks the silence. "My people have always lived here," he says. "Before the men in iron skins, before even the French." He picks at the inside of the cane with a thumbnail. "No one writes it down. We do not have a book about who we are. We speak it. We remember."

Eliza absorbs the words. She thinks of the archives, the endless arguments over whose record is most "primary." She wonders if anyone ever considered that the act of writing down is not always about accuracy, but about power. Here, memory is as strong as stone.

She asks, “How do you remember so much?”

Apochi considers, then gestures at the children weaving a circle around the fire. “We speak. They listen. Then they speak.”

“And if someone forgets?”

He turns to her, face flat. “Then it was not worth keeping.”

She wants to argue, but can’t. There is an economy to this logic she cannot dispute.

In the late afternoon, the entire settlement seems to contract toward the central hearth. Women bring pots of grain and roasted squash; men carry strips of smoked meat and baskets of fruit that she can only compare to persimmons. The food is not portioned; it is placed at intervals so anyone can reach it. She tries to note the rituals of serving—who eats first, who waits, whether there is any sacred order—but finds only a gentle chaos, people drifting in and out, no one policing the boundaries.

Apochi eats sparingly, but often, and shares his portion with a boy who hovers at his shoulder. The boy says nothing, but their physical resemblance is unmistakable. She almost asks, then realizes: the boy is not his son, but his nephew, or cousin, or maybe just another child whose parent is absent. Family here is not about blood, but about proximity.

She feels herself relaxing. The tension in her neck, held since the moment she crossed, dissipates by degrees. She can almost convince herself that the world has not just ended and begun again outside the marsh.

When dusk settles, and the fire turns orange and loud, the voices around her rise in tandem. It is not a song, but a story—one she cannot parse, but which the children repeat in fragments, filling in gaps, arguing over the details. Apochi explains that the story is about a man who became a fish to escape his enemies, but forgot how to become a man again. The children debate whether he wanted to or whether being a fish was a better life.

She sees, in their faces and bodies, the whole of a world that will soon be erased from its own land.

She also sees that this is not a museum. Not an artifact.

It is a community, alive and perfect in its unbroken sequence.

She looks at Apochi, who is staring into the fire as if it contains all of history.

He turns and meets her gaze.

"You see it now," he says. Not a question.

She does.

The fire cracks, and the smoke rises into the air, mingling with the first stars.

Eliza sits among the people she has studied her entire life, and for the first time, she realizes that the record is not enough.

You have to be here.

You have to endure.

The sun sags behind the high pine, flattening the world into gradients of gold and bruise. As if cued by some ancient timer, the tempo of the settlement shifts—children called in by mothers, baskets of fish and root bundled toward central mats, the day's work packed into the neat, circular logic of evening. The air loses the sour tang of marsh and replaces it with the heavy sweetness of boiling grain, woodsmoke, the musk of hundreds of bodies layered together in contented exhaustion.

Eliza sits at the edge of the hearth, her knees drawn up, arms looped around them. The mat beneath her has warmed from hours of use. A pale dog—lean, fox-faced—curls at her side, every so often bumping her calf with its nose, perhaps hoping she will share the next bite. Its fur is rough as a pot scrubber, its tongue pink as sunset.

She tells herself she is here to observe. This is field work. Embedded anthropology, if anyone in her time could appreciate the distinction between "participant" and "living ghost." But the academic urge erodes quickly against the gravity of the scene unfolding before her.

Across the fire, Apochi sits cross-legged, working a bone needle through a torn strip of cordage. He doesn't speak unless spoken to; his attention seems always to be triangulated between Eliza, the slow perimeter of the firelight, and the tasks of the people who rely on him. She has not seen him eat, but each time food appears, he serves himself last, and then only after offering some to her.

Tonight, the meal is different from the noon fare. There's a wooden bowl, deep and carved with the shallow spiral of a snail's shell, half-filled with a porridge so thick it could be clay. Eliza dips a finger, tastes the bright starch of maize cut through with the oily punch of smoked fish. When she returns for a second taste, a small boy beside her grins, as if he's seen a challenge bested.

Apochi watches her eat for a moment, then nods, as if affirming a silent hypothesis.

He says, "To share food is to connect. It is how one makes family, even when blood does not."

She nods, chewing slowly to prolong the experience. "In my world, we make contracts and call them families."

Apochi considers this. “Does that mean no one eats together?”

She laughs, a sound that comes out sharper than she intends. “We eat together, but sometimes it feels like a negotiation.”

He shrugs, neither approving nor disapproving. “A meal can be a negotiation, too.”

Eliza wants to ask what he is negotiating for, but thinks better of it.

Instead, she looks around the hearth, trying to imprint every detail. The women stir the pots with long sticks, their hands deft, practiced, unhurried. A man with hair the color of river mud strips scales from a fish with quick, practiced flicks, the silver slivers catching firelight as they fly. Children pass woven cups of water, careful not to spill, though the effort leaves a trail of damp footprints in the sand.

Above them, night thickens. Stars fight their way through the haze, visible first as a handful of scattered points, then as a slow population of the sky. The village seems to pull closer to the fire’s edge, its borders shrinking in time with the loss of light.

A girl—maybe twelve, maybe older, her age hidden under the sun and the seriousness of her brow—sits down beside Eliza. She points at the pattern of shells stitched into Eliza’s sleeve and asks, “What is this?”

Eliza fingers the edge. “It’s called embroidery. It’s…decoration. Art.”

The girl considers. “Pretty,” she says. “But not strong.”

Eliza is about to argue, then realizes the girl means the thread itself. She shakes her head. “No, not strong.”

Apochi breaks in, his Spanish formal and slow. “In your world, do you not decorate with strong things?”

Eliza shrugs. “We decorate with what is beautiful, not what lasts.”

Apochi nods, as if that confirms something he already knew.

He looks into the fire. “The Spanish decorate with stone. They make walls. They put their names in the stone, thinking it will keep them forever.”

Eliza glances up, uncertain where this is headed.

Apochi continues: “When the walls fall, and they always do, the names are just dust. My people do not need the stone. We decorate with memory. We make the story strong, not the shell.”

He turns to her, his gaze reflecting both the flames and a kind of patient sadness. “This is how we survive when the walls come.”

She feels the weight of the moment. She wants to say: They will come for you, and there will be no shelter. She wants to say: In my world, you are a footnote, a vanished voice, a pattern woven into an artifact case and nothing more.

She cannot. She will not.

Instead, she asks, “Do you fear the Spanish?”

Apochi’s jaw tightens. The shadows from the fire exaggerate the line of his cheekbone, making his face appear momentarily hollow, older than it is.

“We move inland,” he says, gesturing with his chin toward the dark mass of trees beyond the maize beds. “Each season, a little farther. When they come, we watch. When they tire, we return. It is the way.”

Eliza fumbles for another question, something that might dispel the cold pressing into her ribs. “How long have your people lived here?”

Apochi shrugs, the motion both dismissive and absolute. “Always. Before the first canoe crossed the water. Before even the birds knew the rivers.”

His pride is obvious, but not boastful. She sees how, when he says these things, his posture straightens, his hands relax. He is not defending—he is belonging.

She presses: “Do you want to stay?”

He doesn’t answer immediately. He draws the bone needle through the cord again, careful and precise, then says, “What I want is not important. The land remembers us. If we are careful, it will hold us longer.”

She recognizes the urge to believe in this. It is faith, but not the kind that needs temples or Bibles. It is faith in sequence: that if the story is repeated enough, it will outlast the men who carry the swords.

The meal winds down. People begin drifting away from the fire, children clustered in sleepy knots, women cleaning up with minimal motion and maximal efficiency. The old woman with silver hair remains, eyes half-closed, humming a tune as she rocks a baby on her thigh.

Eliza feels the urge to linger, to ask for more, to somehow offer something in return for the hospitality and the accidental wisdom. But every instinct tells her to maintain her boundary, to keep the observer’s distance.

She is halfway to standing when Apochi places a hand on her wrist. Not hard, just enough to keep her anchored.

He says, quietly, "To leave food uneaten is to leave a story unfinished."

She sits again, scooping another bite of the maize porridge. She chews, swallows, and lets the warmth spread out from her tongue.

Apochi releases her wrist and looks back at the fire.

They sit that way, in parallel silence, as the night settles into its new shape.

In the far distance, a line of smoke rises—visible only because it snakes into the stars, black on black.

Apochi follows her gaze. "That is the Spanish," he says, voice flat. "They burn a new camp every few days to clear the land."

Eliza thinks of all the future maps that will not mention this place, this moment, this man.

She thinks of her own city, two hundred fifty years from now, layered with history but empty of all but the names written in stone.

She wonders, again, whether writing things down really makes them last longer. Or if the story must be told, over and over, until the very act of telling is enough.

She finishes her food. She licks the last taste of it from her lips.

She closes her eyes.

And for the first time, the fire inside her does not demand to know, but to remember.

The world beyond the village boundary is black as pitch.

Somewhere in that darkness, predators hunt: the men in iron skins, the animals of claw and tooth, the currents of history already stirring. But inside the perimeter of woven mat and firelight, nothing exists but the story.

The people arrange themselves in a great circle, larger than the one used for meals, larger than any meeting Eliza has ever seen outside a legislative chamber or a football stadium. Children wedge themselves between parents' knees, faces shining with sweat and anticipation. Elders settle onto the most battered mats, the ones whose frayed ends tell a history longer than memory, bodies folded with the comfort of a thousand repetitions.

Apochi takes his place at the perimeter, not among the elders, but in the silent wedge reserved for those who protect and watch. He does not look at Eliza, but she knows the space beside him is meant for her. She settles in, aware of her alienness, but also of the unexpected comfort of being part of the shape.

The oldest woman in the village—her hair a froth of silver, her voice soft but undeniable—lifts both hands and begins.

Eliza cannot hope to follow the words. The Timucua language is a storm of syllables, soft at the edges, but occasionally punctuated by hard, almost violent sounds. It is a voice made for the open air, meant to float and scatter. She catches only the rhythm.

Apochi leans close, translating in fragments, sometimes halting to find the right word.

"She says…" He stops, listening to a long, rolling passage. "Once, before the first people, there was only the sea and sky. The world was empty of everything but salt and air."

Eliza watches the woman's hands. They shape the sea: fingers undulating, palms cupped, now splitting the air with a gesture of division.

“She says the sky wept until the foam became land. The land was lonely, so it grew people out of itself.”

The children giggle at this, recognizing the joke—that they are made of sand and seawater.

“She says the first people tried to walk upright, but the sun burned them. So, they learned to move with the grass, to bend and hide. They became clever, making homes in the shade.”

The listeners hum in agreement. A man near the front grunts a correction, and the woman fires back a rapid reply, the two of them sparring gently over the shape of the old story.

Eliza feels the gravity of the moment. This is not performance, not ceremony; this is as functional as fire, as urgent as the food that will come tomorrow. Every child knows this story, but each time it is told, the edges shift, adapting to the needs of the night.

The tale continues. The first people encounter a “monster of metal”—here, Apochi pauses, as if debating the accuracy of his own translation.

“She means… Spanish. Or maybe not. Maybe French. Long ago. They came with fire in their hands.”

The villagers’ faces go flat at this turn, no laughter now. Even the children sense the importance of the shift.

The story is not a chronology. It folds time, lets the past speak through the present, sometimes contradicting itself. The men from across the water come and go, but the people remain, always learning, always remembering.

The old woman gestures, summoning the wind; her fingers flutter, and her voice drops to a near-whisper. Eliza does not need a translation for this part: it is the story of survival, told in the pitch of the voice and the hush of the crowd.

"She says: when you are too proud, you drown. When you forget, you drown. Only the story floats."

Apochi lets the words settle, not embellishing.

When the story ends, there is no applause, but a low, musical sound—dozens of voices exhaling at once, the communal equivalent of a sigh. The woman bows her head, satisfied.

Another elder picks up the thread, this time a man whose face is marked by burns, his hands twisted at odd angles. He tells of a storm—one so fierce it tore the village from its moorings, lifted the huts into the air, and scattered the people for days.

Eliza recognizes the allegory, the way trauma is alchemized into warning. But as the man speaks, she also hears the humor woven in: the prankster who tied huts together, the child who floated downstream and returned with an armful of stolen fruit. The story does not end in tragedy, but in reunion, in the resilience of people who always return, always rebuild.

Apochi translates only the essentials. "He says: the wind is like the future. You cannot stop it, so you learn to lean into it."

Eliza finds herself nodding, the lesson as valid in her world as it is in this one.

As the stories wind down, children drift into sleep, their heads resting on parents' arms or laps. The fire pops and settles, sending up an occasional spark that draws all eyes upward.

For a moment, there is silence.

Then, from the far side of the circle, a voice calls out in Spanish. It is a woman, her face shadowed but her accent clear.

She asks, "What if the wind is too strong? What if you cannot return?"

Apochi does not translate. He answers in his own tongue, words measured, slow.

Eliza watches the exchange, feeling the pulse of anxiety ripple through the adults. She wonders if they know, as she does, what comes next: the displacement, the plague, the long, slow erasure.

The old woman responds, her voice the anchor.

Apochi leans in. "She says: if you cannot return, you make a new story. You teach it to your children, and then you are never truly gone."

The fire burns lower. The elders begin to sing, low and without words, a drone that is more vibration than melody. Eliza feels it in her chest, a resonance that soothes and shatters at once.

She blinks, and her vision blurs—not from exhaustion, but from the pressure of wanting to remember every detail, the terror that she will lose it, that her own memory will betray her.

Apochi places a hand on her shoulder. The gesture is gentle, not possessive. His thumb brushes her collarbone, a grounding touch.

He whispers: "We build with memory."

She cannot answer, not with words. She leans slightly into his hand and lets herself be still.

The fire dwindles to embers. One by one, people rise, carrying children, gathering sleeping mats. The elders remain until the last, voices now soft enough to blend into the night.

Eliza and Apochi sit alone at the edge of the ring.

He says, "You are not of this story, but you hear it."

She manages to speak. "I wish I could tell it. The right way."

Apochi shakes his head. “You will tell your way. That is enough.”

She stares into the dying coals, seeing not just the story, but the history that will swallow it. She thinks of all the archives, all the databases and plaques, the monuments to people who never got to write their own name.

She thinks of the way the old woman’s hands shaped the sea, the way children laughed at being made of sand, the way every person in the circle knew their own lineage, stretching back to the foam.

She knows, now, that the story is not the same as the record. One survives in stone; the other survives in voice, in repetition, in the stubborn continuity of being told.

The wind stirs, and in it she hears the echo of a thousand unrecorded nights, of voices layered over time like sediment.

Apochi’s hand remains steady as the tide.

Eliza closes her eyes.

She listens.

She endures.

And in the dark, memory floats.

Chapter 9: The Marsh Lesson

Eliza & Apochi — 1565

The marsh is neither land nor water, but a third thing that refuses to be explained.

Eliza learns this the hard way. The moment she leaves the stable margin of pine and palmetto, her boots lose all negotiation with the ground. The mud is not surface but appetite; it gulps each step up to the ankle, sometimes the calf. The warmth of the day lingers in the shallow pools, and as she follows Apochi away from the familiar paths, the water climbs with greedy confidence, first to the knees, then mid-thigh, soaking through layers of fabric that had once meant protection.

She expects the cold, but the water is blood-temperature, almost intimate in the way it envelopes her. What surprises her is the pressure—steady, insistent, as if every drop in the marsh is a hand urging her to turn back. She does not. Instead, she catalogues: pressure, density, the smooth persistence of warm silt seeping through the seams of her pants. The taste of air so thick with green rot it feels alive in the lungs.

Mosquitoes swarm her face, crowding the line between hair and skin. She tries to ignore them, to focus on Apochi's silhouette several yards ahead: bare arms, damp with the film of exertion, the shell cord at his neck bobbing with each surefooted stride. He moves as if the mud is suggestion, not obstacle; he picks his way between cypress knees and sharp-tipped reeds, reading the ground like a familiar text.

She tries to mimic his path and nearly topples. The mud grabs her boot and holds on, unwilling to relinquish its new acquisition. She leans hard on a cypress root, the bark biting into her palm, and manages to wrench herself free with a sound somewhere between a slurp and a curse.

Apochi glances back—not with pity, but with the dry patience of a man who has watched generations learn to swim by sinking first.

“You walk like a buck treading through black-water muck,” he observes, voice pitched just above the insect chorus.

“I'm from a place where the ground holds still,” she replies, wiping her brow and smearing a fresh constellation of dead mosquitoes across her temple.

A flicker of humor in his eyes. “Ground always moves. Only sometimes it pretends not to.”

She wonders if this is the beginning of a lesson or a rebuke.

He gestures for her to keep up, then veers left, stepping onto a series of roots that form a natural lattice above the deeper channel.

She follows, testing each foothold before committing her weight, and soon they are moving in a winding pattern through the marsh, avoiding places where the surface liquefies at a glance.

They travel in silence, punctuated only by the calls of birds—egrets in mid-argument, the distant churring of what might be a rail. The sun is barely above the horizon, its light thickening into gold and copper as it filters through the canopy. Everything glows a little, even the mud.

Eventually, Apochi stops. He waits until she closes the gap and stands beside him on a hummock only marginally more stable than the water itself.

He crouches and gestures for her to do the same. The motion is practical, not ceremonial. Once they are both level with the water, he points to a patch of surface, then to the base of a nearby mangrove.

"Watch," he says.

She watches.

For a long time, nothing has changed. The water is placid except for the ripple of gnats skating its surface.

Then, without warning, the reflection of a branch splits and shivers—subtle, easy to miss. She blinks and sees the origin: a slow, deliberate swirl in the water, as if something large is moving beneath. It is not random. The swirl arcs around the mangrove root and dissipates before reaching them.

Apochi looks at her, waiting for comprehension.

She stares, then shrugs. "Fish?"

He shakes his head. "Not fish. Water itself. See?"

He dips a finger into the current and draws a line that follows the arc of the swirl. The current nudges a piece of broken bark, carrying it smoothly around the root instead of crashing it into place. He hands her the bark.

"Try."

She sets the bark onto the water and watches it hesitate, then roll gently along the swirl before swinging around the root and floating away.

"Every root remembers where the water wanted to go," he says. "Every water remembers the roots."

The meaning settles in slowly, like silt in a floodplain.

He stands and steps into the channel, beckoning. She hesitates, but the look on his face is not open to negotiation. She follows, feeling the water press and tug at her legs.

He stops again, closer to the mangrove, and this time he takes her wrist—careful, measured, without threat. He guides her hand to the submerged root and positions her palm so the water flows over her skin.

"Close your eyes," he instructs.

She hesitates, then obeys.

At first, all she senses is temperature: a uniform, enveloping warmth. But as she holds still, she becomes aware of subtle differences—the way water speeds up on one side of her hand, then slows, then splits. She can almost feel the ghostly outline of the root before her fingers touch it.

Apochi speaks softly: "To move through the marsh, you must learn how the water moves. Water shows you what the mud hides."

She opens her eyes.

He releases her wrist, satisfied, and points farther along the channel, where the water darkens, and the grass thickens.

“Follow the easy line,” he says. “Not the straight line.”

She nods, not trusting herself to answer without betraying either frustration or awe.

They continue, Eliza, concentrating on the currents, watching how each obstacle shapes the water in advance. She begins to predict the shifts: where a log is buried, where the mud will suck hardest at her feet, where the surface merely looks solid. Each time she anticipates correctly, a faint satisfaction flickers across Apochi’s face. When she missteps, he lets her struggle for a moment before offering a suggestion, never a command.

The mosquitoes do not abate, but she notices them less. The rhythm of movement, the logic of the marsh, demands all her attention.

After an hour, or maybe a lifetime, they reach a place where the trees give way to a wider channel. The sun is higher now, lighting the water so it glows from below, rendering every shadow a secret. The earth here is softer, the current slower.

Apochi stops on a dry patch and waits for her.

“You see better now,” he says.

She looks back along their path. It is not a straight line at all, but a series of careful arcs and loops, each dictated by the memory of the water and the shape of the land beneath.

“Water remembers where it has been,” she says, echoing his words.

He nods, pleased.

She wants to ask if it remembers where it’s going, too, but

she suspects the answer.

They stand together in the dappled light, neither quite teacher nor student, but something balanced in the middle.

For the first time, she feels less like a foreign body in the marsh—and more like something the water might choose to carry forward.

Apochi is the first to break the quiet. He points toward a low line of sky where a flock of egrets—white as old scars—lifts from the edge of a channel and wheels inland, their long necks outstretched and indignant.

"Do you see?" he asks.

Eliza shields her eyes, half-blind with sunlight. "The birds?"

He nods. "They do not leave unless the water rises."

She stares, looking for the logic beneath the assertion. "You watch the birds to know the tides?"

A shake of the head, gentle. "We watch everything. Birds are honest. If they move, there is a reason. If they stay, there is reason."

He steps forward, water swirling up to the mid-thigh now, and gestures for her to follow. As she does, her foot lands on something sharper than mud—a shell, a buried fragment of the marsh's long, slow memory. She stumbles, regains her footing, and looks down.

Apochi kneels, ignoring the suction of silt, and scrapes away at the base of a mangrove root. He lifts a single bivalve, split and empty, then tosses it back into the channel. The water claims it instantly.

"There are beds here," he says, "but only after the birds come."

He glances at her, waiting for the implication to land.

It does, eventually: the birds know when the water is right for shellfish to surface.

She says it aloud, testing the idea. "The birds eat when it's safe to eat."

A small, approving smile. "And we eat after the birds."

They move deeper, the land dissolving into a puzzle of islets and winding currents. The further they go, the more the marsh reveals its rules: the earthy tang of rot sharpening in the heat, the distant shriek of a bird of prey, the subtle shift of current as the bottom drops away, and the mud gives place to dark, swirling pools.

Apochi stops her again, this time with a hand on her forearm. He points to the surface where a small commotion has begun: the water erupts in tiny, staccato bursts, as if the air itself is trying to escape.

"Fish?" she hazards.

"Small ones, yes," he agrees. "They jump only when chased."

She watches, tries to see what he sees.

"If there is no big fish," he explains, "there is no reason for the small to run."

He leans close, speaking low. "If you are hunted, you must know what hunts you. You must know the paths they take."

She nods, then frowns, frustrated by the cryptic wisdom.

He continues: "You do not walk straight in the marsh. Not

just because of mud, but because of what hides in it."

A sudden movement: he takes a reed, breaks it off at the base, and drops it in the water. Instead of floating idly, the reed is caught and pulled rapidly toward a hidden bend. The current, invisible at the surface, betrays itself with this single, fragile marker.

Apochi gestures for her to try.

She looks around, finds a broken cattail stalk, and drops it in. It hesitates, spins, and is also drawn toward the same hidden route.

She looks up, triumphant, expecting a nod. Instead, she finds him watching her—intensely, appraisingly, as if measuring not her success but her understanding.

"Your people look, but do not see," he says.

It stings. She wants to retort, but the truth is too raw. She is, after all, trained to observe, but what has she truly seen since arriving?

He softens, just slightly. "When the water is new, it shows its secrets. When the water is old, it keeps them."

She does not ask what he means. She is learning that sometimes the lesson is less about the answer and more about patience.

The marsh shifts as they move again, this time more quietly. Every step Eliza takes is now calculated, each movement of her body designed to minimize noise and splash. She is surprised to find herself enjoying the focus, the narrowing of her attention to the absolute present.

Apochi halts once more, this time without warning. He crouches, tracing a fingertip over a pattern of ripples she would not have noticed if he had not pointed them out. He does not explain right away. Instead, he watches to see if she can puzzle it out.

She stares at the ripples, comparing them to the countless others she's seen today. At first, they look the same—concentric, overlapping. But then she notices that they reflect at a sharper angle, and their point of origin is not visible on the surface.

It's a subtle difference, but enough.

She points: "Something is under there."

He smiles with real approval now. "Oyster bed," he says. "The shell edges break the water before you see them."

She grins despite herself, feeling, for a rare moment, unburdened by the heaviness of history or the gnawing ache of what will come for his people.

They wade a little farther, side by side, the sun higher now and the air pulsing with the layered music of birds and insects. The earthy rot of the marsh is no longer unpleasant; it feels essential, grounding.

Eliza wants to ask more, to have him teach her every secret the water holds. But she knows that the best knowledge is not a thing given but a thing shown, a thing practiced.

They stand for a while in silence, watching the marsh conduct its impossible symphony of survival. A pair of egrets stalks the shallows nearby, elegant and cruel. The sky darkens momentarily as a cloud passes, then blazes back to full light.

Apochi's hand brushes hers, just briefly—a gesture without calculation, just confirmation that they have both seen the same thing.

For the first time, she is not a passive recorder of this world, but an engaged part of its rhythm.

The day presses on, water and memory moving as one.

When the sun crests high enough to flatten all shadows, Apochi leads them to a shallow hummock where the water barely covers the ankles. The ground here is springy, the soil a woven mat of root and old leaf. The air, free of mosquitoes for the moment, feels almost light.

He stops, takes a slow breath, and surveys the circle of open sky above them.

"This is a good place," he says.

Eliza sets her pack down, grateful for a moment's pause. Her shoulders ache with the unfamiliar effort of the marsh, but her mind is alive, humming with the morning's lessons. The water still runs in complex patterns around her boots, and when she closes her eyes, she can almost visualize the unseen shapes beneath the surface.

Apochi stands silent for a long time, as if the next words require permission from the place itself. When he speaks, his tone is altered—not the clipped authority of a guide, but something slower, heavier.

"We build with memory," he says, looking at her to see if she will catch the meaning.

"Not with stone?" she hazards, remembering the morning's offhand phrase.

He gives a tiny shake of the head. "Stone is for men who want to own the land. To put a hand on it and make it say their name."

She thinks of the coquina walls in her own century, remembers the way the oldest buildings in St. Augustine stand half in ruin, battered by every storm but always rebuilt, always with more stone.

"Stone breaks," he says. "Memory bends."

She wants to argue, wants to quote the centuries that have survived on the persistence of monuments, but she senses that would be missing the point. Instead, she asks, "How do you build with memory?"

He kneels, picking a handful of green reeds. "Watch," he says.

With a knife-edge fingernail, he strips the outer layers, then weaves three stalks together, braiding them tight. He shapes them into a small loop, then sets the loop upright in the shallowest trickle of water, anchoring it in the mud. The current pushes at the ring, but it does not collapse. Instead, it flexes, adapting its shape to the flow.

"Fish come through here," he explains. "If you put stone, they turn away. If you put memory, they go where you ask."

She crouches close, fascinated. "Show me?"

He hands her a bundle of reeds. "Make three strong," he instructs.

She fumbles with the material at first, her fingers thick and clumsy compared to his. He watches, then, without warning, moves behind her and places his hands over hers. His touch is warm and dry. He guides her fingers, showing the rhythm of the braid, the right pressure to hold without snapping. For a moment, she is acutely aware of the point of contact—how his skin fits against hers, how the cadence of his breath slows the frantic pace of her own.

Together, they twist the reeds into a loop. Her second try is less perfect than his, but it holds. He sets it in the water, aligning it just so with the current.

"You cannot own the water," he says softly, close enough that she feels the words vibrate through her bones. "But you can ask it to remember you."

She looks at the tiny trap, sees how the current moves through it, how small particles of plant matter catch in the weave. It is ephemeral—a structure that will dissolve in days, maybe hours—but for now, it shapes the water.

"Spanish build stone forts," he says, "and spend their lives defending them. We build memory, and let it move."

He steps back, giving her space. The moment lingers in the air, charged and vulnerable.

Eliza is tempted, painfully, to tell him about the future—the fates that await his people, the erasure in the centuries to come, how even the memory will be almost wiped clean. But something stops her. Perhaps it is the dignity of the moment, or the trust he has offered, or maybe just the sense that this, too, is memory worth protecting.

She reaches for another set of reeds, tries again, and this time her hands move with a steadier purpose.

As she works, Apochi collects more materials, showing her how to knot them together, how to layer the traps to make a line across the shallows. They construct a dozen in silence, each one more confident than the last.

"The tide comes, the tide goes," he says, laying the final loop in place. "We remember its path. And it remembers us."

He stands and surveys their work—temporary, almost invisible, but enough to shape a morning, a lesson, a moment. He nods with satisfaction.

"Will you remember?" he asks, not as a challenge, but a

genuine question.

She meets his gaze. “I will.”

He seems content with that answer.

They rest together on the dry patch, side by side, the effort of the morning settling into a mutual, companionable silence. The marsh is alive with noise, but it feels like a hush, as if the world is holding its breath.

She wants to reach out, to ask if he feels the same sense of connection, the same sense of impending loss. Instead, she rests her hand on the cool mud and waits.

Finally, he speaks. “You come from a far place,” he says. “But you carry storms with you.”

She almost laughs—she has heard it before, from him, from others—but it is not an accusation. He says it with respect.

She wants to tell him the truth, but it feels too dangerous, too raw.

Instead, she says, “Teach me more.”

He nods, smiling, and they stand, walking the edge of the marsh until the sun dips low and the water shifts again, new and old in the same instant.

As they go, Eliza looks back at the line of reed traps, their memory written briefly on the surface of the water.

She promises herself that she will remember this, that she will carry it forward—even if no one else ever knows the name.

In the gathering dusk, the marsh is both what it always was and what it has just become: a place where the water and the past are in constant conversation, each shaping the other, each refusing to be owned.

Above them, the sky is a wild, open archive. The wind lifts, and the scent of salt and life and rot is almost sweet.

They walk home together, the future and the past in unsteady alliance.

Chapter 10: Matanzas Inlet

Eliza POV — 1565

The inlet does not change for history.

Even now, centuries before coquina walls will fossilize the shoreline, the water finds its way, folding up against the sand in slow, predatory increments. Salt breathes in from the ocean, dragging the stink of kelp and something riper—a sweetness Eliza recognizes as the perfume of rotting shell. The marsh grass is shoulder-high, a corrugated mat of green and yellow blades that flattens only where wind has beaten it flat.

She crouches within this blind, legs bracketed by saw palmetto, and watches the Spanish orchestrate their morning.

Apochi is a stillness at her side. He has wrapped his arms around his knees, chin tucked, eyes fixed on the shifting men across the inlet. She tries to mimic his composure, but her heartbeat is a hammer behind her eyes. Every gust of wind flattens her breath against the back of her teeth. Mosquitoes whirl at her ears, land in the sweaty crook of her elbows, bite and die, and are replaced.

Across the sand, the line of French prisoners wavers but does not break. There are more of them than she expected, nearly two dozen, each lashed wrist-to-wrist in crude ropes. Most have their shirts in tatters, bare arms sunburnt to the color of cooked shrimp. Some have bandages around their heads, others limp or half-dragged by the man in front of them. The Spanish have relieved them of all weapons, but a few carry the scars of swords along their ribs and collarbones—a history written in three colors: white for the old, pink for the healing, and red for the fresh and still weeping.

Eliza's eyes skate over the details, recording even as she dreads them. She thinks: This is the moment the city is founded—not by the cross, not by the wall, but by the execution of an idea.

The Spanish captain—a tall man with a saber that catches the morning sun—paces the sand, barking orders. His armor is bright at the edges, but rusted in the seams, sweat-dark under the arms. The musketeers line up in a single, deliberate row, each planting their feet as if rehearsed. None of the faces are familiar, but every gesture is. Violence is a grammar, and she has spent a lifetime learning to parse it.

Apochi murmurs a word, almost inaudible. She does not understand, but the shape of his jaw is set hard enough to mean any of a dozen possible prayers.

The French are made to kneel. Some go willingly, as if to save their knees from the sharpness of the shells underfoot. Others resist, lurching backward until a musket butt or the flat of a blade brings them down. Two of the prisoners attempt to turn, to plead, but their voices are lost in the morning wind.

A volley of Spanish language—sharp and ordered—cuts through the air, followed by the metallic shuffle of muskets raised in sequence. The prisoners bow their heads, most of them, but a few stare at the water, at the sky, at anything but the men about to kill them. Eliza finds herself searching for their eyes. She is desperate for some act of defiance, something to complicate the neatness of the record.

One of the French, a boy barely older than her own students, looks straight ahead. He mouths something—mother, perhaps, or God, or a curse spat at the tide.

Eliza's whole body seizes as the captain gives the order. The word is not "fire," but something longer, almost ceremonial. The effect is the same.

The muskets discharge as one. The sound is not as sharp as she expects; the humidity flattens it, turns it into a low, rolling boom that trembles the air and then is gone. For a moment, nothing happens. Then, as if at the pull of an unseen string, four or five bodies pitch forward into the sand. The others collapse sideways or crumple without grace. One man remains upright for a heartbeat, head tilted, then folds over with a slowness that makes her stomach turn.

Blood spreads out from under the bodies, an ooze that glistens black in the first light. The Spanish move in with bayonets, checking each for signs of life. There is little struggle. Two or three of the wounded are finished quickly, a stab or two, then stillness.

Eliza tries to breathe. Her own hands are clawed into the marsh grass so deeply that her fingernails split the stems. Sweat trickles down her spine in cold, abrupt rivers. She wants to look away, to close her eyes and flatten the event into abstraction, but she cannot. She is here for this—has always been here for this.

Apochi watches her. He does not touch her, but his gaze is an anchor. It holds her in the present, keeps her from dissolving into the violence.

The Spanish captain turns and gives another order. A second file of prisoners is dragged forward. This group is smaller, more broken. One of them sobs openly, a choked, animal sound that carries even over the water. Another recites a prayer in a gasping, trembling French; she can make out "Seigneur" and "pitié," words she last heard in a Paris cathedral.

Again, they are forced to kneel. Again, the musketeers raise their weapons. The ritual is identical, but the effect is more terrible for its repetition.

Eliza feels her throat close as the second volley erupts. This time the sound is muffled, as if the air itself is too thick with memory to carry the noise.

The new bodies tumble onto the old. The sand, which was once pale, is now streaked with blood and matter. She notes the way the tide is creeping up the bank, the water already lapping at the feet of the first to die.

One of the French, perhaps delirious, attempts to stand even after being shot. He rises, listing sideways, and staggers two or three steps before a Spanish soldier runs him through with a bayonet. The body sags, hangs for a moment on the steel, then slumps to the sand.

Apochi inhales sharply, the first sign of emotion he has given since it started. Eliza looks at him, then at the scene, then at her own hands—marsh-green, slick with her own sweat, shaking.

She wants to scream. To run. To force the world to notice that this is not an archive, not a ledger, but a thing happening in a morning that will never be rewound.

Instead, she remains in the grass. Her teeth clamp down on

her lip, hard enough to draw blood. She tastes copper, real and now.

The Spanish finish the work. There is no triumph, no gesture of victory. They begin to dig, the officers overseeing the labor with the same detachment they used to manage the execution. The bodies are rolled into a shallow pit, then covered with a hurried layer of sand and shell. A wooden cross is planted at the head of the grave. The gesture is meant as a sign of piety, but Eliza sees it for what it is: a marker for future generations, a warning, a scar.

The prisoners who remain alive are led away, limping, shoulders hunched. Their faces are already blurred by distance and tears.

The inlet remains unchanged moments later. The tide erases the line of footprints. The wind lifts the edge of the Spanish banner; makes it flicker against the sky. Seagulls settle where the men have gone, picking at what is left behind.

Eliza exhales, and the sound is not a sob, not a scream, but something deeper—a sound that carries from her lungs to her knees to the mud under her boots.

Apochi speaks. His voice is so close it vibrates in her bones.

"You see now," he says.

She cannot answer.

"You carry this," he continues, "but it does not belong to you."

She turns, looking at him through a veil of her own sweat. He is not cruel. He is not even distant. He is simply present in a way she will never master.

She thinks of the years ahead—how this morning will be diluted in textbooks, how the names will be reduced to numbers, the numbers to footnotes. She thinks of the bodies, already hidden from view, and how their bones will become the foundation of something that claims to be civilization.

Eliza wants to change it. She wants to step into the sand, to shout at the captain, to throw her own body in front of the muskets and dare the world to write around her.

But she is not a player. She is a lens—a witness. The historian's curse is to see and remember but never to intervene.

She digs her fingers into the marsh grass, one last time, until the pain is sharp enough to remind her that she is real.

The inlet fills with the memory of gunpowder. The blood seeps deeper into the sand.

Apochi does not move, but his hand finds hers, holding it tight, anchoring her to the moment.

And in the long, cruel aftermath, Eliza realizes that her presence does not redeem the dead. It only ensures that they are not erased.

The tide moves up the shore, patient as centuries. The wind smooths the grass. The morning closes itself around the atrocity, indifferent, immutable.

Somewhere in the future, another wall will be built. Another record written. But on this day, in this marsh, the truth is blood and sand and the ache of memory that will not be washed away.

She does not realize she is about to scream until his hand clamps over her wrist.

Apochi's grip is absolute: not angry, not even urgent, but as steady as an anchor set in stone. His palm wraps around her forearm, fingers digging into the hollow above her pulse, and only then does she understand that she is trembling—so badly that the marsh grass shivers with her.

The execution continues below them, a horror so methodical that it warps time. The Spanish reload their muskets, tamp down the charges with elegant, practiced brutality. The officer paces the line, his words clipped and indifferent, the syllables carried by the wind.

Eliza feels her mouth fill with spit and then dries instantly. She wants to move, to shout, to throw herself down the embankment and collapse the line with the force of her presence. She imagines herself running—her feet slapping the wet sand, her voice ragged as she howls at the men to stop, to look, to see themselves as monsters.

But she cannot move. Apochi's grip does not permit it, and even if it did, the logic of the world holds her in place. She is trapped by the knowledge that the record has already been written.

Her pulse is a drumbeat, frantic and arrhythmic, and she digs her other hand into the mud to keep herself from flying apart.

Below, a Spanish soldier misfires. There is a moment of confusion. The captain backhands him, a ringing slap across the helmet, then gestures for another man to take his place. The replacement steps forward, shoulders the musket, and shoots a kneeling Frenchman in the back of the neck at point-blank range. The sound is louder this time, as if the entire inlet has been waiting for the shock.

The remaining prisoners do not scream. Most are in shock, already half-dead from thirst and terror. A few mumble prayers, their voices no longer language but sound, raw and animal. She hears "pitié" again, and "Madre," and "Mon Dieu," but mostly the words melt in the wind.

The Spanish finish the second group, then the third. Each

time, the pattern is the same: kneel, aim, fire, bayonet. The efficiency is not evil. It is worse—it is indifferent.

Eliza's vision blurs at the edges. She cannot tell if she is crying. The salt in her eyes could be sweat, or tears, or the atmosphere itself refusing to yield.

Apochi leans closer. His lips brush her ear, his breath steady and warm against her skin.

"You cannot stop the sea," he whispers.

The words jolt her back. She wants to spit at him, to say that she is not a coward, that standing by is not the same as surrender. But when she looks at his face, she sees no judgment, only a strange mercy—a recognition that survival is sometimes the hardest thing.

"You cannot stop the sea," he says again, softer now, and it is not an admonition. It is a blessing.

The executions end. The sand is thick with blood, mud, and tangled bodies. The Spanish stand in a loose line, breathing heavily, sweat pooling in the hollows of their armor. They wipe their faces, laugh, and spit into the tide.

Apochi releases her arm. The relief is instant, but it is also hollow—her body is so light she feels she might float away.

The soldiers wade into the surf to wash the blood from their hands. One man strips his shirt, scrubs the stains off his arms, then tosses the rag into the water, where it swirls and darkens before sinking.

The officer plants the Spanish banner in the sand. The priests gather the survivors for a final benediction, their voices hoarse and metallic, a parody of comfort in a place where nothing is sacred.

Eliza remains motionless, crouched in the reeds. Her knees

throb. Her hands are numb. She cannot process the details, cannot reduce the horror to data points or narrative.

Apochi is beside her, silent now. His presence is an anchor—one she did not ask for, but cannot refuse.

Below, the Spanish begin to search the bodies. They roll each corpse over, strip it of anything valuable, then use their bayonets to ensure there are no survivors. The sound is different now: a wet, slapping rhythm, punctuated by grunts of effort and the occasional exclamation. The wind carries the smell of salt, gunpowder, scat.

She waits for it to end, but it does not. The men keep working, keep checking, keep digging, as if the only thing that matters is the completeness of the erasure.

At last, the Spanish gather their weapons, form up, and march back toward the encampment. The marsh is silent except for the ceaseless, greedy pulse of the tide.

Eliza straightens, stands, and watches as the water inches higher, tugging at the feet of the dead. The first body is lifted, rolled, and then carried slowly away by the current. The sand, once bright and raw, is smoothed over in minutes. The inlet reclaims what it can.

She cannot look at Apochi. She cannot look at her own hands.

She understands, in this moment, that memory is a violence too. To witness is to absorb, to be marked, to be complicit. She will write about this—will document, will record, will make sure the truth survives—but she will never be able to cleanse the blood from her own memory.

The tide moves in. The footprints are erased. The blood is diluted, then gone.

Eliza stands in the grass, breathing the salt and the silence, and she knows she will never feel clean again.

Beside her, Apochi watches the water reclaim the day. His eyes are not cold. They are not empty. They are alive, refusing to look away.

"You cannot stop the sea," he repeats, one last time.

And she believes him.

Above the inlet, the wind shifts direction. The grass bends low, as if bowing to the inevitability of it all.

Eliza remains there until the sun is overhead and the world is once again what it was before.

But she is not.

Chapter 11: The Unspoken

Eliza & Apochi — 1565

The heat clings longer than the light.

They walk single file along the high tide line, neither bothering to lead. Sunset glimmers against the scum of floating pollen and bottle-green algae, coating everything in a faint bronze. Each of Eliza's steps lifts from the mud with a sucking, reluctant sound. She feels the ache already in her shins, but she doesn't stop, doesn't risk what might happen if she stands still.

Behind them, the thunder of cannon has given way to the smaller violence of night creatures. Bullfrogs resume their endless complaint. Cicadas rally after the day's bombardment, loud enough that when Eliza closes her eyes, the sound blots out even her heartbeat. If she listens for human voices, she can still pick up the echo of the Spanish: drunken song and shouted order, the distant lilt of something between prayer and threat. But here, with the marsh widening out toward the saltwater, the occupation seems far away.

Apochi moves with a ghost's confidence, never quite touching the ground the same way twice. His ankles are streaked with black silt; above the knees, he's scraped raw from rushing through a thicket Eliza could barely push through. He shows no sign of pain. When he glances over his shoulder, the gesture is so small she almost misses it. But she knows he is measuring the distance between themselves and the fort, between herself and wherever she came from.

She is thinking about distance, too. How does it grow in every possible way?

Eventually, the ground grows firmer and the grass shorter, replaced by a margin of crushed oyster shell and gray sand. Here, the world tilts down into a shallow basin, a tidepool scattered with tiny fish and the occasional stranded shrimp. The sun sets in earnest now, a fast, tropical drop that leaves no time for purple or gold. Only the memory of heat persists, radiating up from the stones.

Apochi slows. He picks a spot at the edge of the basin—a flat rock, rounded by a hundred years of storm, its surface warm from storing up the entire day's sun. He folds himself onto it cross-legged, hands resting on his knees as if anchoring himself to the world by touch alone.

Eliza hovers a moment, then crouches low at the water's edge, her boots sinking into the sand with a soft hiss. She dips her fingers into the water. It is as warm as a body, and as alive: something nips at her cuticle, and she jerks her hand away, startled, shaking droplets into the dusk.

Neither one speaks.

Mosquitoes find them, quick and hungry. Apochi does not swat at them, but Eliza slaps at her bare arm, leaving a smear of blood she can't remember drawing.

They sit there for a long time, silent as fossils. Eliza stares at her reflection in the darkening water. The surface gives her nothing back—her face is a blur of motion, a distortion of the dying sky. She thinks of all the things she has witnessed, all the things she has failed to stop. The record growing inside her: men with their bones crushed by stone, boys whipped for clumsiness, birds dying from wounds inflicted only to pass an hour's boredom. And then the quieter deaths, the memory of entire peoples passing without witness.

She tries to think of the world without monuments, without written names. She thinks of what remains, and what is always lost.

Her shoulders drop, her spine slumping. She lets her hand hang in the water until it stops trembling, then speaks.

"I'm not…" she starts, then falters, the language refusing to cooperate. Her voice is hoarse from a day of salt and not enough water. "I'm not fully from here."

She doesn't look at him, but she can sense his attention pivot toward her, a gentler pressure than the air itself.

"I know," Apochi says. Not unkindly. "I knew when I first saw you."

She tries to smile. It's a grimace. "You make it sound simple."

He shakes his head. "No. It is not simple. But it is not strange to me."

The sky is almost black now. Only a band of orange lingers along the horizon, as if a second sun is biding time. The air has grown heavier, if anything; the world is too damp to cool down.

Eliza pulls her hand from the water, watching it drip. She feels each drop as if it weighs more than the finger it leaves behind.

"I thought I could just observe," she says. "That I could be a ghost, a shadow, and then leave."

Apochi is quiet, waiting.

She huffs out a short, bitter laugh. "But everything sticks. The air, the sound, the things I see. I can't—" Her throat tightens. "I can't let it go, not even when I know I'm not supposed to change anything."

He says nothing. The soundscape shifts: a ripple of water, the clack of something hard underfoot, the slap of her own voice against the silence.

"I saw what the Spanish will do," she says. "I know what's going to happen here."

Apochi studies her face as if he could read the script in her eyes. The last sunray snags in the amber flecks of his gaze, lighting them for a heartbeat before they fade to darkness. He does not reach for her. He does not recoil.

"Do you want to stop it?" he asks. The question is simple and not a trap.

She stares into the water, then shakes her head once, sharply. "I wanted to. But I can't. That's not why I was sent."

"Why, then?"

She doesn't have an answer that fits in one language, or any language.

Instead, she shrugs, letting the gesture carry the entire weight.

They listen together to the sound of water licking the edges of stone.

Eventually, Apochi speaks, voice softer than the wind. "Some things are not meant to be stopped. Some things are tide."

She looks at him then, really looks, and finds no judgment—just a steadiness, a patience, a certainty that does not need explanation.

Eliza closes her eyes, exhausted. The mosquitoes hover at her jawline, persistent and mindless.

"Thank you," she says. She isn't sure for what. But it is the only thing she can think to say.

He nods, a movement so gentle it could be the motion of the earth itself, shifting underneath them, bringing the next tide in.

They sit that way for a long time—her hunched over the water, him cross-legged and upright on the stone—both of them waiting for something neither can name, but both can feel.

Above them, the stars begin to reveal themselves, one by one, each a memory of a sun already gone.

The hush thickens as the sun's last warmth bleeds away.

Apochi does not look at Eliza, but she senses he is watching her through the web of reflected stars and motionless air. There is a kindness in his posture: back straight, hands loose and open, the body language of someone inviting confession rather than extracting it.

It is the opposite of every interrogation she's ever faced. There is no intent to conquer in him—just the patience to witness.

When he speaks again, it is so softly that she must lean closer to catch it.

"I saw the storms in your eyes," he says, as if reciting a truth older than language. "From the first moment. You look at this place as if it is already gone."

The words land in the space between them and stay there, unchallenged. Eliza thinks of the way Cartwright had once said her ideas bordered on "regional romanticism," as if an entire coastline of memory could be dismissed as quaint. She wonders how different her career might have been if someone had once allowed the shape of her pain to take up space instead of flattening it beneath a thesis.

"I'm sorry," she says, not knowing if it's for the world, for herself, or for him.

He shrugs. "You do not need to be. Storms come. They do not explain."

She laughs once, briefly and brokenly. "You sound like my advisor," she says. "Except he thought I was the storm."

He considers this, the corners of his mouth hinting at amusement, or perhaps just recognition. "That is not untrue," he says. "But you are not the first storm, or the last."

The reeds sway with the first hint of a night wind. It isn't cooling; it just moves the humidity sideways. A pair of dragonflies collide above the tidepool, entwine for a second, then vanish in opposite directions. The heron stalks through the water, long legs lifting with impossible patience, its head cocked to catch whatever stirs beneath the surface.

Apochi watches the heron, then looks back at Eliza.

"I do not ask where you came from," he says, "because I know you do not wish to say."

She startles at his intuition, unsure whether it's a simple observation or something deeper. "Is it that obvious?" she asks.

He tilts his head, the gesture neither mocking nor pitying. "You name things with your eyes, even when you do not have words. And you carry memory like a shield."

Eliza looks at her hands, then at the scar on his forearm—an old wound, healed unevenly, a record written in flesh. She wants to ask about it, about all the old wars he's already survived, but the question feels selfish.

Instead, she says, "What happens now?"

Apochi draws a line in the wet sand with the heel of his palm, then another that curves around it, like a river meeting the sea.

"Now?" he asks. "We wait for the tide to change. It always does."

He looks up at her, and for the first time, she sees not only patience, but something like acceptance. "You fear for what comes," he says. "You think it is your fault?"

She shakes her head, too fast. "No. I just… I know more than I can say."

He nods, as if this is the most ordinary thing in the world.

"I have lived by the water all my life," he says. "Sometimes the river gives, sometimes it takes. The fish do not know which day will end their life, or which day will give them a feast. But they swim all the same. Because that is what they are."

Eliza listens to the words as if they are being translated from another element, something denser than air.

"I envy that," she admits. "Not thinking about what comes next."

Apochi smiles, and it is not a dismissal. "We think," he says. "We just do not think we can stop the sea."

For a moment, she believes he might be teasing her, but the earnestness in his eyes makes her reconsider. He is not mocking her urge to warn; he is only questioning whether it can make a difference.

The heron stabs downward, draws out a silvery flash, swallows, and resumes its watch.

Eliza feels her own urge rise again—the need to tell him, to warn him that everything he knows will be rewritten by people who think nothing of his existence, that his entire world will be edited out of history by men with a better grasp of narrative and monument.

She opens her mouth to speak.

He is closer than she expects. His hand lifts, slow enough that she could refuse, but she does not. He places one finger gently against her lips, the touch featherlight, a gesture not of silence but of kindness.

He shakes his head once.

"Some things are not meant to be spoken," he says, his voice so low that it is barely audible over the water.

She closes her mouth, feels the touch linger even after he lowers his hand.

They watch the heron together as it walks the length of the tidepool, purposeful and inscrutable.

For a long time, neither says anything.

At last, he rises from the stone, standing over her but not imposing. "We move with the tide," he says. "Come."

He starts walking, slow and deliberate, and she follows, feeling the mud cling to her boots, the water warm against her calves.

The stars multiply overhead, indifferent to everything below.

Behind them, the heron takes flight, its wings cutting the dusk in a single clean arc.

The darkness softens the boundaries between land and water, body and shadow.

They walk for a time along the shore, the mud cool beneath their feet, until the reeds grow too dense and Apochi stops. He motions for Eliza to join him on a slab of driftwood lodged at the edge of a shallow inlet, half-buried by a century of tide. She sits beside him, closer than before, the space between their knees barely the width of a palm.

Night gathers fast. The air is thick with the scent of damp and the constant whine of insects. But the worst of the mosquitoes has receded, replaced now by a softer, persistent buzzing—less an assault, more an ambient hum.

Eliza draws her knees to her chest, wrapping her arms around them. She feels the heat of Apochi beside her, his presence as tangible as the rough grain of the wood beneath her. The silence between them is no longer heavy, but alive—saturated with all the words neither can say.

They watch as the sky empties itself of color, and the stars begin to map their slow, meticulous geometry across the dome of night. The longer Eliza looks, the more she recognizes—the familiar constellations, the stubborn presence of Polaris, the unyielding logic of celestial navigation. She wonders what the stars will look like to him, whether he sees them as fixed or restless, friend or foe.

Apochi is the first to speak, voice low, meant only for her. "You watch the sky as if you could change it by looking," he says. Not a criticism. Not quite a compliment, either.

She smiles, rolling her forehead against her knees. "I wish I could," she admits. "Sometimes I wish I could just… undo what comes next."

He glances at her, then at the water, then at her again. His hair has dried in wild, uneven strands, fanning out behind him like the roots of a mangrove. He looks less like a ghost now, more like a man who has always belonged to this place and this hour.

He reaches for something beside him, a long blade of marsh grass, and spins it between his fingers with idle precision. "The sky does not care," he says. "It remembers everything, but it does not mourn."

Eliza considers this. "Are you saying we shouldn't mourn?"

He shakes his head. "We mourn. But it does not stop the next day from coming."

A heron calls once, distant, and the echo bounces off the water. The sound is mournful, but not defeated.

She looks at him then, really looks, and sees the gold again in his eyes—a trace of sunset preserved, refusing to dissolve. The silence turns charged.

Without warning, a tear escapes down her cheek, hot and unfamiliar. She hadn't realized she was crying.

Apochi notices. He sets down the marsh grass and leans toward her, his thumb tracing the line of the tear before it reaches her jaw. The touch is so gentle it feels almost imaginary.

He does not remove his hand. Instead, his palm cradles her

cheek, warm and rough.

"The storms in your eyes have grown deeper since I first saw you," he says. "But you see more, too."

She closes her eyes, letting herself rest against his touch. Her breathing slows, steadies.

He moves his thumb in a small, absent circle just beneath her cheekbone. "I have seen many storms," he says. "But never one that tried to hold itself still."

She laughs, or tries to, but the sound catches in her throat and comes out as a gasp.

He pulls her in, not forceful, but as if they are both part of the same inevitable motion—the way the tide gathers the debris of a hundred broken things and arranges them, for a moment, into a new pattern.

Their faces are close, not quite touching. His breath smells of salt and river mint; hers of adrenaline and loss. She feels the line between them go thin and bright, like a filament drawn tight by the weight of what cannot be spoken.

He kisses her, once, at the corner of her mouth. Not a claim. Not even a beginning. Just a moment out of time.

Eliza opens her eyes and finds him still there, watching her.

"I will remember you," she says, and is surprised by the certainty in her own voice.

He nods. "And I will remember you," he answers.

They say nothing else for a long time.

Around them, the marsh slips into a quieter register. The frogs go silent, the wind falls, the water calms to a mirror.

On the far horizon, a faint line of torchlight glows—Spanish camp, distant but insistent, a border of fire pushing back against the vastness of dark.

Eliza wonders how many nights she will have like this. How many before the world reclaims its narrative and she must return, no longer allowed the comfort of being a ghost.

She doesn't want to think about it, so she lets herself lean into Apochi's shoulder, feeling the solid warmth, the grounding reality of muscle and skin.

He wraps his arm around her, not as possession, but as acknowledgment. They fit together awkwardly, perfectly, the way two broken things sometimes do.

Above them, the stars burn on—unmoved by tragedy, unimpressed by love, relentless in their willingness to be remembered.

At the edge of the inlet, the heron returns. It lands in silence, folding itself into the reeds, patient for whatever morning brings.

They stay this way until the torches dwindle and the sky pales with the promise of another day.

Chapter 12: 1763

Eliza POV — British Florida

The Lantern Array does not warn her before it ruptures.

One instant: Eliza stands in a corridor of coquina, the ancient stone humming with the pulse of an entire city's memory. The next, the world buckles sideways—vision shredding into slivers, sound telescoping into a single, blood-shearing note. Her balance goes first. Knees buckle, hips collapse, the self she knows scattering and then slamming back together in a body that isn't hers but is, cell for cell, the same.

She vomits memory into the dirt before she's even fully reassembled.

There is no gentle fade. There is only the liquid violence of arrival: her molecules packing themselves into place with a pressure so intense her teeth hurt. She tastes copper, bile, and the high, burning chemical of her own fear. The air is different—lighter, full of camphor and sea grass, wind laced with the raw sugar stink of distant fire.

She scrapes herself off the ground and staggers. Her palm slams into a wall.

It is the same wall she's always known, the Castillo's face: coquina, pocked with the blunt memory of three centuries' worth of siege. But the wall no longer wears the red crosses and Catholic iconography of Spanish command. The paint is gone, or—no, not gone, just overtopped. A new insignia blooms over the stone: the Royal Arms of Great Britain, freshly stenciled, blue and gold as a bruise.

She pants, sucking oxygen in hard gasps. Her vision sizzles at the edges. Spots crowd in, then recede. Her boots are soaked from the knee down. She looks, and her clothing—the field kit, the woven belt scavenged from 1565—remains. Even the compass at her throat is still there, its laminated case now fractured, water pooled beneath the surface. It is possible, she thinks, that she is dying. The boundaries between times have never liked her much, and now they are actively seeking revenge.

She closes her eyes and flattens her other hand against the coquina, feeling the sugar-cube roughness of shell and stone. It is the only thing that makes sense. She catalogues the wall—sized pores, the variance of grain, the faint warmth it has stolen from the sun. If the universe wishes to come apart, she will go down counting every layer.

Her breath finds a rhythm. Not normal, but less panicked.

She blinks open her eyes. The city is silent—no Spanish voices, no chants, no rattle of prayer. Instead, the low, professional cadence of English orders barked in the clipped rhythm of military occupation. A red-coated sentry passes by, muskets slung loose, the man too bored or tired to notice a new arrival slumped against the wall. The scent of rum and tallow hangs on him as he disappears down the avenue.

She tries to catalog. Tries to understand.

She is in St. Augustine, but it is not the same city she left.

She looks up. Flags whip in the breeze, the Union Jack everywhere she expects the Lion and Castle. The Castillos' upper tier bristles with cannon—fewer than the Spanish kept, but cleaner, newer, as if re-inherited. She touches the compass at her chest; it leaks, a dampness pooling at her collarbone.

The world tilts again, and she nearly falls, catching herself by digging her fingers into the grout of the wall.

She's aware, dimly, that she should be more afraid. That the Lantern Array, wherever it is, has not just phased her forward in time but shattered every rule of containment and recovery. But her mind, always a triage machine, chooses instead to fixate on details: the lime in the mortar, the absence of salt rot, the way the stone seems to have been scrubbed clean of its past as if history could be erased by mere effort.

She catalogues the loss. The shift. The fact that every inch of the fort's old grandeur now belongs to an empire that doesn't even remember what it stole.

She wonders, for a brief and disloyal moment, if anyone remembers her.

Then she steadies herself, breathes, and catalogues the feeling of survival.

She is alive. She is anchored.

She is not sure for how long.

She pulls herself upright, one hand braced against the wall, the other clutching the damaged compass so hard the edges cut into her palm.

If this is 1763, the year the city is handed to the British, then nothing she knows applies. She is a woman in a century that does not want her.

She looks at the wall and wonders how many layers it can bear.

She moves forward, joints creaking, breath still ragged, but already the historian in her is awake and cataloguing. Already she is preparing to observe, to remember, to bear witness even as the world tries to overwrite itself around her.

She walks, because standing still is not an option.

She walks, because it is the only thing that has ever worked.

She walks, and with every step, the city rearranges itself—history piling atop history, each layer less stable than the last.

She keeps her hand on the wall, as if she could absorb the memory of the stone into her bones.

She suspects she will need it.

She slips through the city as a shadow.

The streets of St. Augustine have shed their skin overnight. Gone are the strutting hidalgos, the Franciscan brown robes, the quick, suspicious glances of a Spanish military colony forever expecting siege. In their place: redcoats. English voices, clipped and cold. The syllables punch through the humidity with an efficiency she has never heard in this latitude.

She keeps to the edges, letting the city's new order arrange itself around her.

First, the plaza. Where once the benches were filled with Spanish officials, now English officers occupy the shade, tricorns cocked at aggressive angles, muskets resting in the crooks of their arms. Their skin is already sunburnt, as if Florida rejects their northern blood. She catalogues the ranks and insignia, noting the light blue sashes of the Highland regiments—Scots, mostly, conscripted or exiled by force of empire. They watch the square with wary pride, as if daring the past to reclaim its ground.

She keeps her eyes down and walks with purpose, the way servants or laborers do. The compass at her throat is tucked under the collar, water still seeping from its edge, cool against her skin. Her field pack is heavier now—sodden and smelling faintly of marsh, a relic from a century prior that would raise questions if anyone cared to look.

No one does. The city is too busy changing hands.

Down the side street, she finds what she is looking for: the slow-motion exodus. Spanish families, stripped of authority and now only citizens, are packing what remains of their lives into crates and barrels. Everything not essential is abandoned—furniture left on the curb, religious icons tucked hastily into straw, letters bundled in twine and crammed between linens. A girl of perhaps twelve lifts a caged canary onto a cart already stacked with household goods. The bird sings, oblivious.

A boy, not much older, follows with a box labeled "La Habana." Eliza feels the old anger spark—how history always makes the winners architects, the losers cargo.

A woman, mother or aunt, wipes her eyes and repeats, "Dios

nos proteja en Cuba. Dios nos proteja." The prayer is a threadbare blanket.

Eliza wants to help. To say something. But she is an echo in a century that cannot hear her.

A British officer rounds the corner, boots striking the cobble with theatrical authority. "Clear this street for His Majesty's regiment," he barks, voice seasoned with the threat of power. He glances at the Spanish family and sneers, then signals the redcoats behind him. The soldiers move with mechanical precision, shunting civilians aside with their musket stocks.

Eliza tenses. Her body folds itself small. She steps back into the lee of a stone arch and catalogues:

—Spanish faces tight with fear, jaws set for endurance.

—Redcoat uniforms already fraying at the cuffs.

—Bundles of dried orange peel, a last taste of the old world.

—A girl, no more than eight, clutching a half-burnt candle as if it might re-light all that has gone dark.

She blinks, and the image is burned in, catalogued for some future that might care.

At the intersection, a church bell rings. She recognizes the sound—not the smooth bronze chime of the Spanish mission, but a duller, heavier clang. The church has been re-dedicated to the Anglican rite, its saints banished, the altar stripped to bare stone. The congregation now files in on Sunday mornings with less color, more obligation. She records the difference in sound, in gait, in the weight of unshared tradition.

As she moves deeper into the city, she notes the subtle acts of resistance: a Spanish flag, hastily painted over but still ghosting beneath the new British coat of arms; a child scraping at the paint with a flat stone, drawing out the old crest in secret. In a doorway, an old man carves a small cross into the jamb, then covers it with mud—memory, hidden but persistent.

She turns a corner and nearly collides with a pair of British marines. The men pause, take her in—a woman, alone, with clothing more suited to another world. For a moment, she is exposed. Her pulse hammers in her neck.

One of the marines' grins, showing a mouthful of bad teeth. "A bit far from the wash house, aren't you?"

She lowers her head, mutters in broken English, "Errand for the rector," and pushes past. Her accent is not perfect, but in this city of transitions, no one expects perfection.

They let her go.

She presses on.

At the city gate, she finds a line of wagons—Spanish, French, and a few Creoles. The exiles shuffle toward the future, eyes fixed on the ground or the horizon. The British sentry at the gate checks their passes, scrawls a note in a ledger, then waves them on. The process is slow, bureaucratic, and dehumanizing.

One family is turned away—their pass is not in order. The father argues, voice rising, hands shaking. The sentry remains unmoved. After a brief standoff, the family retreats, huddling at the roadside, unsure where to go. Eliza notes the father's posture: defiant until the last, then folding inward, protecting his children from what comes next.

She thinks of the Timucua, of Apochi, and the layers of erasure that always precede the next regime. Her hands tremble. She grips the compass so hard her palm aches.

She circles back toward the plaza, the heart of the city. There, the British Governor stands on the steps of the former Spanish courthouse, reading a proclamation to a small, mostly indifferent crowd. His voice is sonorous, heavy with self-importance.

"...by authority of His Britannic Majesty, this city is henceforth governed by the laws and customs of England. All residents will swear allegiance or be subject to removal..."

Eliza catalogues:

—The awkward fit of English power in Spanish architecture.

—The new flags, stitched hastily, colors bleeding in the damp.

—The blank faces of men who have changed allegiances more than once, and will do so again.

—A woman, old and veiled, spitting at the ground as the proclamation ends.

She could fill a notebook with what goes unseen: the ledger entries changed, the prayers unsaid, the loss that lingers in the air like gunpowder after a failed volley.

A redcoat passes too close. She flinches, but the man does not notice. To him, she is already part of the background.

For a brief moment, she hates the historian's discipline—the oath not to interfere, only to observe, to bear witness, but never leave a mark. She wants to disrupt something, to remind the world that it does not change cleanly, that every layer of paint leaves its own residue.

Instead, she walks.

Past the plaza, through the gate, into the open. She finds the old fort at the edge of town, its walls now draped in the British banner, cannons aimed not at the sea but at the city itself—a reminder to the conquered that submission is the first and last duty.

She sits at the base of the wall, knees pulled to her chest, breathing the salt and stone, cataloguing the ache in her bones.

She is alone, truly alone, in a century that is neither hers nor anyone's.

She closes her eyes and listens to the voices echo down the avenue: Spanish, English, and all the lost languages in between.

She lets herself catalog the grief, too.

And when she stands, she does so with the certainty that memory is not passive, that to observe is to hold the world in place for just a heartbeat longer than it would have survived on its own.

She moves forward.

The city shifts around her, layer by layer.

The interior of the chapel is all wrong.

She sits at the rear, on a hard, unfamiliar bench, watching the space misremember itself. The pews—recently installed, the wood raw and splintery—are packed with British colonists who smell of wool and sweetened tobacco. Their faces are fresh imports, pale and angular, eyes fixed on the altar with the blankness of obedience, not faith. The old congregation has been erased. No veils, no mantillas, no humid crush of candle smoke, only the clean, rectangular lines of Protestant utility.

Above, the walls are stripped bare. Every niche that once cradled a saint's effigy is patched with lime and whitewash—no stations of the cross, no Madonnas, no bleeding Christ. The only cross is a plain one, made from two beams, hung askew above the altar like an afterthought.

The singing is unfamiliar. Eliza catalogs the hymn as it struggles to fill the vault: the melody is thin, a single voice raised, and the rest forced to follow. The words are in English, but the cadence is wrong for the echo of the room.

"Our help is in the Lord, who made heaven and earth..."

No one harmonizes. No one weeps. The sound is too orderly, too thin to make a dent in the heavy air.

The minister stands at the front, stiff in a black robe that could have belonged to a Spanish priest if not for the starched Protestant collar. His sermon is brief, dense with legal language: "...God's providence in delivering this territory from popish superstitions... the righteousness of His Majesty's rule... the duty of every Christian soul to honor the new order..."

She has heard these sermons before, in every century. The content is always the same—only the accent changes.

Her hands drift to the surface of the pew, feeling the wood grain, rough as unplaned memory. She runs her thumb over a small knot, then glances down: someone has scratched a name here, hastily, in the soft pine. The letters are Spanish, even though the hand that wrote them is gone.

She looks up. The ceiling is a barrel vault, with old cedar beams left from the original church. The Protestants have not yet gotten around to replacing it. The wood darkens with age, and in the right light, she can almost see the smoke stains from candles that no longer burn.

She closes her eyes and imagines the space as it was: a crush of bodies, air thick with incense, the Latin mass washing over believers who recited by rote. A city believing itself eternal.

She opens her eyes. The new congregation fidgets. Several children are present, their feet unable to reach the floor, kicking the air in time with the dull beat of the preacher's voice. She catalogs their clothing, the cut of their coats and frocks, the way their mothers nudge them into stillness.

Behind her, the doors remain propped open, letting in a draft that smells of brine and the sharp undertone of foreign gunpowder. She notes that, too.

When the service ends, the congregation files out in orderly lines. A man with a blue sash helps his wife to her feet, then steers her toward the door without a glance at the altar. The children spill into the aisle, shoving each other in the race for daylight. There are no prayers at the end, no lingering at the rail—the space empties with the efficiency of a military parade.

Eliza stays behind. She walks the length of the chapel, cataloguing the details. She crouches at the altar, fingers tracing the chisel marks where the old Spanish carving has been hacked away. She lingers at the walls, searching for old paint beneath new lime. Near the front, she finds a patch where the whitewash has already begun to crack, exposing a faint halo of blue pigment: the sky behind a vanished saint.

She wonders what the English will do when the lime sloughs off and the old art returns.

She wonders if they will paint over it again or look away.

She sits on the altar steps, listening to the echo of the empty chapel. In the silence, she hears the persistence of memory—the way the old rituals claw their way to the surface, refusing to be erased. She wonders if that is what she is, now: a fragment of something that no longer fits, refusing to fade.

She stands.

On her way out, she touches the edge of the nave, palm pressed to the seam where two centuries meet. She feels a tremor, a barely perceptible pulse. For a moment, she thinks she can sense all the hands that have touched this wall, all the prayers and curses and vows it has absorbed.

She steps outside.

The light is blinding, the plaza almost empty now. The air is cooler than before, as if the city is exhaling after the service's forced reverence.

She walks around the side of the chapel to the corner where the British coat of arms has been carved into the coquina. The edges are sharp, the emblem fresh. But beneath it, the stone still holds the faded trace of the Spanish crest. She traces the old lines with her finger, careful not to draw attention.

Just below the crest, someone has etched a date: "1565," the city's founding, half-obscured by the British markings. She runs her thumb over the numbers, grounding herself in the knowledge that no empire, no matter how meticulous, can fully erase the memory it has chosen to overwrite.

She steps back and looks at the wall as a whole: a palimpsest, one authority written atop another, each layer a record of both power and loss.

For a moment, she feels the fracture inside her line up perfectly with the one in the stone.

She is not of this time. She is not of any time. She is the space between layers, the margin where all the meanings bleed together.

She turns away, feeling both lighter and more burdened.

She walks because there is only one direction: forward.

And as the shadows lengthen in the plaza, she knows she will remember every detail—the splintered pew, the chipped paint, the voices in the wrong language—and that somewhere, in the sediment of centuries, the memory of what was will survive the command to forget.

Chapter 13: Collapse Warning

Gabe POV — 2026

Gabe sits alone beneath a million tons of historical gravity.

The control chamber is never silent, not even at midnight. The Lantern Array breathes through the coquina like a body in fever: a constant, low-pitched pulse that thrums in the soles of your shoes and the roots of your teeth. On nights like this, the stone vibrates faintly under Gabe's hand where it rests on the console, absorbing the hum and transforming it into something almost sentient. The air smells of ozone and limestone and the ghost of brine from the long-dry moat above.

He watches the monitors with the attention of a man tracking both a lover and a live wire. Each panel throws a different slice of data—bio-signature overlay, phase coherence graphs, historical resonance heat maps, and a real-time neural telemetry feed that maps Eliza's mind through the centuries. The first time he saw it all lit up, he thought it looked like the world's most complicated EKG. Now it's just her pulse, amplified across five hundred years.

For hours, she holds steady in 1565. Her waveform sits like a well-anchored buoy, undisturbed by the normal quantum drift. He checks her location every twelve minutes: stable within a kilometer of St. Augustine's founding latitude and longitude. Her vitals stay within range—higher than baseline, but not alarming. Neural readout suggests REM sleep, or the closest approximation available to a mind adrift in a sixteenth-century marsh.

He almost allows himself to unclench.

Then, at 01:47 local, the first spike hits.

It's so abrupt, he hears it before he sees it—an electrical pop through the chamber's sound system. This stutter ripples through the Array and sets the overhead fluorescents into a momentary shiver. On the main panel, her bio-signature jumps three standard deviations off its axis, oscillating like a plucked string.

He blinks hard, reloads the visualization, and rechecks the diagnostics. Not a glitch. The signal is robust, but now it vibrates at a new harmonic—something not accounted for in his last 10 models.

"Shit," he mutters, and punches up the raw log.

The trace is clear: Eliza's position bounces, microseconds apart, from 1565 to a flashpoint in 1763—then 1821, then 1861, and then, impossibly, to 1964—before snapping back to her initial location. The transitions are so fast they leave an afterimage across the display, a quantum echo like a skipped heartbeat.

Gabe's fingers move on the interface before he's finished cursing. He brings the Array's feedback loop into sharper focus, narrowing the error margin and running a full self-check of phase stability. The machine's hum grows louder, the stone vibrating hard enough that he feels it through the seat of his pants. Warning overlays begin layering onto the display: PHASE CONFLICT, HARMONIC RESONANCE BREACH, BIO-SIGNATURE VARIANCE ABOVE THRESHOLD.

He toggles the environmental overlay. The local field is as stable as ever. The problem is not the Array. The problem is her.

He whispers, "Come on, Eliza," to the empty room.

He tries three different stabilization routines in sequence: increasing field density, decreasing it, then staggering the harmonic to ride out the spike. The first two do nothing. The third slows the flicker, but each temporal rebound returns more violently, sending alerts in shrill, overlapping tones.

On the second monitor, her neural telemetry is peaking—cortisol surge, spike in adrenaline, then a moment of paradoxical calm. He recognizes it as the pattern she shows right before taking a professional risk. He remembers the Boston conference. He remembers the moment she called out the entire field for its blindness. That same signature: terror, then the calculated clarity of someone about to gamble everything.

He tries to reset the buffer. The interface refuses. For a split second, the Array's visualizer flashes a warning he has never seen before: ANCHOR POINT UNRESOLVED.

He tries to ignore the sweat forming under his glasses, on his brow, beneath his arms. "Come on, come on—" he chants softly, an absurd prayer to a goddess of logic.

In desperation, he reroutes the Array's power from the secondary stack, pulling energy away from non-critical systems. The chamber lights dim, then flicker in time with the spikes on her feed.

The stone at his elbow is warm, almost feverish.

Through it all, the hum never ceases. It only modulates, rising in pitch, as if the entire Castillo were singing its own warning.

He isolates the oscillation to a set of historical vectors. Every bounce lands on a documented trauma: the Spanish founding, the British handover, the American takeover, the Civil War blockade, the 1964 Civil Rights riot. He watches as her consciousness, or whatever remains of it, skips across these moments like a flat stone.

He realizes, with a clarity so cold it burns, that the celebration above—the endless festival of 250 years—has created a resonance so intense that it's pulling her across every commemorated version of the city at once.

"It's the party," he says, to nobody, to the walls, to the ghosts in the Array. "It's the confounded commemoration."

The next spike is even stronger. The Array draws power so aggressively that the air ionizes, the fluorescent fixtures flickering so fast it feels like daylight on a bad trip.

He's running out of time.

He pulls up her last recorded message, an audio log she left before the jump. It's her voice, steady, professional, threaded with the affection she never admitted outside a crisis: "If anything goes wrong, you know what to do, Gabe. Don't save me if it means losing the city."

He hates her for saying it. He loves her for meaning it.

He adjusts the input feed, trying to match the waveforms to the schedule of events above. He overlays the timeline of the Fourth of July celebration—parades, church bells, Civil Rights reenactment, sunrise at the Castillo. Each event lines up with a harmonic surge in the Array.

He curses again, loudly, knowing the sound will not echo beyond the coquina.

He tries to reset to the last clean checkpoint. The system locks him out—her bio-signature is no longer a single point. It's now five points, pulling equally on the Array, threatening to rip the whole structure apart from the inside out.

He tries to imagine how it feels for her: the world flickering between centuries, senses fractured by the weight of too much memory, too little time.

He tries to imagine losing her. The thought almost ruins him.

The only thing left is the last-resort option: force the Array to pick a single anchor, to collapse all possible versions of the city into one. It's a brute-force solution, risky, potentially catastrophic. If the wrong period dominates, she could be lost entirely. Or worse, overwrite the present with a new past.

He sits, staring at the prompt, sweat freezing on his upper lip.

The coquina wall hums under his touch, asking him to choose.

He types in the command string. His hands are steady, but his heart isn't. He primes the system, ready to activate at the first sign of complete signal loss.

He waits. The hum of the Array builds to a whine, almost musical. The lights pulse with it. Above, a test firework goes off, the sound leaking through stone and history—a muffled boom, and then silence.

The display steadies for a second. Her signature stabilizes in one epoch—1964, the year of the Civil Rights riot.

He sees the note in the margin of the log, a timestamped

annotation from Eliza herself: "Remember the lost names."

He almost sobs.

The next spike is due in ten seconds, when the fireworks finale will test the city grid.

He braces both hands on the console.

"Come on, Eliza," he whispers again, eyes fixed on the display. "Find your anchor point."

The timer counts down.

Nine. Eight. Seven. Six.

The walls begin to tremble. The machinery's hum is deafening.

Five. Four. Three.

His thumb hovers over the EXECUTE button.

Two.

He wonders if she can hear him.

One.

He presses.

The world outside goes blinding white for half a second, as if every year of the city's existence flares at once. Then the hum collapses to silence.

On the main monitor, a single bio-signature glows: 2026, present day, St. Augustine.

He scans the room, wild-eyed, lungs burning. The machinery powers down slowly, the lights returning to normal. The coquina wall under his hand cools.

On the display, her neural feed returns to baseline. Heart rate elevated, but regular.

He slumps forward, arms wrapped around the monitor as if it's the only thing keeping him upright.

"You did it," he croaks, his voice wrecked.

He looks around, half expecting her to materialize beside him, wild hair and all.

But the chamber is empty, save for the fading echo of the Array, the distant sound of the city above, and the steady blue pulse on the monitor that means, for now, she is home.

The chamber does not go silent; it transitions to aftermath.

Gabe lets the chair roll back from the console, the plastic wheels grinding softly against centuries-old limestone. He blinks hard, vision rimmed with a headache bright enough to paint the air. His wrists ache from hours at the interface, but he does not unclench. Instead, he scans the auxiliary monitors, looking for ripples—changes, artifacts, ghosts.

They appear almost instantly.

On the far-left screen, the St. Augustine Municipal Record Archive flickers through a checksum cycle. For one frame, a plaque dedication for the 1964 Monson Motor Lodge reads: "Site of peaceful protest." Next, it says: "Site of incident, details unknown." On another, the 1821 transfer of the Castillo is signed not by the expected American officer, but by a Spanish functionary whose name should have disappeared a generation earlier. Even the earliest records—baptisms, burials, land grants—mutate as he watches, the names shifting by a letter, a syllable, a lineage.

He swallows, dry-mouthed. He knows what this means.

The Array had not simply anchored Eliza to a point in time; it had caught her in the undertow of the city's own memory—each commemorative act aboveground sending a shockwave through the resonance field, each ritual remembrance jostling her anchor. The temporal instability was not random. It was the city's own identity crisis, playing out in every parade, every plaque, every tour group reciting a different version of the past.

He pulls up the master event schedule for the Semiquincentennial: sunrise mass at the Cathedral, a lunch-hour cannonade at the Castillo, historic reenactments in every public park, a civil rights march restaged along King Street, fireworks over Matanzas Bay. Each moment is designed to summon, if only for a heartbeat, the past into the present.

He overlays these on the time-resonance graph. Every spike in the Array corresponds to a major event above. The worse the overlap—say, a church bell tolling at the same moment a reenactor fires a musket—the more intense the phase breach.

Gabe leans forward, elbows on the console, knuckles white. "It's the celebration," he says, barely louder than the hum. "All those overlapping commemorations are tugging at her."

The walls seem to agree. The coquina pulses in time with the warning pings—each low vibration a physical reminder of the city's age and the sediment of its memory. He stands, approaches the rough-hewn wall, and presses his palm flat against it. The stone is warm and vibratory, as if the entire city were trying to tell him something in a language older than Spanish, Timucua, or English.

Another warning pops up: PHASE ALIGNMENT UNSTABLE.

He imagines Eliza caught in the turbulence—every reenacted history a gravitational pull, every lost name a weight added to her. She would be seeing not just one city, but every city layered atop itself, every memory crowding for primacy.

He imagines her alone, holding to the last fact that might save her: that names matter. That remembering is a form of survival.

The stone thrums under his hand, stronger now, the rhythm matching his own pulse. For a second, he feels as if he could fall forward through the wall and land somewhere else—another year, another memory, another version of himself, one who never let go.

He steadies himself.

He knows what he has to do next, even if it terrifies him.

He drags his hand down the wall, feeling the grit of dead creatures and lost voices packed into every inch. "Hold on," he says, not knowing if he's talking to Eliza or to the city or to himself. "Just a little longer."

On the monitors, the records continue to rewrite themselves, history bleeding forward and back in fits and starts. But through it all, one line holds steady—a single, unaltered blue pulse, like a beacon.

He breathes in the charged air and returns to the console.

He has a decision to make.

The final interface is a flat black slab, designed to eliminate hesitation. But Gabe hesitates anyway.

The dual-authorization console sits flush with the old stone, a deliberate reminder of how little separates the present from the past. He places both hands on the touch sensors, waiting for the system to recognize his bio-signature. The room's light drops an octave, every source dimming to a bloodred throb. Above the slab, two virtual keys glow: REINFORCE and RECALL.

He imagines the other hand on the console—the one the Array was calibrated for, the one meant to work in tandem with his. Eliza's print is there, invisible but persistent, a quantum echo like everything else about her.

He knows the theory. Reinforcement will commit the Array's energy to keeping her stable wherever she lands. Recall will initiate forced reentry, locking onto her bio-signature and dragging her back to the present, regardless of intervening physics. The risks are clear: forced recall during phase instability could shatter her body, scatter her memories, even erase the last anchor she has in this time.

He stares at the two choices, his reflection split by the slab's obsidian surface. For the first time in his life, data is not enough.

He reviews the telemetry—her jumps, her dwell times, the brief windows where her pulse and neural pattern lock into coherence. Every one of those moments corresponds to a name, a face, a fragment of human history: the priest who took the confession of a dying rebel, the child who led a protest march on King Street, the laborer who built the coquina wall but died unnamed. Every time Eliza's pattern stabilizes, it's because she has made contact with another person, or with the memory of one. She doesn't just observe history—she connects to it.

"You were right," he says, voice barely above the hum. "It's the emotional component. The Array responds to connection, not just physics."

He thinks about what that means. If he trusts her to find her own anchor, she might land somewhere survivable. If he tries to drag her back, he risks destroying the very thing he's trying to save.

For a second, he almost laughs. It's so obvious. He has spent his life reinforcing systems, defending against chaos, building layers of protection around everything and everyone he loves. Eliza, for all her radical theory and reckless optimism, had always been the one willing to risk erasure for a chance at something permanent.

He looks at the virtual keys again. His thumb hovers, then drops to the console. He inputs a sequence—neither full recall nor raw reinforcement, but a threshold adjustment, a way to let her signal run just loose enough to settle itself.

The Array recognizes the override. The red lights fade to amber. The warning pings drop in frequency, then resolve to a single, steady pulse.

He sits back in the chair, breathless. The room feels lighter, or maybe it's just the absence of imminent disaster.

On the main monitor, her bio-signature lands and holds. Not in the present. Not in 1565. But at a fixed point, unspooling in real time, as if she has found the one moment where every version of St. Augustine can exist together.

He watches as her neural feed stabilizes, heart rate smoothing to a near-perfect rhythm. The monitor paints her signature in gold and blue, an anomaly in the data that doesn't scare him this time. It feels, in some way, like music.

He whispers, "Find your way home," and lets his hand rest on the console, unwilling to break the connection.

He closes his eyes, just for a moment, and in the dark behind his eyelids, he can almost see her—not as a point on a map, but as a person, vivid and complicated and anchored in the exact way she had always wanted to be.

When he opens his eyes again, the room is calm. The Array

glows steadily, the stone silent. The world above prepares for another dawn, the city unaware that its own memory has been, for a breath, held in the balance.

Gabe sits back, shoulders slumping with exhaustion, and watches the monitors. The moment stretches, quiet and unbroken.

He has made his decision.

He will trust her to navigate the storm.

He will not recall.

He will wait.

And when the time comes—when the tides align, when the city has finished telling its story—he will be here to greet her, whether in this life or in the only place that matters: the place where memory becomes real.

Chapter 14: 1821

Eliza POV — American Florida

Eliza arrives in 1821 with the distinct sensation of having fallen up rather than down—a vertigo compounded by the clatter of boots, voices, and the sudden verticality of banners snapping in humid wind. St. Augustine's Plaza de la Constitución opens around her like a bloom in too-bright light: palm trees trimmed, the central gazebo lacquered with fresh whitewash, the square swept clean of anything but history and anticipation.

She wavers; one hand braced on a coquina wall still slick from morning mist. It is the same stone as always, but the air is different—less salt, more tobacco; less rot, more the anxious sweat of men who know they are being watched by a ledger that will outlive them. Her other hand, automatic, checks for the notebook at her hip. The weight is there, blessedly, and she steadies herself.

Across the plaza, a wooden platform has been raised above the flagstones, its planks barely concealing the fresh mud underneath. The platform is draped with a blue banner, one half given to the gold and red of Spain, the other to the crisp, theoretical stars of the United States. On the platform, a line of Spanish officials in blue dress uniforms faces a contingent of Americans so new their boots are still light in color, the leather unscuffed by use or guilt.

Governor José Coppinger, slight and severe, stands at parade rest on the Spanish side. He looks straight ahead, chin set at an angle that says he is already thinking of the next assignment, or the passage home, or perhaps simply the sweet inertia of never having to hear English spoken with a southern accent again. Opposite him is Colonel Robert Butler, the American Commissioner, taller by half a head and already glistening with sweat. Butler's coat is tailored for a narrower man and strains at the buttons each time he inhales for emphasis. The two men are close enough to touch. Still, their hands remain occupied: Coppinger with a velvet pouch of iron keys, Butler with a scroll of official documents he keeps trying to flatten and read, as if their weight alone will manifest the authority they claim.

Spanish infantry stands in neat rows in front of the platform. Their uniforms are battered, the blue dulled nearly to gray in the summer light, but each soldier's boots are shined, and their hats perched at an identical, defiant angle. Some of the men are local recruits, their skin darkened by the same sun that will soon burn them as exiles. Others are veterans from Havana, sent to ensure the proper ceremonial gravity. Their faces are masks of stoicism, but Eliza notes the way some steal glances at the Spanish flag overhead, the tremble in the jaw of the youngest private at the end of the row.

In counterpoint, the American troops are arrayed to the right of the platform. Their uniforms are lighter in fabric and brighter in color; the white stripes and blue coats look almost gaudy against the weathered stone and the city's earth tones. Their posture is less rigid, a parade-ground discipline that still leaves room for curiosity—one sergeant, barely shaving age, keeps sneaking looks at the local women gathered in the shade of the plaza's edge, who in turn observe him as one might a new species of bird.

The crowd is dense at the plaza's edge. Spanish families gather in tight clusters: the women in black mantillas, faces pale and closed, the men somber and stubbled, eyes fixed on the ritual unfolding at the platform. The children watch everything, wide-eyed and unblinking, as if memorizing the new world for later. Behind them, the city's free blacks and Seminole traders stand in loose groups, cautious but attentive. A few newly arrived American merchants hover at the margins, already assessing the angles of the plaza and the quality of the storefronts that ring it.

Eliza's heartbeat settles. She retrieves her notebook and begins to write, her hand steadier now. She records the names: Coppinger, Butler, the chaplain reading from a battered Latin missal, the American officer with the streak of red clay on his trousers. She notes the sequence of the ceremony: the invocation, the reading of the treaty, the translation, halting but official, into English for the benefit of the Americans and into softer Andalusian for the local crowd. She catalogs the expressions—the stoic, the bored, the quietly mutinous.

The keys are transferred with a formality Eliza finds both touching and absurd. Coppinger produces them from the velvet pouch, lifts them overhead for all to see, and then hands them, one at a time, to Butler, who places them on a silver tray held by a boy in American livery. The sound of the iron hitting the tray is deliberate, ceremonial. After the final key, there is a pause, during which the Spanish chaplain blesses the transfer, making the sign of the cross so rapidly that Eliza wonders if it might be meant as a curse.

Then the flags.

Two Spanish soldiers step forward, their movements so

perfectly synchronized that for a moment, Eliza doubts her own sense of time. They lower the red-and-gold banner slowly, folding it with practiced reverence, and hand it off to a waiting aide. In the same motion, two American soldiers unclip the Stars and Stripes from their side of the platform, unfurling it overhead with a flourish and lashing it to the pole in less time than it takes for the drum to roll. The American flag climbs the mast, the drumbeat sharp and slightly ragged—Eliza recognizes it as the first public attempt by these men to claim this rhythm as their own.

The crowd is silent as the flags pass in the air. The silence holds through the Spanish anthem, played by a small, nervous band hidden somewhere behind the platform. When the anthem ends, the Americans begin their own. It is not yet "The Star-Spangled Banner" as history will remember it, but a rougher, earlier song—the tune slightly off, the lyrics half-forgotten by the men asked to sing. A handful of American wives and children join in, their voices outnumbered by the Spanish stillness.

Eliza writes all of it. She notes the American merchants at the plaza's edge, already measuring the distance from platform to nearest storefront, calculating frontage and footfall. She sees the Spanish officials whose faces are stony as they watch the flag they have served for generations come down and another, not entirely real yet, go up. She observes the mixed-race crowd, the African and Seminole families on the margins, watching not with hope or anger but with a cold, calculating patience. They have seen this kind of transfer before.

The official ceremony ends with a handshake. Coppinger and Butler clasp hands, though neither man looks entirely at ease. The Americans step forward to congratulate one another, their voices loud, but not celebratory—more a forced cheer, as if volume alone will smooth over the nerves of conquest. The Spanish linger for a moment, then begin to disperse in small groups, not looking back.

Eliza tucks her notebook into her shirt, the paper already curling from the humidity. She steps away from the coquina wall and joins the current of people flooding from the plaza. She moves with care—observing, listening, recording—but also with a sense that for the first time in hours, she belongs less to the machinery of the moment and more to its sediment, its aftermath.

The transfer is done. The pageantry of empire has been performed.

But as she looks back over her shoulder, she sees the old Spanish flag, folded and carried away by a silent aide, and wonders what will become of the memories stitched into its fraying edge.

Above the square, the new flag flaps, stubborn and bright, in the morning wind.

Below, the stone absorbs another layer of history.

The air in St. Augustine is no longer ceremonial; it is restless, eager, sliced with the shrill calls of commerce and confusion. The ceremony in the plaza barely over, Eliza tracks the pulse of the city as it ripples outward from the center, flooding the narrow streets with a tide of bodies and intent.

She walks with the current, shoulders hunched against the sun and the close press of strangers. To her left, a Spanish family clusters at the threshold of their house, the father's arms windmilling as he tries to herd his brood indoors, away from the eyes of passing Americans. The mother, face shiny with tears, tugs at the collars of her two daughters, pulling them close, murmuring endearments even as her gaze remains fixed on the avenue. Their oldest son lingers on the stoop, hair uncombed, shirt unbuttoned, clutching a handful of coins as if the currency itself might change in the next hour. Above them, a banner still flaps: an announcement for a Spanish-language concert, half torn, its bottom edge curling.

A few doors down, the new order wastes no time. A pair of American soldiers—one with a recruit's acne, the other with the squared-off jaw of a second son desperate for advancement—are nailing proclamations onto the sun-bleached wood. The first poster is English, dense with legalese: All residents are required to register property and affirm loyalty. The second is a crude translation, the Spanish phrasing so stiff that Eliza winces. Beneath these, old Spanish decrees remain, yellowed but legible, now relegated to the background like sediment in a glass.

She notes the layers, scribbles in the notebook, and diagrams the palimpsest of authority.

On the corner, a merchant with a neckerchief the color of overripe mango shouts in two languages, sometimes in the same sentence. He peddles coffee and lemon water, but also offers to buy “any and all valuables” at “the most honest price in the city.” His pitch is interrupted by an American lawyer, who sidles up and begins to argue, in loud and fractured Spanish, about the future of the merchant’s lease. The negotiation grows animated, drawing a small crowd. Someone mentions “the right to pursue happiness,” and the phrase gets picked up and repeated, by locals as a joke, by newcomers as gospel.

On every block, the velocity of transition stuns Eliza. Some Spanish families are already loading trunks and crates onto wagons for the journey to the docks. The luggage is battered, monogrammed with initials dating back a century, the leather worn thin at every handle. The packing is brisk, silent, and determined. In some cases, families are joined by house servants—black and brown, some free, some less so—who bear their own bundles, moving with a dignity that seems impervious to either flag.

Not all are leaving. In a shaded side street, an elderly woman in a black dress and white lace mantilla clutches her rosary beads and pleads with her son at the threshold of a shop. "¿Nos quedamos o nos vamos?" Her voice is reed-thin, but the question slices the air. Her son, hair cropped to American fashion but eyes unmistakably Castilian, stares at his shoes, unwilling to answer.

Eliza sketches the tableau quickly: the stoop, the beads, the tension in the man's jaw. She feels the story behind the image—two centuries of presence, the inertia of roots, the quicksand of loss.

She moves on, past the open windows of a bakery. Inside, Spanish-speaking bakers and American customers collide in mutual incomprehension. The Americans point and gesture, unwilling to attempt the language, and the bakers respond with the universal hospitality of hot bread. The coin changes hands, but so does something less tangible—curiosity, the possibility of absorption. Eliza writes: "They conquer by stomach first."

Farther along, the church bells toll. At the cathedral steps, a Spanish priest in a threadbare cassock blesses the departing families, sprinkling holy water over heads bowed in a blend of devotion and resignation. His Latin is quick, almost mumbled. Some pause for the sacrament, others pass by with eyes averted. A few, Eliza notices, are already wearing small American flags pinned to their hats or shawls—a gesture of either survival or sarcasm, she cannot yet tell.

Just past the square, on a scrap of lawn, an American minister in a black frock coat is distributing pamphlets to anyone who will take them. "Freedom of Worship!" the flyers proclaim in oversized type. The minister hands out the papers with a salesman's optimism, offering a handshake and a smile to every passerby, even those who ignore him. Eliza notes the contrast: the Spanish priest comforts the leaving; the American minister courts the staying.

In the commercial center, change happens fastest. Signs written in Spanish are being repainted—sometimes over the old letters, sometimes right on top of them. One butcher's window reads "CARNICERÍA," but someone has added "Meat Market" in crooked blue below. Next door, a tailor's sign now boasts "Taylor & Sons—American Haberdashery," the paint so fresh it still drips. American merchants, many of them barely off the ships themselves, press faces against glass, measuring dimensions, calculating the profits of the new regime.

Eliza documents the shift with a precise hand. She sketches the sign transitions, the awkward overlaps. She tracks how Americans, in clusters of two or three, walk the perimeter of each property, sometimes with tape measures, sometimes with nothing more than a gaze sharpened by generations of land hunger. She overhears one declare, "We'll put the post office here—perfect sightline from the fort." His companion replies, "First, we'll need a jail."

The Castillo de San Marcos dominates the northern horizon, as always, but today the air around it vibrates with both anticipation and threat. Eliza walks toward it, careful to stay in the shade, and watches as a pair of American officers pace the perimeter. They carry sketch pads and brass rulers, stopping at intervals to make notes and measure the thickness of the coquina walls. At the front gate, two Spanish guards stand motionless, rifles at attention. Their faces are impassive, but the smallest motion—one thumb tapping the rifle's barrel, the other shifting his weight from heel to toe—betrays the strain. The Americans do not address them, but their intentions are clear: the fort is already American property, awaiting only the official word.

A little further up the street, Eliza sees a knot of young men—Spanish, by the shape of their faces and the angle of their gestures—arguing in tight voices. They point back at the plaza, at the flag, at the Americans now scattered through the city. Their leader, a thin man with a widow's peak and a heavy brow, shakes his fist in the direction of the Castillo. The others nod, but with diminishing conviction. Eliza records the faces, the emotion: a complicated braid of loyalty, rage, and something like relief.

At the docks, chaos reigns. Wagons jam the narrow access roads, loaded with everything from grandfather clocks to live hens in crates. The ships are flagged for Cuba, as well as New Orleans, Savannah, and Charleston. Some families weep as they board, some joke in brittle voices, some turn their faces to the wind and do not look back. American customs officers, pressed into service for the first time, try to impose order with ledgers and red tape, but are quickly overwhelmed by the reality of centuries uprooted in a single day.

Eliza watches as a Spanish priest wades into the crowd, offering last-minute blessings and hasty confessions. The American minister follows a few paces behind, pamphlets in hand, undeterred by refusals. Eliza feels the overlap, the mutual refusal to cede the moment.

She sketches the ships themselves: the battered Spanish freighters, patched with new wood and old sails; the smaller, sleeker American schooners, painted in aggressive stripes. She notes the names painted on the bows—San Cristobal, Maria Isabel, Liberty, The New Republic. The names will outlast the paint.

On the way back from the docks, Eliza passes the home of a Spanish noblewoman—a low mansion, its gate flanked by lion statues blackened by age. The courtyard is full of furniture, art, and china, all stacked as if for an estate sale. Inside, the lady of the house sits on a straight-backed chair, a glass of sherry in her hand. Her dress is immaculate, her hair styled as if for a portrait. Around her, a pair of American men in business suits haggle with her steward in three languages, attempting to price the past before it has even finished ending.

Eliza approaches the gate. The noblewoman catches her eye,

and for a moment, the two share a look: not exactly complicity, but the mutual awareness of observers. Eliza sketches her pose and gaze, and tucks the drawing into the notebook.

She returns to the Castillo as the sun begins to slide down the western sky. The American officers are still there, still measuring, but now joined by a civilian surveyor with a stack of maps and a hungry smile. The Spanish guards remain unchanged, but Eliza can see the relief in their posture now—the hardest part is simply enduring.

She walks the outer wall, traces the graffiti carved into the stone: names, dates, the odd vulgarity. She reads a message in Spanish—"Aún somos aquí"—and beside it, a freshly scratched "U.S.A. July 1821." The future is written right on top of the past.

Eliza sits in the shadow of the fort and opens her notebook one more time. She writes: "No one ever leaves. They watch themselves be replaced."

The day ends not with the closure of the ceremony, but with the slow accretion of memory, one sign, one measurement, one argument at a time.

It is not a clean transition, but a layered one.

In the growing dusk, the city buzzes with the unresolved energy of a story still deciding which language it will tell itself in.

Evening in St. Augustine carries a hint of sea chill, even in July. The sun's exit leaves the boarding houses glowing—windows lit from within, the coquina walls exhaling the heat they stored all day. Eliza slips through the door of a house on Treasury Street, the sign over the lintel still reading "Casa de Huéspedes," though someone has hastily painted "Rooms for Gentlefolk" beneath it in a shade of blue that bleeds into the stone.

Inside, the smell of stewing garlic and pimentón collides with the bitter tang of over-boiled coffee. The dining room is crowded: local Spanish families, their children scrubbed and hair neatly parted; American newcomers, their collars starched and optimism set to maximum; a handful of British exiles from the last occupation, content to eat in silence and watch history circle the table.

The proprietress, Señora Alvarez, moves between the tables with regal efficiency. Her dress is black, her hair pinned in a net, her hands never still. She balances three bowls at once, ladling out caldo gallego to a pair of sunburned American clerks who try, and fail, to pronounce it back to her. She corrects them with a smile that is not unfriendly, but which makes it clear that the kitchen—and possibly the city—is still hers.

Eliza slides into an open seat at a communal table. She is flanked on one side by a Spanish matron with an arctic stare and a string of pearls; on the other by a sallow American merchant who polishes his spectacles with a nervous compulsion. Across from her sits a British widow, one elbow resting on a dog-eared ledger, and an elderly Spanish gentleman whose goatee and courtly gestures seem relics of another century.

Conversation builds in waves. At first, the language of the room is Spanish, with a gloss of polite English when an American turns to speak. As the stew is served, the chatter shifts—Americans louder, their vowels broadening, the Spanish growing softer, more insular.

Señora Alvarez hovers, catching every nuance. “Eat, eat,” she instructs, but when the American merchant hesitates over his bowl, she leans in. “It is only pork,” she tells him, “Not, as you say, ‘strange meat.’” Her accent is thick, but her wit is diamond sharp.

The merchant laughs nervously, spoon clattering on

porcelain. “No offense meant, Señora,” he says. “Only, back home, we don’t stew our food this way. It’s…rich.”

“You will get used to it,” she says, then to the table at large, “Everyone gets used to it here. Even the English.”

A ripple of laughter, and the British widow lifts her sherry glass in tribute.

The conversation deepens as the table fills: two American officers, dress coats traded for rougher linen, arrive late and sit without asking. They draw immediate attention, the Spaniards glancing sidelong at the cut of the uniform, the Americans eyeing the food with suspicion. One officer—Lieutenant Stevens, by the monogram stitched on his shirt—wastes no time in declaring, “We aim to make this city the jewel of the new Florida. Trade, law, schools—all in English, of course.”

The pearls-wearing matron draws herself up. “Spanish was good enough for three hundred years,” she says in careful English.

Stevens grins, unoffended. “A new start means a new tongue. English is the language of liberty.” The word “liberty” hangs in the air, a challenge and a promise.

The elderly Spanish man lifts his spoon with the gravity of a judge. “Liberty speaks all tongues,” he replies. “Otherwise, it is merely conquest with better slogans.”

The table holds its breath. Eliza records the exchange with her eyes, then writes it verbatim in her book, the letters dark against the page. She watches as tension ebbs and returns, as people decide whether to laugh or take offense, as the evening’s mood teeters on the edge of something more brittle.

Señora Alvarez diffuses it by bringing out a second course—a dish of rice and seafood, the saffron scent slicing through the awkwardness. "Here, we eat together," she says, "no matter which flag hangs outside." She serves Stevens first, then the matron, then Eliza.

One of the Americans—an engineer, by the ink stains on his fingers—asks Alvarez if she intends to keep the boarding house now that her husband has "elected to return to Havana."

She pours him coffee with the poise of a duchess. "I have run this house since my second child. My husband went to Havana only because he prefers his mother's tamales to my stew. He will return as soon as he runs out of patience, or rum."

The room laughs, even the engineer.

Eliza asks, quietly, if many families are leaving.

"Some," Alvarez says. "Mostly those with business in Cuba, or who fear what the Americans might bring." She glances at Stevens, then back to Eliza. "But this city, it has seen Spanish, British, Spanish again. Now, American. The walls remember all flags, even when the people forget."

The British widow adds, "I have never seen a place change hands so often and remain so much itself. The shops close for a day, then open again, same shelves, new signs. Even the ghosts must be exhausted."

Stevens—less brash now, slowed by the weight of food and sherry—admits that he cannot tell the difference between the old regime and the new, except for the proclamations and the flags. "But give it time," he adds, "Americans will paint this place in their image soon enough."

Eliza looks around the room: Spanish lace on the windows, English teacups on the sideboard, American newspapers folded into triangles and used to prop up an uneven table leg. She sees the

American children in the corner, learning Spanish from their playmates faster than their parents can say "states' rights." She notes how the Americans adopt Spanish words when it suits them—"plaza," "matanzas," "castillo"—even as they lecture about the purity of English.

She writes, "The new regime absorbs the old not by force, but by hunger. They eat the food, marry the daughters, hire the craftsmen, learn the names of the streets before they change them."

The table empties slowly, people lingering for dessert, for gossip, for the pleasure of not going out into the dark just yet. In a lull, the Spanish matron leans toward Eliza and asks, "Which do you prefer—the new or the old?"

Eliza considers, then answers honestly: "I prefer the parts that survive. The memory."

The matron nods as if this is both expected and a little sad.

Outside, dusk has surrendered to darkness, and the only lights are the oil lamps in the windows. The city is quiet for the first time all day, the air holding the last traces of sherry and garlic and unresolved argument.

Señora Alvarez, clearing plates, pauses to watch the room a moment. She catches Eliza's gaze, and with a small, knowing smile, lifts her chin toward the window.

"Tomorrow, you will wake, and the world will be changed," she says. "But you will still need to eat, and to laugh, and to argue about nothing. The flags are for the soldiers. The rest is just life."

Eliza closes her notebook. She thinks of the fortress, of the measured walls, of the city's layers—how each regime leaves its mark, and each mark is softened by the next.

She leaves the boarding house with a full belly and a head

swirling with voices, confident that when the Americans finally remake the city in their own image, it will look a lot like what came before, only painted in stripes.

Above her, the new flag flutters, defiant and bright, but the stone beneath it remains unchanged, waiting patiently to be layered with tomorrow's memories.

By the time Eliza reaches the waterfront, dusk has settled in layers—lavender over indigo, the river's surface burnished in metallic bands by the setting sun. The air smells of tar, tobacco, salt, and the quiet panic of those who know their horizon is about to change forever.

The docks are a tangle of wagons and stevedores, the planks thrumming underfoot with the weight of trunks, crates, and the final sweepings of old estates. Eliza pauses at the edge of the fray and surveys the drama of departure: families pressed together, every gesture weighted with the possibility that it might be their last; children corralled by nurses, wide-eyed and silent; men standing with the hunched, expectant posture of those who would rather fight than cry.

She spots the family she has been tracking all day: the matriarch, black lace now limp with sweat and grief, the father directing the loading of trunks with clipped authority. Their daughters—three in all—cluster at the edge of the pier. The youngest clings to her mother, her face splotched with tears. The eldest, already wedded to a minor Spanish official, stands apart, jaw set, hands in white gloves that tremble as she tries to remain composed.

The middle daughter, Eliza, notices, wears the dress of an American merchant's wife: lighter fabric, brighter color, a ribbon the blue of Fourth of July bunting. Her new husband, an awkwardly tall man with a sunburnt scalp, hovers behind her, unsure whether he belongs in this moment or not.

Eliza drifts closer, notebook open, careful not to intrude but hungry for the truth of the parting.

The loading is slow. American customs officials pick through every trunk, checking for contraband and unpaid duties. They do so with neither malice nor hurry, as if they are the arbiters of a world in which time is a renewable resource. Behind them, Spanish priests make the rounds, offering last blessings, sometimes in Latin, sometimes in the soft dialects of the islands.

A cluster of women from the town gathers by the seawall. They speak in urgent, hushed Spanish, exchanging addresses and promises, the word "Cuba" repeated like a chant. One woman passes a handkerchief to another, then both weep openly, the relief of letting go stronger than any national loyalty.

At the dock's far end, a group of young Spanish men, stripped to the waist and glistening with sweat, work the ropes and the winches. Eliza notes how their shouts and laughter have the defiant edge of those who know they are being watched by history and refuse to go quietly.

The ships themselves are monstrous and inert, their hulls painted with the crests of Spanish provinces, their decks stacked with the material remains of entire lives. Sailors, mostly Cuban and some French, perch in the rigging, making jokes in at least three languages.

Amid the commotion, Eliza witnesses the core of the day's paradox: parents embracing grown children who have chosen to stay, the parting hugs so fierce they border on violence. The matriarch of the family clutches her Americanized daughter, whispering a string of rapid-fire prayers in her ear. The daughter's new husband stands a respectful distance away; his gaze fixed on the horizon.

"Es sólo por ahora," the mother says, her voice choked. "Solo por ahora." She touches the blue ribbon at her daughter's waist, as if this is the true wound.

The daughter, in halting Spanish, promises to write, to visit, to send photographs. "It won't be forever," she says, "when things settle." She looks at Eliza, briefly, her eyes wide and unguarded, then turns away, her husband's hand now lightly at her back.

Eliza's notes catch the irony: "They leave with the conviction of return, knowing in the bones that they will not."

The sun drops lower. A queue forms at the edge of the dock, passengers waiting for the boatman to call their names. Customs officials check the manifests, ticking off names and ages in a language none of the departing really claim. Some families crowd forward, eager to leave. Others lag, as if every moment on the dock is one more heartbeat of the life they are abandoning.

Near the seawall, a different ritual. Eliza notices an old woman kneeling at the base of the coquina. She is gray-haired, stooped, but her hands are steady as she digs a small hole in the sand. She removes a bundle wrapped in blue silk from her purse and buries it in the earth, patting the sand flat with her palm. Eliza draws closer, careful not to startle.

The old woman looks up and, recognizing the question in Eliza's eyes, speaks in a whisper. "Para que me recuerde. To remember me."

Eliza records the gesture, the words, the way the old woman lingers a moment before rising and smoothing her dress. As the woman boards the skiff, she never once looks back at the shore.

The ships fill. Gangplanks creak. The voices of sailors rise as they prepare to cast off. On the pier, the families left behind watch with a mixture of envy, loss, and calculated hope. Eliza notes how, in this moment, even the language changes: the farewells shouted to the decks are a blend of Spanish, English, and the fractured hybrids that have always flourished in border places.

On the Castillo's ramparts, fresh chalk lines mark where the Americans will install new cannons. The old Spanish guards are gone, replaced by a handful of American soldiers with mismatched uniforms and an air of disbelief at their own authority. One sits on the seawall, legs swinging over the edge, chewing a stalk of grass as he watches the ships depart. He has the look of someone who has never lived by the ocean and cannot believe how many people the world can hold.

Eliza walks the length of the seawall. She runs her hand over the rough shell-and-lime surface, reading the layers of labor and time embedded in each stone. At the base of the wall, she spots more buried tokens: a glint of a coin, a faded ribbon, the corner of a leather-bound prayer book. Each one is a refusal to sever completely, a final anchoring in the land that will soon claim a new flag.

She writes: "There are more ways to belong than to own."

As the last of the sunlight fractures on the river, the ships begin to move—sails rising, the crews shouting orders, the crowd on the docks waving and weeping, but also already turning toward home, toward the future.

The coquina seawall, now etched with the fresh graffiti of American soldiers, stands unchanged in substance. Above it, the flags of two nations: one being lowered into memory, one straining toward the wind.

Eliza closes her notebook, the pages swollen with ink and damp.

She lingers at the waterfront, watching the sails shrink and vanish. She thinks of the names that will not make it into the history books, the tokens hidden in the earth, the mothers and daughters now divided by a waterline and a politics neither truly understands.

In the darkness, the old and new merge. The shouts of sailors blend with the laughter of American children, the prayers of the priests with the laments of the left-behind.

Eliza writes her final note for the day:

America does not begin cleanly. It accumulates. Each regime drapes its flag over the last and calls it the foundation. But the sediment—what resists, what endures—remains, and sometimes, if you listen at the water's edge, you can hear all the voices at once.

She stands at the seawall, notebook pressed to her chest, and lets the weight of the place settle.

Then she walks home in the new American darkness, ready to remember for those who cannot.

Chapter 15: 1861

Eliza POV — Civil War, Florida

She lands hard this time.

Not onto marsh or cordgrass, not into the soft yield of centuries past, but onto the ribcage of a street—narrow, cobbled, the stones radiating August heat through the soles of her shoes. It's as if the world wants to eject her outright: she slams into the present with a jolt so clean it erases her breath, sending her careening sideways into the rough embrace of a coquina wall.

Her hands slap against its surface, scraping across fossilized shell and oolitic grit. She tastes iron at the back of her teeth, and it takes a second to realize it's not blood but cannon smoke drifting through the thick, wet air.

The city has changed again. She knows it before she opens her eyes.

The buildings are taller now, two and three stories, their wooden galleries blackened by sun and salted by the memory of ocean. The shutters are painted in the unsteady blues and greens of cheap pigment; half of them are closed, as if the houses themselves have something to fear. Somewhere close by, a dog barks, then stops abruptly, the sound strangled as if smothered by a hand.

A new flag snaps overhead—a different geometry of red, white, and blue, the stars in a ring this time. Soldiers in gray march past, their uniforms streaked with dust and sweat. Their faces are too young or too old, almost nothing in between. Their boots thud unevenly on the stones, as if none of them are walking quite in time with the century they've been given.

Eliza leans back against the wall and tries to breathe, but the air is so dense with combustion that it feels like inhaling a lit match.

The Lantern Array flickers in her mind, a faint but constant undertow. It's a reminder: she is an observer, not an actor. She is here only to witness. To record.

A memory overlays the scene: a decade ago in the Castillo, a docent explaining how the fort had changed hands five times, how each new flag was sewn by the women of the town and hoisted in a ceremony always attended by children and priests. She had smiled politely. Now, she wonders how many of those children lived to see their next ceremony.

A group of Confederates clusters at the end of the street. They are hauling down the Union flag from the Castillo de San Marcos, the blue canton and stars folding over itself like a shroud. The motion is brisk, almost casual; one of the men spits onto the dirt as he ties the rope off at half-mast.

Another group raises the new banner—white field, blue cross, red stars, stitched hastily but with care. The men cheer. Someone fires a pistol into the air, and the sound ricochets off the stone walls, startling a flock of birds into flight.

Eliza feels herself splitting: part of her is locked in the sensory present, the rest spinning out along timelines and annotations, trying to remember whether the city fell bloodlessly or if this was just the first act in a longer tragedy. Her hands tremble, not from fear, but from the voltage of transition.

She follows the soldiers as they move toward the plaza, their boots dragging small avalanches of shell grit along the way. The civilians emerge from their houses, tentatively at first—women in dark cotton, children barefoot, men with rough, unshaved faces. Some hang back, others step boldly into the square, their postures defiant or defeated, but never neutral.

The soldiers make a show of it, parading the captured Union colors in a slow circuit before dumping them at the foot of the courthouse steps. The officer in charge—a man with a pale, almost luminous beard—delivers a short speech, his voice booming with practiced Southern grace. She cannot catch every word, but the gist is clear: Victory, honor, the cause. The crowd splits cleanly down the middle—half raise hats and cheer, half stand silent and stone-faced, arms folded tight across their chests.

It is the silence that feels louder.

The aftermath ripples through the plaza. A group of young men, more boys than men, begins singing a makeshift anthem; their voices crack on the high notes. A cluster of women in faded black holds hands and prays quietly, heads bowed. Two small children play at the edge of the square, running a stick up and down the battered statue of Ponce de León, as if they could gouge meaning from the centuries with nothing but wood and persistence.

A pair of eyes finds her in the crowd—an elderly woman with hair white as salt, her dress neat despite the stains at the hem. She moves with a limp, but her expression is knife-sharp as she approaches. Her hands are clenched at her sides, knuckles bone-pale.

She passes in front of Eliza, pauses, then spits with precise venom at the feet of another woman standing a few paces away. The target is broad-shouldered, stiff-backed, with a Confederate cockade pinned to her collar.

"My son died at Manassas for your so-called cause," the old woman hisses. Her voice is not loud, but it cuts through the other noise like a wire.

The Confederate sympathizer recoils, but only slightly. Her own face is tight with grief, and for a second, Eliza wonders if she is about to cry or retaliate. Instead, the woman turns her gaze away—past the soldiers, past the flags, past everything—and fixes it on the fort, its silhouette black against the bruised sky.

The tension doesn't break, but it mutates: resentment, shame, the kind of pain that knots itself around the tongue and refuses to be spoken.

Eliza's palm is still pressed to the coquina wall. She tries to imagine how many words these stones have heard, how many times they have outlived the men who built and battered them.

She walks the perimeter of the plaza, notebook in hand. She catalogs:

- The soldiers' faces, flushed and slick with sweat.

- The texture of the wall is dry and brittle at the surface but cold and damp below.

- The way the children mimic the marching, their steps uneven, uncertain which side they belong to.

- The way the old woman holds her ground, as if she is the last anchor to a world already swept away.

She writes: “Families once united are now their own nations.”

The flag in the square flaps fitfully, the fabric already beginning to fray at the edges.

Eliza closes her notebook, fingertips gritty with shell dust. She leans into the wall again, steadying herself.

It occurs to her that these are the same families—same bloodlines, same houses, same names—as those who watched the Spanish surrender to the British, who watched the British depart for the continent, who watched the Americans raise the Stars and Stripes for the first time. Now, they watch each other, and it’s not clear who is the foreigner.

The city doesn’t blink. It endures.

She stays until the plaza empties, until the officers finish their cigarettes and the last echo of singing fades into the bay.

Only then does she allow herself to move, following the curve of the ancient street, the pulse of the Array steady in her head, the future and the past braided tighter than ever.

Somewhere, a dog barks again.

This time, the sound is not cut short. It carries on, stubborn and alive, into the humid dark.

Night at the inlet is absolute.

The horizon disappears, the black water indistinguishable from the black sky except for a sliver of phosphorescence where brine churns against the shallows. Eliza crouches low in the cordgrass, knees deep in cold mud, the spines of sawgrass biting her thighs through thin fabric. The marsh breathes in the dark—snapping, humming, popping with the sound of tiny jaws and nervous life—but the only thing that matters is the narrow, oil-dark channel winding through the shoals.

She hugs the ground, keeping her head lower than the highest marsh blade. Mosquitoes find her instantly, swarming around her ears, but she does not slap them away. Movement would betray her. Even here, even now, she feels the residual warning: stay unseen.

Out on the channel, a boat—no, a streak of moving shadow—slides toward open water. The hull is barely visible, painted the color of wet slate, but the splash of a muffled oar betrays its presence. At the prow, a single lantern glows, hooded and swaying with the boat's pulse. The light is the color of old teeth.

Eliza's eyes adjust. She counts five men on deck, one at the rudder, two crouched low in the middle, one standing at the bow with a long pole, and the other, she assumes, below deck, tending cargo. The men are all shapes—stooped, angular, arms and hands corded with tension.

A voice, sharp and urgent, cuts across the marsh: "¡Rápido, muchachos! Push off!"

The men dig in with the pole, shoving the runner into deeper water. Another voice, this one pitched higher and speaking English, whispers: "Too loud, dammit. You'll wake the whole coast." The two languages tangle in the air, the command and the complaint almost indistinguishable in their anxiety.

A flash of color at the stern—a Confederate officer's sash, cheap red ribbon banded around a blue frock coat. The officer holds a revolver against his thigh, pointed downward, but his attention is on the horizon. His hat is gone, revealing a strip of pale scalp where hair once grew.

The crew moves with the choreography of desperation. Crates and barrels—marked with crude crosses and painted numbers—are lashed down, the men working by feel, not light. The cargo smells of gun oil and salt-cured beef. Still, Eliza knows from the records that the critical contents are medical: quinine, laudanum, the last reserves of anesthetic for a hospital overrun by fever and infection.

"Douse that light, fool," hisses the officer. "Union cutter's just beyond the sandbar."

The lantern vanishes, and for a split second, even the boat itself disappears—an absence so total that Eliza wonders if the Array has glitched, skipped her to a moment when the boat had already passed.

But then: the sound of a Union searchlight, a sweep of white across the inlet, scattering blue shadows up the marsh grass. The cutter is close now, so close Eliza can hear the slap of boots on its deck, the crisp calls of "Ready port!" and "Steady on!"

The blockade runner freezes. The men press themselves flat to the deck, faces buried in the crook of an arm or the curve of a knee, bodies straining not to move, not to breathe.

Eliza's own breath stutters. Her pulse pounds at the base of her skull, matching the rhythm of the distant surf.

The searchlight sweeps past, missing the boat by a margin so fine it feels preordained. A gull shrieks overhead, and for a second the marsh is pure sound—wings, water, blood.

The cutter's engine rumbles, then fades as it turns its attention up-coast. The runner's crew waits five heartbeats—Eliza counts them, deliberate and slow—before resuming movement. The oars slip into the water, wrapped in rags to silence the pull, and the boat edges forward like an animal trained to flinch from pain.

At the shore, two men emerge from the shadow of a palmetto, pushing a skiff loaded with more crates into the shallow. One is barefoot, his ankles painted with bites and sores. He helps drag the skiff through the reeds, splashing silently, his body angled as if expecting a bullet at any moment.

The officer on the runner hisses them aboard, his voice brittle with relief and rage. The two men scramble on, nearly capsizing the boat, but the runner rights itself. The cargo is hauled aboard in seconds; the skiff is pushed away, left to drift or sink.

For a moment, Eliza feels the absolute fragility of this moment—how the entire supply chain for a city, a cause, a war can depend on the patience of mosquitoes and the blind luck of cloud cover.

The runner pivots into the deeper channel. The crew works in silence now, their faces invisible. One man removes his hat and holds it against his chest, lips moving in what she can only guess is prayer or apology.

A Confederate private stands on the bank near Eliza, so close she can smell sweat and tobacco. He leans in to his companion—a boy barely old enough for a beard—and whispers: "If they don't make it, Augustine's done by next week." The boy nods, jaw clenched, eyes fixed on the slip of darkness that is the runner's wake.

Eliza notes it all: the staccato hush of breath, the play of shadow over the water, the absolute stillness of every living thing until the boat is gone. She tries to memorize the sequence, knowing full well that no record will remember it this way—no monument, no commemorative marker, nothing to note the lives and hands that scraped and bled in these marshes.

The runner is nearly invisible now, sliding into the curve of the inlet, the men's voices lost to distance.

A sound behind her—a single, wet cough. She pivots, careful not to rustle the reeds. An old woman stands in the mud, her feet planted solid, arms folded around a canvas sack. She wears a faded blue dress, patched at the elbows, and her hair is pinned in a way that says "yesterday's news." She watches the boat disappear, then spits into the channel.

"Waste of good quinine," she mutters. "Better off with the Yankees. At least they'd pay for it."

Eliza almost laughs, but the moment is too sharp, too brittle.

The woman turns, her eyes passing over Eliza as if she were a ghost or a hallucination—then keeps walking, each step sucking at the mud with the resignation of someone who knows the future is a long, slow attrition.

The cutter's searchlight returns, but it sweeps harmlessly across empty water.

Eliza holds her position until the marsh settles again. The bugs return; the frogs resume their chorus. The pulse of the Array fades into a distant, mechanical hum.

She stands, knees aching, and wipes her hands on the damp hem of her shirt.

Above the inlet, the stars flicker in their indifferent patterns.

Below, the runner is gone, but its path is marked by the slow, secret churn of the tide—memory that cannot be blockaded, only briefly diverted.

She walks back toward the town, boots squishing in the night. Every step is a catalogue, a ledger entry in the history no one will write.

But she has seen it. She will remember.

The next morning, the city will wake to the knowledge that its fate is balanced on the edge of a midnight gamble.

Eliza, alone in the dark, carries the sum of it in her bones.

By morning, the rumor has already outpaced the news.

A column of Union blue—more faded than the illustrations ever allowed—appears at the city's northern gate before the Spanish moss even dries from overnight dew. Their boots are caked in mud, but their rifles glint in the flat, hard light. They do not march so much as trudge, shoulders set for disappointment, but the absence of resistance is its own kind of welcome.

Eliza walks with them—not in uniform, not in step, but parallel, a shadow observer cataloguing every reaction the city offers.

The streets are suddenly, preternaturally clean. Shutters snap closed at the first sight of the Stars and Stripes. A man in a straw hat leans against the post office, arms folded, expression studiedly blank. Three women in morning dresses peer out from a second-floor window, one of them quickly retreating when a Union drummer glances up and grins.

The plaza is nearly deserted.

The blue column splits at the square, half continuing toward the fort, half holding position in front of the courthouse. The commander, a captain whose hair is as silver as his buttons, gives a short, functional order: "Standard, up. Colors on the wall."

It is more ritual than necessity—there's no one here to cheer or to contest the transition. Eliza finds herself drifting with the current of Union men toward the Castillo.

The fort has changed again. Its battered flagpole, freshly splintered, lists slightly to starboard. The Stars and Bars hang limp, no wind to send it flying. Cannon scars ring the lower bastions, black as thumbprints. The walls—never truly white—are pitted and gray, crusted with the residue of salt and sulfur.

She watches as two soldiers haul down the Confederate flag, folding it with a care that surprises her. A third man takes the Stars and Stripes, this one patched at the corner, and hoists it skyward. The colors unfurl slowly, sluggish, the cloth heavy with the memory of other hands.

From the upper terrace, a pair of children peer over the wall—one clutching a homemade Union flag, the other with a ragged cockade sewn to his sleeve. The first boy brandishes the flag, waving it in tight, eager circles. The second tries to snatch it, and for a moment, the two are locked in a silent, physical negotiation. The smaller boy wins, jabbing his opponent in the ribs, then running along the parapet, triumphant.

Eliza blinks. The war is everywhere, and everywhere it is a different war.

She turns back toward the city, following the slow drift of people emerging from their homes. A group of men—Black, barefoot, each wearing a shirt white as new bones—stands at the edge of the square, uncertain whether to move closer. Their postures are wary but upright, heads held high.

A Union sergeant beckons them forward, then climbs the steps of the courthouse, reading from a sheet of paper in a voice that wobbles but does not break.

"…and by order of the President of these United States, all persons held as slaves within said designated States and parts of States, are, and henceforward shall be free…"

The words echo across the plaza, the legal language foreign and immense. The men at the edge of the square do not cheer, nor do they collapse in relief. Instead, they stand in silence, listening to the end of the reading, then slowly disperse, one or two at a time, as if afraid of waking from a dream.

At the fort, a young Black woman walks up the ramp with her head uncovered, her eyes fixed on the new flag. She stands at the base of the wall and reaches out to touch the stone, as if needing proof that the world has changed. Her fingertips leave a smear of red brick dust on the ancient shell. She whispers, "These stones have seen Spanish, British, and now this. They'll see more yet."

Eliza stands behind her, hands deep in her pockets. She wants to say something—anything—, but nothing she could say would be as true as what the woman has already spoken.

A gust of wind finally finds the new flag, sending it into a full and vigorous wave. The Union soldiers stand at attention. The fort watches with the patient indifference of a structure designed to endure.

The war is not over. Not here, not in the world, not even in the hearts of the men and women who have just witnessed its latest inversion.

Eliza walks the city's perimeter, tracing the boundary between past and future. She passes a house where the window is open, another home is boarded up, and a sign nailed to the door: Gone to Georgia, Will Return. In a shaded alley, she sees the two boys again, this time sitting together, sharing the flag between them, the contest of morning already forgotten.

Her own heart aches with the knowledge that none of this is finished—that the American project is not a matter of banners or declarations, but of the slow, painful process of deciding who is permitted to belong.

She stops at the wall, the one that has anchored her through centuries. The coquina is warm beneath her hand, alive with the breath of the ocean and the memory of everything it has witnessed.

She presses her palm to the stone and lets herself feel it—the weight of history, the tightness in her chest, the inescapable knowledge that there is no single moment of victory, only the slow accumulation of truth against the bone.

A new flag flies, and the city lives.

She turns from the wall, determined to remember all of it: the war, the witness, the weight of memory.

There is work yet to be done.

Chapter 16: 1964

Eliza POV — Civil Rights St. Augustine

Eliza arrives hard.

It is not the drag of marsh or brine this time, but an instant, shattering reassembly that fizzes at the cellular level—static, skin, sweat, a double flash of sodium in her mouth. Air compresses around her, not the open Atlantic sky but a crust of atmosphere both hotter and more contained. The very molecules of the present shove her inward.

She lands, the soles of her shoes scuffing the concrete. No, not concrete. Brickwork. Red and brown, pocked and sticky in the heat. A low wall of coquina stone at her back, its surface worn smooth from centuries of hands—Spanish, British, American, and all the unrecorded. Overhead, the sun blisters against the flagpoles and casts geometric shadows through the heavy green of the live oaks. She does not fall, but for a heartbeat, she is certain she has been hit. The impact comes from every direction, including above.

Plaza de la Constitución, St. Augustine, Florida. June 1964.

Noise slams her next. The plaza roars. It is not the animal sound of muskets or thunder, but the massed, polyphonic cry of a modern protest: call-and-response, thousands of throats raised together, syllables she can almost make out but not quite. Her ears ring with it, but already her mind is searching for the pattern, the rhythm that will let her float on the surface without sinking.

She takes three rapid breaths, tries to slow her pulse, and only then realizes her hands are locked white-knuckled around the strap of her field notebook. The canvas bag at her side is battered, caked with the dust of five centuries, but she is present enough to check for the pen she keeps tucked in the spiral.

She lifts her gaze.

The plaza is choked with people. Black and white together, unevenly mixed but unmistakably together, the bodies shifting and clumping as the crowd flows like tidewater around the statue at the center. Some hold signs: "JESUS LOVES ALL," "INTEGRATE NOW," "FREEDOM AND DIGNITY." Others link arms or clap hands to the rhythm of the voices; the movement so coordinated it seems rehearsed. The marchers are young and old, men in Sunday suits already wilting in the wet heat, women in dresses with collars starched flat, their heels digging holes into the soft brick. Children and teenagers, faces shiny with sweat and terror and something else—something that looks like hope.

Beneath it all, the ancient coquina walls that have held up every regime and every riot in this city's long life.

She can smell the day: fried food from a street cart, the sting of aftershave, the salt of human fear. Someone has dropped a bottle of Coke, and it runs sticky over the bricks, drawing bees in a slow spiral.

Eliza blinks. Her brain fights to contextualize the moment, to find the invisible seam between memory and record. She tries to place herself within the time: The Civil Rights Act is still months away. The Voting Rights Act is a rumor, a future yet unwritten. In the margins of this demonstration, police stand with billy clubs already at the ready, white hands gripping black wood so hard the veins pop blue under skin. The patrol cars are parked in neat lines, the old St. Johns County crest stenciled on each door.

She opens her notebook with one hand; the movement is so practiced it is nearly unconscious. She begins to write—not in full words at first, just impressions, fragments. Crowd density: est. 1200. Ratio, Black: white: 4:1. Police: 26 visible, 14 in riot formation—hot, humid, 95°. No wind. Anthems: "We Shall Overcome," "This Little Light," plus others unIDed.

She is jostled from behind; a man in a navy suit moves past, his elbow catching her ribs. She turns to apologize, but he is already gone, his face set in the half-smile of someone trying to project calm and not quite making it. The crowd surges forward, then stops. In the stillness, Eliza can finally make out the words: "What do we want? Freedom! When do we want it? Now!"

She watches as a group of protestors approaches the front of the crowd—a mix of college students and older women, each with a sign, each scanning the police line as if daring them to move. There is tension everywhere, but it is held in check by a strange, almost choreographed discipline. The marchers do not touch the police, and the police do not yet touch them.

Eliza finds herself drifting toward the edge of the crowd, as if proximity to the coquina wall might anchor her to something solid.

She catalogues the texture of the stone: the tiny fossil shells compressed into the surface, the way the mortar seeps between blocks, the hairline cracks that run like fault lines. She wonders, not for the first time, whether stone can remember what blood is.

A ripple moves through the massed bodies.

He is not tall, but he is visible instantly—the way he carries himself, the way the space in front of him seems to clear before his stride. Dr. Martin Luther King, Jr. moves to the front of the plaza with three men in dark suits at his side. He is not smiling. The effect is not grim, but deeply focused, as if all the energy in the plaza has congealed around him. Behind him, a woman in a white dress clutches a Bible to her chest, knuckles pale.

Eliza cannot breathe for a moment. She does not remember what she was supposed to do upon seeing him, only that she must not interfere. She writes anyway: MLK arrives at 11:32 am. Flanked by two aides (Abernathy? Young?). Voice low, not raised. Authority is spatial, not vocal.

Dr. King pauses at the base of the statue, not quite centered, and raises his hands. The crowd falls silent, the echo louder than the protest had been. He speaks—not a prepared speech, but something urgent, ad hoc, designed for the moment.

"We are here," he says, "because justice has not yet reached St. Augustine. We are here, as brothers and sisters, because every American is entitled to dignity."

The crowd answers, a wave of amens and affirmations.

"We are not here," he says, "to shame or to fight. We are here to bear witness."

He glances at the officers massed along the curb. His gaze is clear, unwavering, almost soft.

"We have chosen," he says, "to walk in the path of peace, no matter how many times we are struck. Because our cause is just, and our hearts are not hardened by hatred."

He steps back. The words hang, fragile and perfect.

The crowd surges again. A woman, tall and elderly, steps to the front, her sign held high: "I AM A MAN." She locks eyes with a policeman standing ten feet away. He looks away first.

Eliza writes it all down. She is sweating through her shirt, the ink beading and smearing on the page. Her heart races, but her hand is steady.

The police move.

It is not sudden, not a riot; it is the slow, deliberate march of inevitability. The officers fan out, forming a human line, their nightsticks held upright, not yet raised but present.

Across St. Augustine—from the Plaza to the Monson Motor Lodge—the demonstrations have taken on this same quiet discipline. What happens here is happening everywhere.

The demonstrators do not scatter.

They have been taught not to.

A young man at the front steps forward. He places his hands behind his back, eyes open, chin level. Two officers take his arms. He does not resist. He is led away, and another protester steps forward to replace him.

Again.

And again.

The pattern reveals itself: not chaos, but intention. A choreography of surrender that refuses humiliation. Each arrest is answered by another body stepping forward, not in defiance, but in resolve.

Eliza feels it before she understands it.

This is not a reaction.

This is a strategy.

The line advances. The sound of cameras clicking through the humid air. Somewhere behind her, a reporter murmurs into a microphone, his voice low and urgent.

Dr. Martin Luther King Jr. stands among them.

He does not move first.

He waits.

He allows others to go before him—students, ministers, residents—each one offering themselves to arrest with the same quiet steadiness. When the space opens, he steps forward.

No announcement.

No hesitation.

Just a step.

The officer in front of him pauses, only for a fraction of a second. The cameras shift. The air tightens.

Dr. King brings his hands together, wrists aligned.

"I'm ready," he says quietly.

The officer nods and takes his arm.

There is no struggle.

Only movement.

Eliza leans forward, writing faster than her hand can manage, trying to capture not just the words, but the tone—the absence of fear, the deliberate stillness. She is no longer sure she is breathing.

As he is led away, the space he leaves does not collapse.

It fills.

A woman begins to sing—soft at first, then gathering strength:

"We shall overcome…"

Another voice joins.

Then another.

The song rises, lifting above the police line, above the tension, above the watching crowd.

"We shall overcome someday—"

It is thin and human, but it carries.

Eliza lowers her pen.

She watches the arrested being guided toward patrol cars, their posture upright, their movements unhurried—no one fights. No one runs. The resistance is not in force, but in refusal to surrender dignity.

She thinks of St. Augustine's civil rights protests of 1964—how this city, older than the nation itself, has once again become a place where the country is forced to look at itself.

The plaza has seen violence before.

This is something else.

This is exposure.

Above her, the coquina walls do not move. But the light catches them, and for a brief instant, they seem to shimmer.

History is not changed.

It is not even repeated.

It is endured.

And in the plaza, for this hour, no one can pretend not to see.

She moves with the current.

There is no time to process, to catalog, to even think about the passage from the Plaza to the Monson Motor Lodge. One moment, she is in the massed, singing crowd, notebook alive in her hands, the next, she is swept down King Street with a hundred others. Their march is ragged, off-pace from the singing now, more about urgency than choreography.

The heat intensifies as they near the motel, a slab of white and turquoise so aggressively American it seems to mock the bodies outside. The pool glistens in a perfect rectangle, fenced with aluminum, the surface smooth as oil. On the sign: "NO COLOREDS." On the door: a cluster of nervous white faces, peering from behind drapes.

A line of police waits at the curb, arms folded, nightsticks looped in holsters. Their faces are blank, but their stance is clear: We are ready.

Eliza is pressed to the edge of the group, but her field of vision is unbroken. She tracks the lead demonstrators—a tall Black teenager in a yellow collared shirt, a pale woman with dark bobbed hair, an older man in a borrowed suit three sizes too large. They move with the deliberate calm of people who have decided that pain is inevitable, but humiliation is not.

At the edge of the pool, they hesitate, only for a second, and then: shoes off, socks balled and tossed to the deck, feet slapping cold against the tile. The boy jumps in first. The splash is small but seismic. The woman follows, her limbs pale as milk, water closing over her head. Then the rest.

Within seconds, ten bodies bob in the water—arms linked, faces turned skyward, shirts ballooning and skin slick with chlorine. The Black boy shouts something, triumphant, and the crowd on the deck answers with a cheer, less from joy than from the terror of having already gone too far to turn back.

Eliza watches the surface tension shiver. She makes notes. "First Black-white swim-in. Bodies: 10. Response: delayed. Authority: unprepared?"

She is wrong.

The hotel manager storms out, red-faced and shaking. He is a man of about fifty, bald at the crown, with the physique of a high school coach who has not kept up with his own legend. His mouth works, but for a moment, he cannot find words. The crowd is silent; every pair of eyes is fixed on him. He glares at the swimmers, then at the police.

"Get them out!" he shrieks. "They're trespassing! This is private property!"

The officers do not move. They wait, just as the demonstrators wait, for something to escalate.

The manager pivots and disappears inside. The pause is brief, but Eliza feels it physically, a shift in air pressure, an omen. She tightens her grip on the notebook. She could recite, if forced, the lines of the coming event from memory—she has read the accounts, seen the black-and-white photos, even the grainy TV footage. None of it prepares her for the live edge of the moment.

He returns with a gallon jug. Its label reads: Muriatic Acid. He unscrews the cap as he approaches the pool, sloshing the liquid so it splatters over his forearm and onto the concrete. The crowd draws back, one body at a time.

He leans over the edge and tips the jug, sending a thin, clear stream into the water. "I'm cleaning the pool!" he shouts, the words ragged. "You want filth in there; I'll clean it out!"

The swimmers jerk away, thrash toward the shallow end. Two go under. The acid reacts instantly, a plume of chemical white blooming outward like a drowning ghost. The stench of hydrochloric—sharp, medical, burning—overpowers every other smell—the surface bubbles. Screams tear loose: not performative, not disciplined, but raw.

The Black boy tries to lift the woman out, but her arm slips from his hand. Her head goes under. Two men on the deck pull her up, but her face is splotched red, already blistering. Her eyes are open, shocked wide. The older man tries to scramble up the ladder, slips, and smashes his knee on the metal rung. Blood slicks the step and turns pink in the swirling water.

The police act now—quick, efficient, not to save but to contain. They haul the swimmers from the pool, one by one, then move down the line, zip-tying wrists behind backs with practiced ease. The woman coughs, then retches, acid-tainted water running from her nose—the boy staggers, clutching his arm, which is streaked with angry red lines.

Eliza cannot move. She stands at the edge of the chemical kill zone, pen gone slack in her hand. She watches the white faces in the hotel windows—children, mothers, men with cigarettes—some horrified, some leering with open delight. A cheer goes up from the far side of the fence, the wordless howl of men who are relieved to see their world restored.

She wants to move. She wants to speak. She wants to throw herself between the manager and the swimmers, wants to grab the acid bottle and hurl it into the street, wants to slap the cigarette from the cop's mouth as he drags the Black boy away. But her feet are welded to the deck.

She is not a historian now. She is a witness, and that is all.

Brock—the manager—walks the perimeter of the pool, checking for anyone who might be left behind. He grins, wild and victorious. The police let him pass, one even clapping him on the back.

Eliza sees, for a second, the flash of centuries: Brock in his short-sleeve shirt and badge of authority, smiling as he enforces the order of the day; the Timucua warrior watching from the marsh as the Spanish drive another spike into the earth; the British governor issuing orders to burn the town to contain "the fever of rebellion." Every generation invents its own justification for cruelty, and everyone believes itself original.

She is shaking. She has not felt this hollow since Matanzas.

Her hands tremble, but the impulse to record returns. She scribbles: "Muriatic acid. Manager: Brock. Cops: passive. Protesters: burned, arrested, faces gone blank. Public: divided (cheers, tears, indifference). Violence: chemical, not just physical. Pain is the spectacle now."

The swimmers are led away, some limping, some in shock. The crowd on the deck disperses, tension spent. Brock gives a statement to a young reporter, his face already losing the flush, settling back to pale. "We had to do it," he says, "for the safety of our guests. They forced our hand."

Eliza looks at the pool. The water is still bubbling, foam gathering at the sides. Chlorine and acid and blood and sweat, all swirling together, impossible to separate.

She turns away before she is sick.

The sidewalk is slick with spilled soda and tears. She walks, unsteady, until she finds herself in the shadow of the ancient city walls, the coquina stone cool and rough under her palm.

She presses her forehead to the wall, as if it might anchor her to something that does not burn.

She does not write for a long time.

It takes an hour for her hands to stop shaking.

She sits on a bench cut from the same stone as the city walls—coquina, ancient, its color somewhere between bone and sand. The heat has not let up, but the air is quieter here. She stares at her own fingers, watching the tremor reduce from earthquake to breeze.

When she can finally unclench her grip, she opens the notebook. It is damp with sweat and chlorine, and the cover is warped. She blots her palm, then begins to write.

The first line is shaky, slanted. "Pool incident, Monson Motor Lodge. 16:45 local. The manager used muriatic acid to forcibly evacuate the integrated group. Protesters: 4 Black, 2 white, 1 Hispanic, 3 observers. Burns: moderate to severe. Police: response time 4 min; method, physical restraint. Onlookers: 25-30, divided. Cheering audible."

She forces herself to add the detail: "Acid: clear, no odor until water contact. Surface film: white, greasy, opaque. Protesters' eyes: pain, but no retreat. Officer's dialogue: 'You asked for this, you got it.'"

Her pen tip scratches the page, pausing only when she cannot decide whether to record the sounds of the crowd or the smell of the pool first.

She glances to her right.

A young Black woman sits two benches down, hair tied back with a scrap of white fabric, arms mottled with red chemical burns. She is not crying. She leans forward, elbows on knees, breathing in slow, deep pulls like a runner after the finish. Her gaze is fixed on the plaza, where the last few police cars idle, doors open, the arrested being processed or packed away.

"They think this stops us?" the woman says, not looking at Eliza, not needing a response. "This just proves we're winning."

Eliza watches the woman's hands. The skin is peeling in thin, ragged strips, but the knuckles do not shake.

A group of teenagers walks by, one of them limping, the others supporting him. They circle up on the grass, compare wounds, and begin planning the next action. Their voices are low, but the urgency in them is unmistakable: "They'll expect us at Woolworth's. Let's try the city offices instead. No, better to split—some go for the bus terminal, the rest hit the church."

Eliza records it: "Protesters regroup. No withdrawal. Strategy: adapt, diffuse, escalate elsewhere."

She sees it now—the battle is not for the pool, or the hotel, or even the plaza. It is for the right to occupy the city as citizens, to claim a patch of sidewalk as legitimate ground.

A breeze stirs. For a second, the air smells of coming rain.

She returns to her log. "Atmosphere post-incident: electric, not mournful. Sense of victory in endurance."

She flips back a few pages. There is her note about the Plaza: "Frederick Douglass statue here, in the future. 2026: will stand on this spot. Today: battle for the meaning of the same space."

She wonders if Douglass could have imagined this. She wonders if anyone can.

On the far side of the wall, the sun begins to sink. Shadows lengthen. The city's colors deepen from heat-shocked glare to the long, bruised blue of evening. The plaza empties, fills, then empties again.

She feels the exhaustion seep into her bones. There is no pain, only a distant ringing, like the silence after a gunshot.

She flips to the end of her notebook and finds a blank page.

She writes: "Field Log, St. Augustine, June 18, 1964. Freedom remains a fight in every generation. The violence at Matanzas in 1565 and the violence today—separated by centuries but connected by the same human struggle for dignity."

She lets the pen rest in the spiral.

The woman on the other bench stands, stretches, and leaves. She glances at Eliza for the first time, and her eyes are not bitter but alive, hungry for the next thing. Eliza wants to thank her, but it is not the time.

The air is full of echoes now: a car horn, a shout, then, somewhere, the rising sound of "We Shall Overcome," slow and unsteady at first, then building, the voices finding each other in the humid dusk.

Eliza stands and walks to the wall. She runs her hand across the rough surface, fingers catching on the places where centuries have worn the coquina unevenly.

She wonders if the stone remembers every voice that has passed, every name shouted or whispered here.

She thinks: The city will not forget. I will not let it.

As the last light fades, she closes her notebook and lets herself listen, just for a moment, to the sound of hope refusing to dissolve.

Chapter 17: Back to 1565

Eliza POV — Return to Apochi

The marsh receives her as if it had never let her go.

Eliza lands hard, heel slipping from a root and pitching her forward into the rank spongy loam. Her palm strikes a cypress knee, splinters biting flesh, the shock so immediate and ordinary that it steals the meaning from the moment: one second, she is light; the next, she is the sum of all her weight. Gravity is local, unforgiving. She exhales mud and memory in equal measure, rolling off her wrist to clutch her ribs and stifle a shout. If there is a seam in time, it is not an elegant opening; it is a fracture, a join so abrupt it leaves her teeth ringing.

She is not alone. A dragonfly startles from the air above her, iridescent wings thrumming against her cheek before darting up into a column of gnats. The insects do not acknowledge her at all. Life in this place is relentless, attentionless. She draws her legs under her, tries to orient, and finds her shoes already soaking through, the familiar itch of marsh water rising up her ankles.

Everything is the same as it was, but nothing inside her is.

She steadies herself with both hands against the cypress, head bowed, breaths shallow. The Lantern Array's aftershock still vibrates inside her: not a physical sensation, but a sense that her molecules are slower to obey her commands, as if lagging behind the moment by a half beat. She swallows, tasting a memory of blood and brine, and wonders if this is what it means to age a hundred years in a day.

She checks her arms, then her face. The skin is unchanged, if a little paler than before. Her shirt is torn at the elbow, and her left knee is caked with black sediment. The compass pendant at her chest sits askew, still cold from the crossing, the metal biting through fabric to press against her skin. She fumbles it upright, the motion more ritual than repair.

Behind her, the marsh stirs.

She senses him before she sees him. Apochi does not announce himself; he emerges through the screen of reeds as if conjured from the water, step so silent it might be the land itself moving. He is leaner than she remembers, or perhaps her own perspective has thickened with all she's carried back. There is a new set to his shoulders, a wariness that was not suspicion but something more internal, as if he's spent her absence in conversation with his own ghosts.

He looks at her for a long moment. His eyes, always dark, now reflect a brief glint of sky: a blue so intense it looks manufactured, the marsh's one concession to extravagance. He blinks. The expression that crosses his face is one she cannot name—relief tangled with the disbelief of a man who knows the tide will always return, but is still surprised each time it does.

"You are whole," he says, and his voice is not a question but a test of reality.

She attempts a nod and nearly topples forward. The ground is less stable than it was in her last memory, or maybe she has lost her ability to compensate. She braces herself again, this time letting her back rest against the cypress knee, a posture that is equal parts defeat and stubbornness.

He closes the distance, stopping just at the edge of her reach.

"You were gone," he adds. It is the most he has ever said in one breath.

"I..." she starts, then finds she cannot finish the sentence with anything resembling truth. The array of possible lies—mission, accident, fever—cycle through her head. None will pass his scrutiny.

Apochi studies her the way one studies weather. His gaze does not linger on her face, but instead flicks between the minute evidence: the tremor in her left hand, the line of mud across her thigh, the way her boots settle deeper into muck than before. He notices the newness of her wounds and the oldness behind her eyes. He notices everything.

"You are changed," he observes.

Eliza tries to answer, but finds the words have gone slippery.

"Travel does that," she manages, her voice raw.

He does not smile. He considers this as if sorting the claim against a catalog of his own migrations.

"Travel where?" He points not at the city or the sky, but at the patch of marsh where he last saw her. The implication is clear: there is nowhere to go, not for people like them, unless it is away from everything.

She wipes grit from her cheek, then traces a line in the dirt with her finger: a curve, a return, a doubling back. She is not sure if the illustration is for him or for herself.

He crouches at her side, knees flexed, feet steady on the slick ground. He does not reach for her. Instead, he plucks a fragment of moss from a nearby branch and presses it into her palm. The gesture is not caretaking so much as insistence: the world remains tactile, and therefore survivable.

She looks at the moss, then at his hands. His fingers are stained ochre, probably from some ceremonial pigment, or perhaps from the residue of the river. There is a new scar on the side of his thumb, raw and red. She wonders how many days she has missed and what has transpired in the world while she was lost in another world.

He asks her again, quietly, "Where did you go?"

She meets his gaze, and for a split second, she wants to tell him everything: the centuries, the city that will rise, the names that will vanish, the impossibility of loving anyone across time. But all she can manage is the simplest truth.

"I was lost," she says.

This time, he does smile—an infinitesimal softening, almost a grimace, as if loss is the most universal state available to any animal in this marsh.

He rises, extends his hand—not as an invitation, but as leverage. She takes it. His grip is warm and unyielding, and he lifts her to standing as easily as if she were hollow.

She steadies herself, aware now of the subtle differences between this moment and her last in the marsh. The birds are quieter, but the water moves faster. A storm must be coming. Or maybe it is already here.

Apochi releases her hand, steps back, and gestures toward the thicker reeds to their left.

"We should move," he says. "They will come soon."

She does not need to ask who.

She follows, boots squelching with every step, and for the first time since her return, she feels the gravity of this world as something to be embraced rather than escaped.

She glances back only once, to the cypress knee, the moss, and the faint disturbance in the mud where she landed.

In her wake, the marsh closes around the memory of the moment, folding it into the long, patient ledger of what endures.

And together, they disappear into the reeds, carrying with them a silence that is neither peace nor surrender, but the necessary hush before everything else begins again.

The light shifts toward the hour when the marsh becomes less a place and more an event. Late afternoon, and the sun is slantwise through the mangrove, making every surface a contest between gold and shadow. Apochi chooses a path that winds through pools of reflected sky, threading them with practiced certainty, always a pace ahead but never out of reach.

Eliza struggles to keep up. Her body is heavier than it was, though not with fatigue; it is as if the water itself has learned her shape, and now each stride is a negotiation with the silt below. Her boots pull free with a muted pop, sometimes losing a piece of sole to the suction. She is conscious of every step, each one echoing with the knowledge that this is not just her body, but the culmination of all the bodies she has ever inhabited—her own, and those she has borne witness to across time.

Apochi halts at a fallen log, half-submerged in mud, the surface polished smooth by countless seasons of rain and rot. He gestures for her to sit. She hesitates, but her legs do not, and she drops with a gracelessness that makes him smile, just briefly, as he crouches beside her.

He produces a container woven from reeds, filled with water darkened by the river's tannins. He holds it out; she takes it with both hands. Their fingers meet—first by accident, then by intent. The touch is not electric. It is humid, deliberate, charged with the static of everything unsaid.

She drinks. The water is tepid, smoky with the memory of things that have decomposed in it, but it is clean enough, and after the brackishness of her last memory, it tastes like arrival. When she finishes, she holds the vessel between her palms for a moment, as if uncertain where to return it.

Apochi watches her with the patience of someone who knows that all things become clear if left unstirred. She feels the heat of his scrutiny as a physical thing, pressing against the side of her face. She is self-conscious, suddenly aware of the way her hair has fallen loose, the streak of mud on her arm, the ragged line of her torn sleeve. But there is no judgment in his gaze, only a keen attention.

"You have seen the other side of the water," he says.

It is not a question, but she answers anyway, lowering her eyes to the mess of her boots. "I have traveled."

"Traveled," he repeats, as if tasting the word for the first time.

"Not far," she says, which is a lie so obvious she wonders if he will call her on it. He does not.

Instead, he leans in, so close that she can smell the woodsmoke in his hair, the clean sharpness of sweat. "You do not move like one who has rested," he observes. "You move like one who is hunted. Or who is returning from war."

She laughs, a single dry burst. "A war with myself, maybe."

He nods, as if this is the only kind that matters.

There is a sound, then, from the far side of the marsh—a low, rolling boom, too regular to be thunder—Cannon fire. Eliza freezes, and the water in the cup trembles, sending a ring of small ripples outward. She sees Apochi notice this, and wonders if he is measuring the time between her flinch and the sound.

"You fear their thunder," he says, and now it is a question.

She answers honestly. "It follows me. No matter where I go."

He rests his hand over hers, gently pushing the cup down to the log. His palm is rough, the pressure more comforting than restraining. "They are not here, not yet," he says. "Only the sound. The sound cannot hurt you."

She wonders if this is true, but nods anyway, grateful for the assertion. For a moment, she lets herself lean into the space between them, the gravity of his presence anchoring her.

He looks away, toward the horizon, where smoke rises in uneven columns. "They build walls to keep the world out," he says. "But the walls do not last. The stone remembers every hand that tries to shape it."

She finds herself echoing his words. "You build with memory."

He turns back to her, surprised. "Yes."

She clarifies, more for herself than him. "In my time, people built to last. Stone, steel, things that are meant to defeat the years. But your people—"

"We build with what is at hand," he finishes for her. "With reed, with shell, with story. The storm comes, and it falls. But the memory moves forward."

She thinks of the Lantern Array and how even the most sophisticated machinery is just sediment waiting to be repurposed by the future. She thinks of all the monuments she has ever studied, and how their grandeur is always at the expense of someone else's memory.

She wants to say something profound, something that will bridge the chasm of centuries between them. Instead, she says, "I'm sorry I left you."

He considers this for a long time, then shrugs. "You did not go far. The marsh does not lose what belongs to it."

She feels the heat rise in her face and knows he has seen it. He shifts his hand, lacing his fingers through hers, the gesture at once accidental and total. There is nothing performative in it; it is not a claim, but a mutual anchoring.

"You are not from here," he says, low and close. "But you have learned to carry it with you."

She looks up, meeting his gaze directly.

"I have to leave again," she admits, the words out before she can regret them.

He squeezes her hand, but does not let go. "Then do it knowing you are not alone in the crossing."

The second cannon shot is closer now. Birds lift from the reeds, a thousand wings beating in panicked synchrony.

Eliza leans into him, her forehead pressing against the side of his head, the contact both grounding and exposing. She closes her eyes and breathes in the smell of water and woodsmoke, memorizing it.

"Your eyes," he says, so softly it is almost a secret, "they carry more storms now."

She cannot tell if this is praise or a warning.

"You have seen far beyond this moment," he adds. His voice is not mournful, but heavy with the weight of things already decided.

She opens her eyes, and for a moment she sees herself from the outside: a woman out of time, clinging to a future that can never include this. She wants to explain it to him, to warn him that she is only a fragment, that she will always leave, always return, never settle long enough to be anything but the memory of herself.

Instead, she holds tighter to his hand, refusing the impulse to let go.

Above them, the sky is pink with the last light of day. The marsh hums with the awareness that it will soon be night, and with it the predators that do not care for history or memory or the fate of two people sitting on a log, holding hands against the encroaching dark.

She looks at him, and in his face, she sees not resignation, but a kind of pride.

"You are not weak," he says. "You are not lost. You are many things, all at once."

She laughs, genuinely this time. "That's not what my people would say."

He shrugs, and the motion is almost affectionate. "Your

people are not here. Only you. And that is enough."

The log creaks beneath them as she shifts her weight, pressing closer. He does not resist. Their shoulders touch, and for a while neither speaks.

In the stillness, the world contracts to the point where their two pulses merge, beating in time with the distant sound of war, the nearer rush of wind, the insistent call of something alive in the reeds.

She knows she will leave him. She knows he knows it, too.

But for now, in the suspended present, she is not just a witness, not just a traveler.

She is here.

And that, impossibly, is enough.

Dusk turns the marsh into an argument between color and shadow. The air is heavier now; the heat traded for a moist chill that creeps along the skin. In the distance, mosquitoes swarm so thick they sound like static. Even the birds—so raucous at sunset—have grown reverent, their calls brief, elliptical, as if unwilling to interrupt what the evening is about to deliver.

Apochi leads Eliza to the water's edge. The path is neither trail nor accident; it is simply where the land gives up and lets the tide take over. Each step down the embankment is deliberate and measured, as if the sand and shell might withdraw their permission at any moment. Eliza keeps pace. Their feet sink just enough to remember the body's weight.

They walk together in a hush that is not uncomfortable, but dense with all the words they have chosen not to say. In the space behind them, the water fills their footprints, erasing evidence almost as fast as they can make it.

Across the expanse of brackish water, fires are already burning. The Spanish have lit theirs on the shore closest to the bay; the light bounces off polished armor and makes ghosts of the men who tend it. On the far horizon, a more scattered set of embers marks the Timucua camp—smaller, but steadier, the fire light seeping into the low-lying mist.

For a time, they walk parallel to the shore, shoes and bare feet leaving alternating prints. Eliza notices that Apochi's stride is more confident on the uneven terrain; he navigates the soft spots and ridges as if he can hear the memory of every past step.

She looks up, and the sky is a collision of colors she cannot name—lavender, rust, a blue that borders on violence. The sun is already gone, but its afterlife lingers on every surface, painting even the reeds in a kind of longing.

Apochi pauses near a pile of drift, bends down, and picks something from the tangled roots. He holds it up: a shell, wider than his palm, its surface marked with intricate notches and grooves.

He turns it over in his hand, then offers it to her.

She takes it, and the tips of their fingers touch—brief, but enough to send a current through her, a surge she cannot write off to nerves or nostalgia. The shell is cool and surprisingly heavy, its surface textured like braille.

"What is it?" she asks, voice low to avoid echo.

He moves closer, until their arms nearly touch.

"It remembers the tides," he says. "Every mark is a season. Every groove, a flood, or a dry year. My father taught me to read them when I was small."

She runs her thumb along a line so deep it nearly splits the shell. "This one?"

"A storm," he says. "A bad one. It changed the river for two years."

She is silent, tracing each scar, each spiral, until the shell seems less an object than an archive.

"We do not carve names into stone," he says, "but we remember. We make marks on what will not last. When the shell is gone, the story stays."

She wants to tell him that she has held so many names, has carried them across centuries, and that every one of them felt as urgent as this. She wants to tell him that in her time, the only thing more reliable than forgetting is the illusion of permanence.

Instead, she presses the shell to her chest, the edge cool against her clavicle.

"You can keep it," he says. "It is not from this world alone."

She smiles, or tries to, but the motion is unstable. She is suddenly aware of the centuries separating them—not as a concept, but as a living force, a river rushing between their two bodies.

Apochi reaches for her free hand. Their fingers tangle, this time on purpose. She lets the shell fall to her side, unwilling to break the contact.

"You will leave again," he says. The words are not accusations, but acknowledgments.

She nods. "Yes."

He turns her to face him, both hands now wrapped around hers.

"But you are here now."

She blinks against the sudden heat in her eyes.

"I am," she says.

He releases her left hand, and with the other traces a line from her wrist to the shell, then back, as if memorizing the shape of her.

"That is how the world remembers," he says. "Not with walls or stone. With touch. With the way something moves through you, and leaves a mark."

She does not trust herself to speak.

He leans in, forehead resting gently against hers, and they stand that way, two beings out of time, the only thing bridging the gap a shared gravity. The air is thick with the promise of rain, but neither moves.

On the distant horizon, the fires flicker, and the first hints of storm play across the surface of the bay.

She lets herself imagine, just for a moment, a world where this is enough: the tide moving in, the shell cool and real in her hand, the memory of his skin pressed to hers.

When they finally part, it is not with regret, but with the understanding that some things are too large for the ledger of stone or story.

She looks at him one last time, memorizing the pattern of shadow and light on his face.

"Goodbye," she says, and the word is less a departure than a spell.

He lets go, stepping back into the rising darkness, his outline soft but steady.

The shell in her hand grows warm with the memory of his touch.

She watches as the water rises, swallowing their footprints, and wonders whether the next time she returns it will be to a world that remembers, or to one that has already forgotten.

For now, she is content to stand at the edge, held between what endures and what must inevitably go.

The sky closes over, and the first drops of rain hit the bay with the soft certainty of history repeating itself.

She breathes in the scent of wet earth and lets it anchor her here for just a moment longer.

Chapter 18: The Choice Revealed

Eliza POV — 1565

At the river's edge, the world narrows to a strip of pale sand and the endless chatter of children inventing games with sticks and half-cured leather. Eliza kneels on a slanting shelf of earth above the water, the ground cool beneath her, and she draws lines with the tip of one finger. Spirals, then grids, then crosshatches—each pattern an unconscious echo of something from her old life: the margins of a conference program, the hash marks of ancient parish records, the cell walls in Gabe's resonance models. Sunlight has lost its cruelty at this hour and slants through the treetops as a warm, yellowed wash, igniting the glitter of gnats and the brief glint of scale on river fish. On the far bank, palm fronds shiver in the onshore breeze, and a flock of white ibises descends in near-perfect formation, stabbing for snails in the muck.

She has not slept. Her eyes ache with the pressure of holding in tears she will not let fall. The historian in her runs the timeline over and over: the build-up, the flashpoint, the aftermath. There is no logic in reviewing the evidence; she has always known how it ends. But the brain, having learned to obey, replays it anyway.

In the records, Apochi's death is a line and a half, barely inked: "He fell at the river crossing, struck by a ball, witness to none but the enemy and the bay." No mention of his clan, his people, the precision of his hands, or the fact that he could listen to a marsh and predict the weather three days hence. No mention that his loss will rupture the fragile truce and trigger the Timucua withdrawal into deeper territory, fracturing the lines of kinship until even the language itself begins to erode. No mention that after his death, the river here will change its course three times, obliterating the very sandbank on which she now sits. The historian's code requires her to bear witness, not to rewrite. The human in her wants to scream.

She picks up a pebble and skims it into the shallows. The water accepts it with an indifferent slap.

Behind her, the village is awake but subdued. Elders sit in a loose circle, hands busy with nets or mending baskets, their voices a low counterpoint to the shrill pleasure of the children. Even at a distance, she can feel the ambient tension: the arrival of a French trader three days ago, the rumors of Spanish scouts to the south, the slow migration of game out of the lowlands. Every face she sees is a face she's already grieved for, once, twice, a hundred times, names drifting upward like pollen and then—so often—vanishing. She tries to memorize the moment: the dampness of the grass, the snarl of voices in two dialects, the cloying sweetness of fermented palm sap that stains the air.

A new line appears in the sand: a shadow, tall and sharp-edged, falling over her shoulder.

Apochi.

He stands just behind her, so close that the air between them seems charged. She knows this without looking; it is as if her body has mapped his presence into its own electrical grid. He does not say her name. He does not ask if she is well. Instead, he sinks to a crouch, folding long legs beneath himself, and draws his own line next to hers—parallel, then diverging, then looping back.

She is the first to break the silence.

"Is there news?" Her voice is stripped to the skeleton.

He hesitates, then nods once. "The men with iron skins follow the river. Two days, maybe less."

She studies the grains of sand between them, their hands nearly touching.

"I heard the runners," she says quietly. "It will be at the crossing by the burnt cypress."

He tilts his head, observing her as if she were a rare bird, a species about to vanish. "You know the place?"

She does. At this time, the cypress is a fresh scar, blackened by a lightning strike. In her century, it is gone, drowned by the river's slow, methodical rerouting.

"Yes," she says. "I know it."

He is silent for a long time. The children's laughter spikes, then recedes as they chase one of their own into the high grass. The village soundscape resets, and for a moment, it is just the two of them, the river, the ticking of distant insects.

"You are afraid," he says at last.

She forces herself to meet his eyes. They are brown but catch glimmers of amber and gold where the light finds them, the same colors she has seen in the sediment of ancient shells.

"Not for myself."

He touches the sand again, draws a circle around one of her spirals. "You know many things before they happen. But you grieve them all the same."

She wants to tell him everything. That in the world to come, his people will be a footnote; that the ceremonies she's witnessed will survive only as mispronounced words on commemorative plaques; that the riverbank on which they now sit will one day be paved and walled, the water renamed, the memory of this place replaced by a sculpture made of laser-cut steel. She wants to warn him, to arm him, to defy her own code.

Instead, she says, "Your children are beautiful. They know the river better than I ever could."

He accepts the compliment without pride or deflection. "They are of the place. Not only the blood."

A small boy stumbles up the bank toward them, clutching a wriggling mud eel. He stops short at the sight of Eliza, hesitates, then grins and presents the catch to Apochi with both hands. Apochi murmurs something—softer, unrecorded language—and the boy flees, laughing.

It is so ordinary it hurts.

The sun lowers behind the tree line. Shadows reach longer, the river turns from gold to bruised purple, and the first fire for the evening meal crackles to life behind them.

Apochi glances over his shoulder at the village, then back to Eliza. "You will leave after tomorrow?" he asks.

She hears the real question: Will you run from the hurt you already know is coming?

She shakes her head, barely. “I will not go.”

He smiles then—only a flicker. “Storms stay,” he says, “until the sky empties.”

A log cracks in the fire, sending sparks tumbling into the dusk. Her hands have gone numb. She cannot let herself reach for him.

He shifts closer, so their shoulders almost touch.

“If I do not return,” he says quietly, “tell the children it was not for nothing.”

The words gutted her. She cannot breathe.

She wants to grab him by the shoulders, shake him, tell him to hide in the reeds, to take his people and vanish into legend. But she knows, with the same certainty that has always haunted her, that this is not how history works. Events are not changed by passion alone.

“Is that enough?” she asks, voice breaking.

He shrugs, a small, hard motion. “Sometimes.”

She wants to hate him for his fatalism. Instead, she aches for it. To move forward without hope of changing the tide.

A wind shifts upriver. The torches along the shore ripple, shadows spinning across the sand. Children are called back for supper, and the laughter dissolves. In the new quiet, the river seems to inhale, the weight of the future settling on its surface like dew.

Apochi rises to his feet and brushes the sand from his palm. He does not offer her a hand, knowing she would not take it. Instead, he watches her, waiting.

She stands, knees stiff from so much crouching, and wipes her hands on her pants. The dusk is now deep enough that her shadow and his are fused into one.

He leans close and speaks softly, so none but her will hear: "If you must see, then watch well."

Then he is gone, striding up the bank toward the fire and the noise and the last meal he will ever eat if history is not remade.

Eliza remains on the riverbank, alone. She looks down at the lines they have drawn in the sand—one looping, one straight, then both erased by the first sweep of incoming tide.

She kneels and traces a final circle in the wet margin, a memory with nowhere to go but under.

Above her, the sky darkens. In the village, a mother calls for her child. Somewhere downstream, a bird screams, startled from its nest.

Eliza listens to all of it and wonders, for the first time, whether she has the right to let the day end as it is written.

The night is a living thing. Smoke from the cook fires coils between the huts and drifts in low, blanket-like clouds above the sleeping children. The insects have reclaimed their soundscape, and the frogs near the estuary belt out polyrhythms that pulse through the night. In the heart of the village, Apochi sits with the elders in the hush that comes after a meal, eyes half-closed, hands resting on his knees. He speaks very little, and when he does, it is to answer with calm certitude the questions put to him by men decades older.

Eliza lingers at the perimeter. She cannot make herself

approach. The line between observer and participant has never been more treacherous—she can feel the rift inside her, splitting wider with every passing hour. The air is sweet with burning pine, but she tastes only the bitterness of impending loss.

She circles the fire, then circles again. Apochi's gaze follows her, not with accusation but with the patience of someone who has already made peace with being misunderstood.

Finally, she gives in and walks to the edge of the light, where the fire's reach brushes his feet.

"You are restless tonight," he observes, not looking up.

She laughs, but it shatters. "Is it that obvious?"

"You walk as if you are hunting something that hunts you back."

The phrase is so precisely Gabe—so much like an equation turned inside out—that it nearly undoes her.

She stares into the fire. The logs collapse inward, sending up a flare of orange and a fresh plume of sparks. Her words are small, almost childlike: "I don't want you to die."

Apochi doesn't flinch. He is quiet for a long time.

"Do you believe it is already decided?"

She shakes her head. "No. Yes. Maybe. I—I know things, and I don't want them to be true."

He watches her then, really watches, eyes dark and reflective.

"You are not like the other ghosts," he says quietly. "They never bring warning."

She looks up sharply, startled. "You think I am a ghost?"

He considers. “Not in the way the priests speak of them. But you belong to more than one place.”

Her throat tightens. She cannot speak for a moment.

He reaches out, sets his hand on her forearm, palm warm and steady.

“You have brought good things,” he says. “Food, when we were hungry. News when we were blind. Even laughter.” His mouth twitches. “The children make new words to describe you. None of them is bad.”

She tries to smile, but her face betrays her.

“You are not afraid of the Spanish,” she says, almost accusing.

He shrugs. There are many. They are armed. They are strangers to this place. Fear does nothing to change that.”

She shakes her head, fiercely now. “You’re more than a name in a ledger. If you go to the river tomorrow—” Her voice cracks. She cannot finish.

Apochi lets the silence ride for a long breath.

“You are a woman who carries storms,” he says. “But you cannot keep rain from falling.”

Her hands are shaking again. She curls them into fists and tucks them under her legs.

“Why do you accept it?” she asks, voice barely audible.

He does not answer directly. Instead, he glances toward the huts, where children’s laughter has turned to the sleep-muted singing of lullabies. “They remember only the living. They will remember me that way, not as someone who ran from his duty.”

She grits her teeth. “Duty is a story men use to die in larger numbers.”

He tilts his head, the shadow of a smile flickering again. “And yet, you would have me run?”

The question is a trap. She sees it too late.

She blurts, “I would have you hide. I would have you anywhere but the crossing.”

His eyes go sharp at that—focused, searching.

“Why the crossing?”

The lie is right there, but she cannot say it. Instead, she stares into the flames and lets the truth hang between them.

A runner appears from the dark, breathless, clutching at his side. Words tumble out in a rush: “The iron men—they camp at the broken sycamore. They are more than before. And they watch the river, even now.”

The elders confer instantly, voices overlapping in panic and calculation. Apochi stands, his motion so fluid it seems rehearsed. He listens to the runner, asks two sharp questions, then turns to the assembled men.

“We move the families at dawn,” he says. “The able will meet them at the crossing and lead them north.” The orders are simple, unadorned.

A new, urgent choreography ripples through the village. Bundles are packed, children roused from beds and wrapped in dry skins, the oldest men given spears and stones to carry. No one cries, not yet. The sound is in all directions, all motion.

Apochi returns to Eliza, standing close, firelight gilding the planes of his face.

“You will stay with the children,” he says.

She shakes her head, mute.

He reaches for her shoulder, and this time she grabs his wrist, her fingers digging into his pulse. The gesture is desperate and unplanned.

“Please,” she says, “don’t go to the eastern crossing. They’ll be waiting there.”

He freezes.

There is a new distance in his eyes—a suspicion, or maybe a sadness.

“How do you know?” he whispers.

She tries to look away but cannot. “I just do. I always have.”

He looks at her as if seeing her for the first time, truly seeing. The storm in her eyes is not lost on him.

She loosens her grip, but he holds her hand now, gently.

“You believe it,” he says. “So, I believe it too.”

There is no more to say. The commotion of the village has risen, and he is needed elsewhere.

He brushes his thumb once across the inside of her wrist—just as he did the first time, he steadied her, days and years and centuries ago.

“If memory builds anything,” he says, “let it be this: I listened.”

He leaves her in the orange hush, her heart pounding, her hands empty.

All night, Eliza paces the village margins, watched by the old women who sense her unease but do not name it. She listens for the river, the runners, the rise and fall of human plans in the face of a certainty no one wants.

In the small hours, before even the frogs have tired, a single lantern—Apochi's—glows by the riverbank, its flame trembling but upright.

She does not sleep.

Tomorrow is written, but tonight, for one brief moment, she holds the pen.

Dawn comes hard, the sky bleeding from the horizon in a seam of ragged red. The marsh is hushed—birds silent, water unmoving, even the wind thick and damp with anticipation. Eliza moves in the half-light, her breath shallow, her body tuned to the memory of every footprint, every snapped reed, every time she watched this moment play out on a page and now finds herself inside it.

She follows at a distance, letting the Timucua men believe her part of the rear guard, a harmless observer, more of a burden than an aid. Apochi leads from the front, his body low and urgent, two boys at his flank who can barely keep up. He glances back once, catches her eye, and she sees again the look from last night: the knowing, the acceptance, the barest ember of hope that maybe—just maybe—today will not end as it must.

The river is high, swollen from two days of hard rain upriver. Mud slicks every surface. They advance through a clutch of cypress so ancient it feels like a memory of land before time, and the water here is deeper, black as oil, hiding everything it wants to keep.

She positions herself behind one of the oldest trees, bark thick and mottled, a vantage point that gives her a view of both the water and the embankment beyond.

The crossing is a disaster waiting to happen. The fording point is a strip of pale earth, no cover, the ground sloping down toward the river with nothing but grass and two thin trunks for shelter. On the far side: nothing but open, waiting marsh. Every nerve in Eliza's body screams—there, there, that is where it happens, that is where it all goes wrong.

She looks for the Spanish. For a moment, there is nothing—then a flicker of movement: helmets, the brief glint of pike, the flash of a blue-and-gold banner. They have dug themselves in among the palmetto, perfectly camouflaged if not for the arrogance of flags.

The first group of Timucua families wades across, women and children waist-deep, baskets on their heads, children gripping at thighs, chins, anything to stay above water. Apochi is in the thick of it, guiding, calling out softly, not a single shout wasted.

The Spanish wait. They wait until the first family hits the far bank, until the men have almost believed they made it.

Then the guns fire.

Noise ruptures the air—a sound so much larger and hotter than any textbook could convey. The echo swallows everything: bird, wind, even the scream of a child who is hit clean through the arm, blood fountaining onto the water.

Chaos is immediate. Timucua men run for cover that does not exist. Children scatter. Apochi yells for the rest to go back, go back, but now the second volley comes, and he is knocked to his knees by the concussion alone.

Eliza acts before she knows she's moving. She is out from

behind the cypress, the bark leaving a stripe of wet on her sleeve, running low and silent along the shore, the world compressing to the circle of her own pounding pulse.

She sees the Spanish soldier aim, twenty meters away, his musket braced on a makeshift fence of sharpened saplings. She sees the line it draws through Apochi's back, sees how perfectly it aligns with the wound she has read about in so many accounts.

She does not think. She moves.

She launches herself forward, hands scrabbling for the end of a branch, and hurls it at the shooter's line of sight. The soldier is surprised, jerks the gun up, and the shot goes wide—except it doesn't. The ball catches Apochi high on the left shoulder, spinning him off his feet and into the water.

Eliza is there before the splash finishes. She slides down the embankment, mud to her hips, and plunges both arms beneath the surface. Apochi's body floats, just barely, the blood already ribboning into the current. His face is underwater, eyes open but blank.

She drags him up, hands slick and useless, and slaps him once, hard, across the cheek. Water explodes from his mouth. He chokes, then gasps, then makes a wet, animal sound she has never heard before.

She presses him against the root of the cypress, shoving moss and wet cloth against the wound. The blood pours out in pulses.

"Hold still," she hisses, but he is barely conscious.

Above them, the battle collapses. The Spanish have broken cover, charging with bayonets to mop up the stragglers. Timucua men fall back, taking cover wherever they can, but it is hopeless—this is not a fight, it is a message written in flesh and iron.

Eliza scans the perimeter. No one is watching. She rips a strip from her own shirt, ties it tight above the wound. Apochi's skin is fever-hot, the bullet's path close enough to kill but not, not yet, not today.

He opens his eyes and focuses on her face.

"You knew," he says, and it is not a question.

She nods, shaking. "Yes."

He tries to sit up, but can't.

"You changed it."

"Yes."

He laughs, then chokes. The sound is wet, awful, and alive.

"You're not a ghost," he says, slurring the words. "You're a liar."

She wipes his face with her palm. "I'll take it."

The noise of the skirmish recedes. She holds his hand, thumb against the inside of his wrist, feeling the fragile, relentless beat of his heart.

For a long moment, nothing else in the world exists.

Then the sound of boots—the Spanish, closing in.

She yanks Apochi up, half-dragging, half-carrying him into the deeper shadow behind the cypress. They collapse together in the muck, the smell of blood and marsh and gunpowder fused into one impossible memory.

He is shaking now, and she knows he could still die, that infection or loss could claim him anyway. But he is here, and she is here, and for one moment, the tide has failed to erase what it intended.

He looks at her, and there is a new clarity—some blend of fear and wonder and calculation. He grins, weak but genuine.

"They will come again," he says.

"I know," she says.

"You'll warn me?"

"Yes," she says.

He closes his eyes and lets his head fall back against her shoulder.

The Spanish sweep past, searching for survivors. She tucks herself against the tree, shielded by roots and shadow, and waits for them to move on.

When they do, the only sound is the river, sliding steadily toward the future.

She holds him until the tremor in his hands subsides, until the blood stops pulsing out and the red has turned to brown, to rust, to the color of memory.

"You can let go now," he says softly.

But she doesn't.

Not for a long, long time.

Chapter 19: The Decision

Gabe POV — 2026

The old stone beneath the Castillo is restless tonight.

Gabriel Navarro leans over the control array, cheekbones blue-shadowed in the monitor glow, every muscle tuned to the sub-bass hum of the system at idle. Aboveground, St. Augustine is a spill of sodium light and tourist applause, the receding echo of a day spent in self-congratulation. But down here, the coquina walls seem to breathe, or to absorb it all—sound, tension, exhaled failure. The microclimate is always a little too damp, and he can't stop smelling salt.

The Lantern Array cycles through its calibration routine, gold bands on the main display stuttering through a heartbeat's worth of harmonic drift before snapping back into place. Gabe waits for the triple-chime of confirmation, then turns his attention to the bank of secondary screens. There is, for once, no human pulse signature in the matrix—Eliza's readings went silent at 4:17 a.m., replaced by the indifferent flatline of "user at rest."

He'd almost prefer the drama of an emergency, but not like this.

On the top-left screen, his own custom dashboard: a wall of city data feeds, public works overlays, and municipal event calendars. The city, as quantified and predicted by the infrastructure that nobody but people like Gabe and a few department heads ever bother to monitor.

A notification pings: bold orange, bottom right.

He almost ignores it—most city alerts are garbage, or promotional, or the kind of spam that accumulates when committees forget who is actually responsible for digital hygiene. But the color is wrong for the routine.

He clicks.

The permit for the Fourth of July fireworks, the showpiece event of the St. Augustine Semiquincentennial, is flagged "cancelled—unresolved." He stares at the line of text. Refreshes. The permit is just gone.

A muscle jumps in his jaw.

He toggles to the official city interface, scrolling back through the approval queue, searching for the signature he expects (because he remembers it: Eliza, insistent, refusing to let the city lowball on a "milestone moment"). Nothing. Not a trace of her approval, or of the committee, or of any secondary signatory. It's not just cancelled. It's erased.

Gabe's fingers drum a nervous pattern on the desk. He checks the time: 10:03 p.m. He debates texting Eliza, but then he thinks better—if she's asleep, she needs it. If not, he'll know soon enough.

He calls the city clerk's office. The phone rings twelve times before a voice answers, sleep-thick and incredulous.

"City of St. Augustine, after-hours. Who is this?"

"Gabe Navarro. Technical liaison for the Semiquincentennial committee. I need to check on a permit—"

There's a grunt. "Did you try the portal? Our system's been down since six, IT says it's a memory leak. What do you need?"

He skips ahead. "The fireworks display. There's no record of the permit on my end."

Pause. Keystrokes in the dark. A cough.

"Huh," says the clerk. "It's not here either. But it was processed. I saw the application. Signed and everything. I printed it out."

Gabe closes his eyes. "Can you scan the paper copy and send it?"

A longer pause, as if the idea of paper existing off-site is suddenly unthinkable. "I'll do it in the morning, Mr. Navarro."

"We might not have a morning," Gabe says, voice flatter than he intends. "Try now."

The clerk relents, muttering, "Hang on." There's a shuffle, a drawer, the rustle of actual pages. Then: "I have it. But the system says nothing was ever filed. Weird."

"Send me the scan," Gabe says. He hangs up without waiting for a reply.

He watches the mailbox. Five minutes. Ten. It arrives: a blurry, off-kilter scan of a single page, blue-ink signatures stacked at the bottom. And a post-it, visible in the scan, written in round, nervous letters: "Is this a test?"

He forwards the scan to his own secure server. Then he checks the digital event calendar again. Now the event listing itself has vanished. The fireworks, the food truck festival, the speech by the mayor—all gone, as if scrubbed by an algorithm with a grudge against public displays.

He checks the parade permit. Same story: deleted, orphaned, only referenced in a handful of half-cached documents that no longer load. Gabe's breath goes tight. He switches to the vendor applications, the ones Eliza had spent three weekends reviewing for historical accuracy. He recalls her on the couch, hair loose, legs curled under her, muttering about the ethics of "anachronistic snack foods" at a city birthday party.

Vendor approvals are gone, too. In their place are the old entries from the previous year: the ones with hot dog stands and the "America the Beautiful" cover band from Palm Coast.

Gabe leans back, staring at the screens. The control chamber is suddenly too quiet, save for the soft tick of the wall clock and the unchanging white-noise hum of the Array's failsafe power loop.

He flips to the commemoration subdirectory, searching for the digital proofs of the new city plaques. Eliza had insisted on a rewording of the Civil Rights marker by the bayfront, scrubbing the sanitized euphemisms in favor of direct language. The plaque was to be cast, installed, and unveiled tomorrow. Gabe had the original text in his inbox.

He opens the city's press release page. The updated plaque wording is gone, replaced by the prior version, the one that smooths over the violence and leaves names as statistics.

He pulls up the historical database and cross-references the change logs. Nothing.

He cross-checks the British Florida page. He remembers the date—October 2, 1763—because Eliza had spent a week convincing the city archivist that the source was wrong by seventeen days. But the database now reads "October 19."

He feels a sweat bead at his temple, even in the cold.

The Array beeps, a soft but insistent two-tone.

Gabe swivels to the main display. Temporal instability readings spike in the margin—subtle, not yet catastrophic, but accelerating. He recognizes the pattern. Not the violence of a person out of time, but the slow, silent gravity of all records folding inward.

He types in a diagnostic command, then a second, forcing the Array to cross-reference against physical city sensors—coastal magnetics, sediment temperature, even noise levels.

The system returns a string of numbers. The harmonics are skewing toward collapse.

He rubs at his eyes, hard, as if pressure will focus him.

What is missing? Not just a name, or a date. The celebration itself. The gathering, the ritual, the thing that tells the city—and maybe the timeline—that it persists.

He starts talking to himself, low, controlled. "It's an anchor. A physical event to mark the layer."

He recalls Eliza's words—"America did not begin cleanly in revolution. It accumulated. It's layered." He thinks of the crowd last year, pressed shoulder to shoulder against the bay, all eyes up and mouths open. He thinks of the camera drone feeds, the way the city glowed under a pulse of communal awe.

Gabe's hands move faster now, pulling up correlation charts from his own research, overlaying them with the newly corrupted city data. He watches as the pattern emerges: every missing or altered record is tied directly to the event, or to the memory of it. The resonance spikes coincide with the disappearance of public documentation.

He looks up at the ancient stone above him, the way it seems to lean in, eager to see if he'll solve the puzzle or join the sediment.

The alarms escalate: red, insistent, across every monitor.

Gabe stands, pushing back from the desk so fast that his chair wobbles and nearly tips. He paces a quick loop of the small room, counting out loud, as if the motion can keep the ideas from escaping.

"Memory is the anchor. No memory, no event. No event—no anchor."

The next logical step drops into place: "Without a focal point, the harmonics dissolve. The past unspools."

He stops at the console, palms braced on the edge, and stares into the center display. The model is clear. If the fireworks don't go off, the resonance that keeps the city—no, maybe the entire Atlantic coast—stitched together, will shred.

And if it shreds, he will lose her. Not just Eliza, but the her that remembers him. The her that exists because the future has a place to land.

He types in a single override command, fingers steady now.

He speaks to the coquina walls, to the Array, to the accumulated centuries and their appetite for error.

"The celebration is the anchor point," he says. "Without it, there's nothing to hold the timeline together."

He takes a breath, eyes stinging, and braces for the next notification.

It arrives in a minute, maybe less.

A cascade of event cancellations, each more urgent than the last.

Somewhere in the city, the fireworks are being offloaded from a rental truck. The showrunner is probably double-checking the ignition sequence, assuming he's still on payroll. The mayor's speech is, as of now, unwritten.

Gabe has to act before the cancellation is real, before the anchor dissolves completely.

He toggles the comm system, punches the city clerk's number again, and this time doesn't wait for the ring.

"We have to get that permit back in the system," he says, voice cracking with urgency. "Now."

And in the microseconds that follow, before the system answers, before the world agrees or refuses, he dares to hope that the city itself remembers how to be whole.

He is through with intermediaries.

Within seconds of hanging up, Gabe is inside the city's back-end: his emergency clearance bypasses the usual handshakes, the screens blinking protest at each escalation, each flagrant override of municipal IT procedure. His hands move faster than his mind can catch—search, query, compare, export—driven by the urgency of a man who knows the world is narrowing in real time.

The coquina walls press in, not claustrophobic, but hungry for an answer. The air is charged—less with humidity than with the residue of everything the Array has ever recorded, ever failed to hold stable.

He pulls up the city archives: at first, it's just the surface changes. Missing permits, shuffled event logs, and an altered point-of-contact for a vendor who, according to the audit trail, has never even been registered to do business in Florida. But then it gets stranger.

A batch job runs overnight to compare city records with the National Register of Historic Places. The report, generated at 2:13 a.m., shows the Civil Rights plaque at the bayfront as "reinstated"—the older version, the one with the milder language, scrubbed of individual names. The newer, sharper language—the one Eliza had championed—isn't just reverted; it's absent, never existing, as though the memory of that change never made it past conception.

Gabe checks the British Florida files. Yesterday, the database showed "October 19, 1763" as the transfer date. Now, with each new refresh, the date lurches later: "October 24," then "November 2." He flips through the change logs, sees his own user credentials attached to an entry he knows he never made, a phantom of himself writing history in absentia.

His palms slick with sweat, he wipes them on his jeans. The Array's status board pulses again—this time, the harmonic signature is less a blip and more a rolling tremor. He feels it in the soles of his feet, through the stone, like the slow advance of a tide.

He calls up the city's personnel directory. Half the event staff have vanished from the directory, their employment dates retroactively terminated, or shifted to other departments. He checks the mayor's bio; the section about her as the "first Latinx leader of the oldest city in America" is missing, replaced by a tepid two-line blurb about fiscal responsibility.

He checks the archives for Eliza's own name, expecting—

dreading—a similar erasure. Instead, he finds something else: her earliest public presentation, the one from the Boston conference, now lists her as a co-author, not as primary. It's as if the record has been edited to downplay her agency, to reduce her to a footnote in her own life.

He almost laughs, but the sound is more of a snarl.

On the room's central table, a speakerphone begins to vibrate, a delayed echo of his earlier call. He stares at it, at the way the device shudders in place, then ignores it.

Instead, he pivots back to the Array's custom logs, this time pulling up the cross-temporal harmonics. There, in the noise, he can see the pattern: Each edit to the city's history is mirrored by a spike in instability. A small edit—a date, a name—ripples briefly, then self-corrects. But major erasures, the communal events, send out echo waves, destabilizing not just the Array but every linked system in its network.

He runs a calculation, the numbers chunking away on the screen. He tracks the anomaly back to its first significant spike: 1964, St. Augustine's own Civil Rights mass arrest. The record there is clean, untouched, but every subsequent commemoration of the event has been scrubbed, minimized, downplayed. Even the Wikipedia entry has shrunk to a single paragraph. He checks the web cache, finds the old versions, then sees them slip away, page by page, as the new algorithm overwrites them.

He leans closer to the monitor, sweat dripping from his brow. "It's not the history," he says aloud. "It's the act of remembering it."

The next test is brutal but effective. He types in a synthetic event—one that never happened, but might plausibly have occurred in a St. Augustine where the Spanish never established a Catholic parish. "1765: First Protestant service held at Castillo de San Marcos." He submits it to the municipal records via a dummy user.

Instantly, the Array spikes, the harmonic bands lurching into the red. Then, a second later, it self-corrects: the entry is purged from the system, and a warning email is sent to his real inbox about "unsanctioned alteration of historic record."

He exhales, hard. The system is now actively defending its own memory.

He sits back, arms crossed, mind racing. The Array was never just a time machine. It was a validator—a polisher of the past, meant to witness, not to intervene. But with each collective ritual erased, the mechanism is starved of the resonance it needs to hold the present together.

He thinks of Eliza, of the way she'd gone silent. He wonders if, in some perverse echo, her own memory of this place is being rewritten, the anchor points of her return dissolving as the events themselves are erased.

He runs another script, this one collating every major public commemoration in the city over the last hundred years. The parade, the fireworks, the commemorative plaques, the oral history nights at the library. As each is erased or altered, the Array's timeline grows less stable, the window for safe retrieval narrowing to minutes.

He scrolls down, reading the raw event feed, watching in horror as the next major event on the calendar—the very celebration that had brought him and Eliza together in the first place—flickers on and off, its details rewritten with every passing second.

He says it again, softer now. "Collective memory creates temporal stability."

The room vibrates, the walls almost pulsing in agreement. He wonders if the old stone, so porous and patient, is trying to warn him: without the ritual, the walls themselves will collapse.

He checks the clock. There are twelve hours until the fireworks are supposed to go off. But at this rate, he suspects, there will be nothing left to commemorate.

He opens the retrieval protocol for the Array. The system warns him: "Temporal anchor points are in flux. Retrieval subject may be unrecoverable."

He ignores the warning, enters his override credentials, and preps the system to drag Eliza back before the timeline finishes eating itself.

His hands tremble, but not from fear.

He looks at the stone, at the way the light from his screens stains it blue, then gold.

"We're not letting you be a footnote," he mutters, punching in the last commands.

In that moment, the city above pulses, as if in agreement, or defiance.

The Array spins up, a hungry whine building from the depths of the chamber.

Gabe breathes in, and the taste of salt is stronger now than ever.

He's ready. For once, there is no calculation, no hesitation.

He commits to the course.

The Array is not a tool tonight. It is a crucible.

The instant Gabe pushes the retrieval sequence, the control chamber explodes into warning: yellow strobes blind him from every display edge, the consoles bellowing in alternating high and low tones designed to signal "imminent system failure" to anyone with a survival instinct. But Gabe disables his—focuses on the screens, on the numbers that mean life or loss.

The system asks for authentication; he palms the reader, smears sweat and possibly blood onto the glass.

"Biometric match: Navarro, Gabriel. Protocol override confirmed."

He types with the speed of a man who no longer cares about protocol. His fingers trip over the keyboard, retyping commands, doubling them for redundancy. The warnings keep coming: "Anchor Point Drift—Critical." "Temporal Memory Event—Unrecoverable." "Resonance Instability: Cascade Imminent."

He recodes the harmonic target by hand, pulling Eliza's last known signature from backup, cross-referencing with the city's now-vanished event schedule, feeding the Array every microsecond of her presence it can scrape from the archives. He tells it, in the language of machine logic, that she is still here, that the city still remembers, that the celebration is not yet lost.

The Array bucks at the command—a physical pulse of energy ripples up through the floor, nearly knocking him off balance. For the first time, the old walls themselves seem to resist, the stones trembling, dust sifting from the ceiling.

A new error: "Subject Location Unknown. Retrieval Unsafe."

He doesn't care.

He slaps the secondary override, the one he and Eliza built in case they were ever trapped out of phase—intended for emergencies, never for something this desperate. The Array demands a dual signature. He keys in Eliza's biometric, fakes the confirmation with a snippet of her heartbeat pattern, now burned into his own memory.

The chamber's blue LEDs ignite, deepening until the room is awash in the color of a bruise. The column at the heart of the Array shudders, its gold filaments coruscating with impossible speed, twisting around an axis that isn't fully in this world.

Gabe speaks aloud because the room expects a voice.

"I'm not losing you to a timeline collapse," he says, and his own voice is savage, unrecognizable.

The system runs its checks. There is nothing left to check.

The Array begins to count down, slow at first, then picking up tempo, the numbers blurring together on the display.

10

A whine builds in the chamber, almost like a scream.

9

The smell of ozone, salt, and iron—his own blood? —fills his mouth.

8

He sees the error logs filling the leftmost screen: each line a different version of history, each version less like the one he remembers.

7

He holds to the memory of her—Eliza at the podium, eyes lit with defiance; Eliza under the cold lights of this very room, fingers ink-stained and trembling with possibility; Eliza in the afterglow of another failure, her laughter never mean, always rising to meet his.

6

The walls vibrate now in open rebellion, the stones remembering centuries of siege and storm and refusing to collapse just because a few electrons can't agree.

5

The blue light intensifies. Every panel on every monitor is shot through with blue, then white, then something that isn't a color at all but the afterimage of looking at the sun.

4

He braces himself on the control desk. The old coquina cuts into his palms—real, not simulated.

3

He thinks of the celebration, of the anchor, of the fireworks that will never launch if this fails.

2

He thinks of her name, a name that must not vanish.

1

The Array initiates.

In the blinding flash that follows, Gabe is everywhere—across the city, in every moment he has ever held her hand, in every echo of memory she has left behind. The harmonic field collapses, then expands, then collapses again. For a split second, he can feel Eliza: not a projection, not a ghost, but the actual presence of her consciousness, pressed against the membrane of the present, fighting to return.

He shouts her name, not caring who hears it.

"Eliza!"

The system responds.

A roar of blue fire fills the chamber, the energy eating all other sound. The column splits, light fracturing and reforming around a center that isn't entirely empty. A wind tears through the room, flipping pages, rattling loose every unanchored object.

He keeps his eyes open, even as the light shreds his vision.

He sees, in the heart of the Array, a single point of gold. Then a hand, curled as if grasping for purchase.

He reaches for it.

The world judders, the blue fades, and everything goes silent except for the soft, continuous beep of the Array's heartbeat monitor.

There is a shape on the floor of the control chamber, curled and gasping for breath, hair loose and wild, every inch of her shaking with the effort of being. She smells of salt and marsh and something older than either.

He kneels beside her, not touching yet, not trusting the miracle.

Her eyes open. The look she gives him is both centuries away and right here.

She says, in a voice so thin it's barely a word, "Home?"

He nods; the word stuck in his own throat.

She reaches for his wrist, two fingers finding his pulse, and holds it.

He clutches her hand, never letting go.

The blue fades, replaced by the steady gold of the present.

The city above, for the moment, remembers.

And in the quiet that follows, there is no collapse. There is only the possibility of holding on.

Chapter 20: The Confession

Eliza & Apochi POV, intercut with Gabe POV — 1565 / 2026

The inlet is a wound.

Salt carves at the cutbanks, and every few minutes the sun finds a patch of standing water and sears it into light so sharp even the marsh grass recoils. Eliza stands with Apochi at the edge, toes over the liminal zone where mud softens into blood-warm brack. Above her, the sky is white, not blue—burned out by heat and the reflective glare of a thousand unblinking eyes.

Across the sand, the Spanish are making ready.

There is a method to it, a choreography refined by centuries of practiced horror. The prisoners—some two hundred, most in shredded linen, a few still in doublet and hose—are herded forward in batches of ten. Their hands are bound, not in front, but looped behind in a configuration that makes both defense and flight an afterthought. Each group is flanked by two soldiers and trailed by a priest. The effect is less a procession than a disassembly line.

Eliza can't stop seeing the faces. Some of the French have already made the crossing, eyes vacant and skin parched to the color of old paper. Others look everywhere but at the line, as if the world beyond the beach—coquina palisade, smoke from the Spanish cook fires, a lone gull dissecting a fish head—is more likely to grant reprieve than the men with muskets.

Apochi stands at her left, weight balanced perfectly over bare feet, his gaze unwavering.

"Is it always like this?" she asks, though the answer is built into the ground beneath her.

He does not turn. "It is always this," he says, as if the difference matters.

The Spanish commander walks the line. Not Menéndez himself—he is above such manual tasks—but a man with the bearing of small authority and the impatience to match. He stops at intervals, barking a question in French-accented Spanish, but receives mostly silence or exhausted prayers. After each interaction, he signals, and the soldiers close the gap around the next set of bodies.

On the far side of the inlet, gulls have gathered. They punctuate every silence with their ragged calls, a counterpoint to the priests' low, chanting hum.

Eliza's hands are empty, and she feels the absence like a phantom limb. Her notebook is tucked deep into her waistband, but for the first time in her life, the impulse to write is subordinate to the need to survive this moment. She tries to remain the observer, to catalog, to recall every layer of violence with the distance her training requires.

But distance is a fiction here.

As the Spanish readied their muskets, a boy broke from the line. He is not more than sixteen, and he runs with the reckless clarity of someone who knows the penalty is the same either way. He doesn't make it past the second soldier; a blow to the face, the crack of a musket stock against bone, and he collapses into sand already pocked with the spatter of earlier executions.

A priest mutters a last rite. A soldier spits into the dirt.

The Spanish commander lifts his hand.

"Fuego," he calls.

The sound is not the thunderclap of modern gunfire. It's a staccato, uneven, half-muffled by powder not yet dry and barrels not yet modern. Some guns misfire, and the soldiers correct by stepping forward and clubbing the downed men. The ones who fall instantly are lucky. The rest are dispatched with an efficiency that makes Eliza's teeth ache.

The air goes chemical—sulfur, iron, wet stone.

The bodies are dragged to the water's edge, and the tide is already at work, foaming up around ankles, painting delicate fans of red and brown that stretch and dissolve with each pulse.

She finds herself counting. It's a way to organize the moment, to survive the data surge. She catalogs the sequence: shoot, drag, submerge, repeat. The process is more reliable than the weapons themselves.

At her side, Apochi says nothing, but his hand flexes in time with each volley. She wonders if he is counting, too.

Another group is herded forward. This time, one of the

prisoners calls out—not for mercy, not for God, but for the name of a woman. The syllables are so raw, Eliza feels them in her own mouth.

The cycle repeats. There is no crescendo, no escalation. Just an unbroken rhythm of violence rendered down to the muscle memory of men who will later tell themselves it was duty, or history, or fate.

Her historian's training rebels. She wants to scream, to lunge, to write herself onto the scene not as a witness but as a barricade. She wants to believe in the power of observation, but the bodies are piling, and the water doesn't care what she remembers.

She takes a step forward before she can stop herself.

Apochi's hand closes around her wrist. Not gentle, but not cruel either. He applies just enough pressure to keep her in place, thumb pressing lightly over the artery. He doesn't look at her.

"You cannot stop the sea," he says, so quiet the words are nearly lost beneath the wet, briny hiss of the tide.

The Spanish are down to the last batch. The beach is a palimpsest of red and black and white, the shells grinding under boots and bare feet alike. The priests have run out of prayers; the soldiers, out of patience.

Eliza stares at the line, at the way each body is made less by the act of dying than by the certainty that it means nothing. She wants to look away, but Apochi's grip holds her in place, his other hand grounding them both in the now.

A gull lands near the edge of the carnage. Picks at an ear, a strip of skin, a patch of blood-matted hair. Its call is the only thing alive.

The last shot echoes. The commander gives a perfunctory salute, then turns back toward the makeshift fort. Soldiers wipe their hands on grass and sand, reloading, already forgetting.

Eliza breathes in through her nose and out through her teeth, willing herself to catalog. To remember. To become more than just another machine for documenting atrocity.

Apochi lets go of her wrist.

She feels her own pulse—racing, wild, not academic at all.

"Did you know them?" she asks.

He shakes his head. "No more than you do."

"But you watched."

He meets her gaze now. "So did you."

The tide begins to reclaim the inlet. Bodies bob, then sink, then become part of the slow-moving slurry headed out to sea. In a few days, there will be nothing to mark the place but the memory of those who refuse to let it fade.

Eliza stands in the receding hush, every nerve ending raw, her notebook still untouched.

"History will record this as necessary," she says.

Apochi considers this.

"Then you must not let history win," he replies.

The words settle between them, denser than the air, more persistent than salt.

The massacre is done. The record is not.

She turns toward the water, the brine thick in her mouth, and promises herself that she will write until the memory of it all outlasts the bones in the sand.

The violence recedes, but does not vanish.

Eliza moves down the length of the inlet, boots heavy with brine and a skin of black sand that seems impossible to remove. Each step leaves a shallow trough, instantly flooded by the creeping tide. Behind her, the Spanish work parties set to the grisly calculus of aftermath. Some drag the dead to a pit already shored with split palm, shovels cleaving the soil in harsh, off-beat rhythm. Others kneel along the beach, scrubbing muskets clean, hands quick and indifferent.

Smoke drifts in lazy snakes across the water, carrying the tang of burning meat and wood not meant for fire. Over it all, the low sun bleeds orange and copper across the surf, reflecting so brightly that, for a moment, the blood seems to glow. In a hundred years, no one will remember the color—only the legend.

Apochi walks at her side, his posture unchanged by the carnage. He does not avert his eyes, nor does he dwell on the spectacle. He observes with the same absolute calm as when he studies a change in the weather or a shift in the river.

Eliza does not speak at first. She is unsure what language would suffice. Her mouth is dry with salt; her lungs packed with the sediment of the last hour.

Apochi is the One who breaks the silence.

"They will not stay," he says, gesturing toward the Spanish as they labor. "They kill, and build, and kill again. But the river waits for them to tire."

"They'll last," she says, and hates herself for how certain it sounds. "They build walls that last for centuries."

Apochi shrugs. "The river is patient. The tide erases all."

They reach the far edge of the killing ground. Here, the sand is less trampled; the residue of violence is in the water, not the soil. Eliza stops and looks back. The smoke, the scattered feathers, the slumped geometry of men who, moments ago, sang hymns to themselves—none of it looks like history worth remembering. But it will be because she is here to write it down.

Her boots sink a half-inch with each step toward the water. She lets the next wave overtop the leather; lets it sting the wounds where broken shell has cut through the ankle. The sensation is raw, clarifying.

She faces Apochi, who stands a little way off, silent now, the wind moving his hair against his cheek in a way that makes her want to touch it.

"My people will forget yours," she says, and the words leave her mouth before she has time to hate them. "We will erase you. We'll pretend you were never here."

Apochi's face does not change. He listens, as if she is describing a future storm rather than the truth of centuries.

He steps forward, closing the distance between them. He reaches out, not abruptly, but certain, and lets his hand rest at her cheek.

"You have storms in your eyes," he says, thumb tracing a single arc beneath her lower lid. "But you are not the wind. You are not the tide. You are just a woman who can remember."

Eliza blinks, and the tears come unbidden, mixing with salt already on her skin.

"If I don't," she whispers, "if I let it happen—"

"Then you are the same as them," he finishes. The words are not a wound, but a diagnosis.

She shakes her head, but he is already pulling her into a loose, deliberate embrace. His other hand settles at the base of her skull, grounding her. She breathes in, and for the first time since childhood, she allows herself to collapse into another body—not as escape, but as the only place left to bear weight.

The air between them is humid and thick, but it feels cleaner than anything she has breathed since her arrival.

She looks up, into his face, and finds not judgment, but expectation.

"Then remember," he says again, softer now.

Her hands find his shoulders, his collarbone, mapping the surface as if she is afraid of forgetting even this.

The sun drops closer to the horizon. Shadows stretch long and segmented over the sand. In the distance, the Spanish begin to sing, or at least make noise enough to cover their work.

Eliza lets her forehead rest against Apochi's.

"I don't know how to remember without changing things," she admits.

He draws her in, their chests pressed close, and she feels the steady, tidal beat of his heart.

"You do not need to change what is. You only need to hold it until the tide comes for you, too."

She exhales, and the sound is half-laugh, half-choke.

He holds her until the cold drives them back up the beach, where they sit side by side, shoulders just touching, watching the last of the smoke flatten itself over the inlet.

Memory, she thinks, is nothing but the residue of survival.

And in this residue, she will build something that cannot be so easily undone.

In the control chamber, time is counted not in hours but in cycles of light.

The Array glows a pale gold at the center of the ancient vault, illuminating the stone in shifting patterns that echo the tides above. Gabe sits at the console, eyes rimmed in red from hours of surveillance, hands hovering over the interface with the delicacy of a surgeon too tired to trust his own flesh.

The monitors pulse with data: waveforms, bio-signature readouts, harmonic densities mapped in real time against the centuries. Eliza's signature—the one he has come to recognize as intimately as his own fingerprint—flashes steady at the core, its amplitude broader than ever, but less volatile. The patterns, once erratic and near collapse, now hum in a new, unlikely coherence.

Gabe does not understand.

He has run the numbers a dozen times. He has cross-referenced every known artifact of quantum bridge instability, every theoretical failure mode. Emotional feedback, especially at the magnitude now recorded, should have destroyed phase alignment. Instead, the Array is more stable than the prototype models ever predicted.

He leans forward, fingers tapping the screen in an unconscious rhythm that mirrors her biometrics. At first, he thinks it is an artifact—noise in the system, a bug in the neural telemetry. But the signature only strengthens, layering in new complexity. He watches as the Array harmonizes with her pulse, her breath, even the micro-tremors that denote acute emotion.

This is not a collapse.

It is an anchor.

He brings up the last fifteen minutes of telemetry, overlays the field resonance against the emotional spectrum, and watches as the two merge. The data suggests—no, proves—that the more Eliza invests, the more the bridge is reinforced. Her connection, not detachment, is what allows her to stay.

He sits back, stunned.

Human connection is not the liability. It is the architecture.

The realization is so simple he almost laughs, but the noise would not fit the gravity of this chamber. Instead, he lets it settle, sinking into the coquina as surely as every previous failure. He thinks of Boston, of the times he chose silence over solidarity. Of the ways he believed that care was best expressed as distance.

He thinks of her, now—so far, but closer in the mathematics than ever before.

He reaches out and places his hand on the monitor, where her vital signs form a steady, living trace.

"You are not alone," he whispers.

The data, impossibly, intensifies.

He watches it for a long time, letting the hum of the Array fill the space between beats.

They had built the machine to watch history. What they failed to understand was that history was already watching them.

He does not look away.

Chapter 21: The Event

Eliza & Apochi — 1565

The Matanzas marshland offers no refuge, not in the season of pursuit.

Spanish soldiers move in gleaming order through the water, the sun catching on their breastplates and burning into every eye that dares to look back. Their boots displace great vortices in the tannin-black channels, but their discipline is unnerving: each step measured, each man aware of the others, every musket and blade lifted clear of the water. Even here, in what should be the domain of the indigenous, they bring the geometry of empire with them, right angles and lines of sight enforced by years of command and the promise of more.

Apochi is the last to break from the cover of reeds. Ahead of him, the women and children are little more than shadows—backs bent, arms entwined, feet slipping on roots and mud. The marsh will devour the weak, but his people are not weak; they have learned the ways of every trick, current and sudden drop, every hillock of floating grass that passes for ground in this world. Even the youngest know how to move quickly and quietly.

But the Spaniards are faster than history records. Their vanguard pushes with reckless confidence, the edge of steel gleaming through sawgrass. When one falls behind, he is prodded back into line with the flat of an officer's sword. Even now, their language is harsh and unwavering: Adelante, adelante, rápido, por la gloria de Dios.

Eliza keeps to the low side of a hummock, flattened against mud so foul it could pass for old blood. She has never before seen the moment of a massacre from this angle; the history books always showed it as a fixed point, clean and abstracted, but here it smells like brine and sweat and the terror of children breathing too loudly. In her mind, she counts the seconds. She calculates the ground to be lost, the water to be crossed, and the precise number of paces between Apochi and the lead soldier.

In the books, this was the end of him. Apochi: executed by order of the Adelantado, body unburied, legacy a parenthetical in the Spanish parish register. No witness. No monument. Only the negative space left by his name, never again appearing in the records after this day.

But the records do not mention her.

She sees him through the curtain of reeds, his arms guiding two small children—a girl with hair matted to her cheeks, a boy so light he must have been born last summer. Apochi says something to them, a word so soft it never rises above the hiss of the marsh. The children hesitate, then dart forward, joining the others as they slip into the next thicket of willow and cypress.

He turns. He is alone.

The Spanish officer raises his hand. The first rank halts; a pair of men kneel, leveling their weapons. One is an arquebusier with the red band of the King's marksmen, the other a conscript with a musket so long it could skewer a man from two paces away. The officer points directly at Apochi.

Eliza's mind fractures into competing imperatives.

If she stays hidden, history holds. Apochi dies, and the pattern continues. The colony consolidates. Timucua resistance shatters. She, in the future, will read about it in a sanitized, palatable line of type, made palatable for classrooms.

But the Array is thrumming in her bones now. The old rules are no longer safe. The containment window is gone.

She weighs the physics: angle of fire, the wind, the density of summer air, the unpredictable refraction off water. In one timeline, he falls here and is lost. In another—

She moves.

Not a run. Not a lunge. Just enough to snap a cattail stalk, to disturb the membrane of silence that has held since sunrise.

The Spanish notice. One man swivels his musket to her, but the officer does not deviate; his target remains Apochi. The shot is inevitable.

The explosion of powder is absolute—noise, smoke, and fire all at once. The crack of the musket shreds the air, and the concussion is so close it rattles her teeth. Eliza throws herself flat as a plume of grey-black smoke billows over the water.

Apochi staggers.

For an endless second, he does not fall. He reaches for his side; his hand pressed to the slick curve of his ribs. There is no exit wound. He turns toward her—not by choice, but as if the impact has pivoted him on the axis of history.

Then he pitches forward, face-first into the shallow pool, arms spread wide. His body floats for a moment, then rolls to one side. His head is submerged; the rest of him bobs on the surface, blood fanning out in a thin pink cloud.

The Spanish officer lowers his arm, satisfied.

"Está hecho," he says, loud enough for all his men.

A corporal wades forward, pokes at the floating body with the muzzle of his pike. Apochi does not react. The soldier looks back at the officer and shakes his head once. The unit resumes its forward march, now fixated on the remaining fugitives threading their way through the far end of the marsh.

Eliza cannot move. The sound in her ears is not the musket; it is the emptiness that follows.

She watches as Apochi's body is caught by a gentle current, drifting toward a tangle of water hyacinth and sawgrass at the edge of the channel. He is not dead—not yet, her mind insists. He cannot be. The shot was off; she saw it deflect. But the water is opaque, and the blood is spreading too quickly for her to measure its source.

The Spanish recede. The marsh regains its voice: insects rise, frogs resume their tireless chorus, the very air seems to exhale.

Eliza presses her palm against the pain in her chest.

She waits for any sign of movement, any flicker of breath, any reason to believe that a single split-second intervention was enough.

Nothing.

She crawls backward, away from the open water, afraid to be seen, afraid to make it worse by failing again. The Spanish are gone, the women and children unseen, the world contracted to a single point of loss.

She marks the exact location in her memory. She writes the details into her bones.

Above her, the late light turns the marsh to gold, and the surface of the water stills, as if waiting for a new instruction.

For the first time since crossing, she doubts whether any witness can truly change what matters.

The body floats, face down. Time moves forward. And the tide, uncaring, begins to close over everything.

It is not the sound of pursuit that brings Eliza out of her hiding place, but its absence.

The Spanish are gone, their shouts replaced by the animal sounds of a world already moving on. The air above the water is thick with gnats, and the surface shivers with reflected sky. Nothing marks Apochi's resting place but the slow expansion of a bloodstain, pink uncoiling into the brackish swirl.

She hesitates at the edge of the pool. Her calves lock. She cannot remember ever entering water for any reason other than cleansing or research. Now it is a necessity, raw and without theory. The mud sucks at her boots, the skin of her knees stings where salt has found a cut she never noticed.

She steps in anyway.

The water is colder than she expects, the silt rising around her with every panicked step. She reaches Apochi in five strides, though the effort of it nearly doubles her pulse. She kneels beside his body, arms shaking, and turns him over with more force than she intends.

For a moment, he does not move. His face is slack, lips blue at the edges, hair streaming away in dark filaments. Then, a spasm—violent and brief. His back arches, and he coughs. A gout of water erupts from his mouth, flecked with blood and spittle. He gasps once, then again, eyes rolling back before they fix on hers.

"Eliza," he manages. The voice is the raw scrape of sand against wood.

She swallows a cry. Her fingers find his neck, check for a pulse. It is there—erratic, but alive. She rolls him further onto his side, lets him cough and spit until the spasms subside. He retches once more, then lies still, breathing hard through his nose.

The wound is bad, but not the worst she has seen. The bullet tore through muscle and skimmed the rib; it had not entered the cavity. Blood mats his side and soaks into the woven cloth at his waist. The smell is metallic and bright, overriding even the marsh's normal decay.

He tries to sit up, nearly collapsing. She holds him, one arm around his back, the other pressing hard against the bleeding.

"You should stay down," she says, though she doubts he understands the words.

His eyes are clear. He studies her with an intensity she cannot meet.

"You were not there. Then you were." He says it like a riddle, or a curse.

She ignores the implication because there is no language for this.

She tears the hem of her shirt with her teeth and rips a long strip from her underskirt. The fabric is filthy, but it is all she has. She bunches it against the wound, then wraps his chest tight, knotting the makeshift bandage with fingers clumsy from cold.

He groans once, but does not resist.

When she finishes, she looks at her hands: they are slick with blood and shaking. She wipes them on the grass, smearing red across her thigh, and wonders how many futures can be stained this easily.

They stay in the open water for less than a minute, but it feels like the entire afternoon has passed them by. When his breathing slows, she helps him to his feet. Apochi is heavier than she thought—solid as a tree root, but weak now, leaning on her for balance. Together they stumble toward the edge of the pool, into a clutch of reeds thick enough to conceal them from anyone not looking.

They collapse in a tangle, half-hidden by palmetto fronds.

For a long while, neither speaks. The sounds of the marsh fill the space between: water sucking at the roots, birds cackling in the distance, the unhurried chorus of frogs and insects never once considering that history had come this close to ending.

Apochi is the One who finally breaks the silence.

"You changed something," he says.

She turns, startled. His voice is stronger, though still ragged.

He touches the makeshift bandage. "The bullet. It was not true. I should have died."

She blinks hard, unable to answer.

He studies her, eyes dark and unreadable. Then he smiles, just a flicker at the corner of his mouth.

“I have seen death,” he says. “It does not hesitate. Yours does.”

She cannot look at him. She examines the water instead, the play of sun on its surface, the slow reclamation of blood into the greater tide.

He lifts a hand, places it over hers—his fingers sticky, the warmth both reassuring and unspeakably sad.

“If you do not belong to this world,” he says, “then you are a better ghost than most.”

She laughs once, a sound that startles both of them.

A distant gunshot echoes, but it is not aimed at anyone here.

She feels something shift in her mind: a pulse, a ripple, an aftershock. The Array, perhaps, or just the universe adjusting to accommodate a new outcome.

In that moment, Eliza realizes the experiment has worked—not in the sense of proof or publication, but in the knowledge that she has intervened just enough to nudge the world without breaking it.

Apochi will not be recorded in any Spanish ledger after this day. But somewhere, in a line not yet written, his descendants will walk the land.

She looks at him then, and he meets her gaze without question, without fear.

The marsh resumes its ordinary rhythm.

They sit together, blood drying on both of them, the quiet between them less an absence and more a new kind of bond—one not described in any history she has ever read.

Above, the late sun fractures through the reeds, painting the water in veins of gold and rust.

For the first time, Eliza wonders what it means not just to witness history, but to become part of it.

She does not move. She lets the world resume around her, and listens to the small, defiant sound of two bodies, alive, refusing to be erased.

Dusk falls, and the marshland flattens into a world without horizon.

The water mirrors the sky's bruise, and the reeds stand sentinel, each blade a blackening silhouette against the loss of light. The Spanish voices are distant now, fractured by fatigue and the camp's logistics. Their work is done for the day; the killing has been accounted for. Fires flicker on the higher ground, their smoke drifting sideways, slow and indifferent.

Eliza and Apochi remain where the current left them. The alcove among the reeds is damp, but the air is warmer than before. Apochi's breathing has slowed to a steady, if shallow, rhythm. His eyes are open, focused. At intervals, he tests the bandage, checking for new blood, but finds only the crusted remains of the initial shock.

They listen to the world: frogs, an owl, the chirp of insects undiminished by human events.

When the last rays of the sun have been wrung from the sky, Apochi sits up with effort. He wipes his mouth with the back of his hand and looks to the north, gauging direction by the swirl of birds settling in the distance.

"My people will go to the second meeting place," he says quietly, as if the words are for the reeds and not for her.

She nods, though he isn't watching.

"We make a pattern, every time they come," he continues. "The Spanish never see it. They chase the empty path. The real path is always underwater."

Eliza processes this slowly. In his words is the survival of generations, a code written into the landscape rather than any ledger. She marvels at its clarity, at the self-sufficiency that has endured centuries of pursuit.

She shifts her legs, and the motion catches his attention.

"You hurt," he observes.

"I'm fine." Her voice is steadier than she expects.

He considers the answer, then accepts it. "We go," he says, pushing himself upright with a grunt. The effort costs him, but he does not complain. He uses the reeds for leverage, moves in slow increments until he can stand unsupported.

Eliza moves to help, but he gestures for her to go back. "Only if I fall," he says, with a crooked smile.

They start moving, one cautious step at a time, through the knee-deep water. The reeds brush against their arms, sometimes parting for them, sometimes resisting. There is no path, only the way forward and the memory of what lies behind.

They do not speak of the gunshot, or the intervention, or the strange fracture in the day's logic. Apochi sometimes glances at Eliza, eyes bright in the half-light, as if trying to measure her shape against the world he knew before.

She steadies him more than once, slipping under his arm when he wavers. Her body is stiff, and the cold seeps through her boots and up her bones, but she does not let go.

As darkness deepens, stars emerge. The sky is clearer than she expects—without the orange haze of cities, every point of light is sharp and infinite. The path through the marsh is marked not by landmarks, but by the position of constellations and the sound of water.

When they stop to rest, Apochi leans against a deadfall, his breath visible in the cooling air.

He says, "You did not let me die."

She wants to deny it, to cloak it in observation or accident, but the lie will not hold.

"I couldn't," she says.

He studies her, the way one studies an animal caught in a snare—sympathetic, but with distance.

"Why?" he asks.

She thinks of the millions of reasons—of timelines and consequences and the sheer impossibility of letting a life end when it could be saved. She thinks of the children who ran ahead, and the pattern his people have kept, and the way the world tries to erase everything not written in stone.

"Because you remember," she says. "Because you are not meant to be forgotten."

He seems to understand, or at least to accept it.

They walk again. The night is total now; the only way forward is a guess at best. But Apochi's steps grow stronger, his weight lighter against her side.

They reach a place where the marsh opens into a wide channel, and the stars reflect double on the surface. Apochi stops. He kneels, scoops water with both hands, and drinks deeply. Some of the water runs down his chin, tracing a new line through the dried blood. He offers her a cupped palm; she drinks without hesitation.

When they are both finished, he says, "My people will remember this place. Not the Spanish, not the priests. Us."

She nods. Her heart beats strangely—fast, then slow, then a kind of steady calm she has never known before.

They continue along the edge of the channel, the sound of the Spanish camp now nothing more than a memory of violence.

Neither of them speaks again until the reeds thicken and the ground rises under their feet. At the edge of the marsh, Apochi stops. He faces her fully.

"You changed the tide," he says, low and reverent.

She shakes her head. "No one owns the tide."

He smiles, and it is the first real one she has ever seen on him.

They stand together in the darkness, the night alive with every sound except the one they have left behind.

In the morning, the Spanish will wake to find the marsh empty. They will mark a single death in their record and move on.

But in the unrecorded world, Apochi's lineage will return to the water, guided by the patterns only they know.

Eliza stands at the boundary of land and tide, knowing she has preserved something vital, even if the world will never recognize it.

Above them, stars burn in silence, and the marsh closes gently over their passage, sealing it away like a secret that refuses to drown.

Chapter 22: The Sacrifice

Eliza POV — 1565

The aftermath clings to everything. Blood, salt, the musk of death, the kind of violence that doesn't subside when the weapons are quiet. The Spanish soldiers have already vanished back to their encampment, leaving only the blackened stain of gunpowder and a handful of distant, guttering campfires. The sky over the inlet is red, fading to bruise, and the sand is marbled with tidewater and blood. The gulls have come back, arguing over the leavings.

Eliza stands at the edge, close enough for the foam to soak her boots, close enough that she has to fight the urge to step in and let the sea erase her, too. She is whole, but only barely; her knees threaten mutiny every time she shifts her weight. Her notebook is gone, waterlogged pages ripped and scattered by the day's wind, but she doesn't care about that now. All the documentation in the world won't help her breathe.

She exhales and waits for the usual snap of pressure at the base of her skull: the crossing, the quantum field, the Lantern Array's invisible leash. But the familiar vibration isn't there. Not gone, exactly, but lessened—a memory of tension, not the thing itself. She closes her eyes and leans into the sensation, as if testing a wall she'd forgotten could collapse.

She remembers how it felt when she first arrived in 1565—every molecule on edge, every cell clamoring for instruction from another century. The Array's guidance was a constant: keep your anchor, watch for drift, trust the return protocol. It had been background music, annoying but necessary, the way the hum of a city never truly recedes.

Now, it is quiet. Not dead, but waiting.

Her body responds first: a slow release in her shoulders, a shudder she tries to pass off as cold. She forces her fingers to open and close, expecting the tremor that's defined her since the first night, but it's gone. She can feel her heartbeat—a miracle in itself—pumping steadily instead of jackhammering panic through her chest.

The tidal surge inches up the sand, almost greedy. It pulls at the threads of what remains. Broken reeds, scraps of uniform, the long red trail of something once human—Nature's archivist, as relentless as time.

She looks down at her hands and flexes them. No shaking. No threat of fracture.

For the first time since the crossing, Eliza is not a ghost trapped between centuries. The field around her is not an imperative. It is, absurdly, a choice.

She laughs, the sound dry and startling in the hush. The

marsh absorbs it without judgment.

The realization blooms: Gabe is not trying to pull her back. She knows it with absolute certainty, a sense deeper than any protocol. She pictures his hands, off the console, willing her to finish what she started or abandon it on her own terms. The thought makes her dizzy—not from longing, but from the absence of rescue.

She breathes in, counting. One. Two. Three. Air is sharp with ozone and decay, but breathable. Every inhale is easier.

Across the inlet, the Spanish fire has gone to embers. The dead are already slipping from the record, washed by the tide and by the indifference of the survivors.

Her hands curl at her sides. Not out of fear. Out of readiness.

Eliza turns from the water and faces the darkening land. The marsh is quiet now, but full of potential. She knows she should be thinking of protocol, of cause and effect, of the consequences of letting herself unmoor from the future.

But for once, the calculus feels simple.

She is not divided. She is not under surveillance.

She is a body—present, agentic, alive in a moment that never should have admitted her.

She takes a step away from the surf, boots heavy, the sand dragging at her heels as if testing her commitment. The night wind moves through her hair, wild and salt-stiffened, and she lets it. She walks, one foot after another, into the territory that will one day be mapped, paved, walled, and named a hundred times over.

She does not look back at the water. The past will always claim what it needs.

But for the first time, she chooses how to face it.

The chamber beneath the Castillo doesn't know how to be silent. Even when the Array is powered down, even when the thick walls muffle every outside sound, there is always the hum—a layered, living frequency that threads through coquina the way blood moves through a vein. Gabe has grown used to it, as much as one ever can. Tonight, it vibrates at a pitch he doesn't remember programming.

He stands in front of the primary array, arms folded, watching the cascade of gold and indigo light as the system recalibrates. Each band of color sweeps across the ancient stone, illuminating mortar and shell, the sedimented memory of a thousand years.

On the display, Eliza's bio-signature flares and recedes with a pattern he has come to know like his own pulse. But tonight, the pattern is different: a steadying, a flattening of the spikes that usually accompany every significant event. He watches the numbers level, the data aligning as if the world finally decided to let them.

His hand hovers over the retrieval override. The button glows softly, tempting, urgent, everything it was designed to be. It would take less than a second—one press and the containment field would reassert, the present would reclaim its lost historian, and all the variables would collapse into the safety of a single outcome.

He does not press it.

Instead, he flexes his fingers and lets them rest at his side. He can feel the shift in his own body: the burning in his chest as adrenaline finally drains, the ache in his jaw from teeth he didn't know were clenched. He inhales, tasting the recycled air, the sharp ozone of a system working at the edge of possible.

The light in the chamber intensifies for a moment. Gold bands thicken, indigo pulses layering over them in a slow, synchronous wave. The coquina walls respond, reflecting the color into the space, wrapping him in the physics of his own invention.

Gabe leans into the resonance, eyes closed, and lets it move through him.

He remembers the first time he saw her run a model without a net. The recklessness that wasn't really recklessness at all, just a refusal to let fear dictate which futures were worth exploring. He had always admired that about her, even as he tried to keep the edges clean.

Now, he wonders if the edges matter.

On the monitor, Eliza's signature grows brighter—steady, anchored, nothing at all like the wild oscillations of near-dissolution. He studies the curve for a long moment, then steps back from the console.

The chamber is alive with quantum energy, the hum so intense it almost feels like a song.

He whispers to the room, to the past, to the woman standing at the edge of a massacre five centuries away: "It's your choice now."

The monitors spike—briefly, beautifully—then settle into a slow, even rhythm. The field has registered its decision. The machine will not act until she is ready.

Gabe closes his eyes and lets himself feel the relief, the fear, the gratitude. He is not good at letting go. But he is learning.

For the first time since the project began, the Array holds without his intervention. The system sustains itself. The present and the past, in equilibrium.

He opens his eyes. The chamber glows, not with the threat of failure, but with the possibility of something earned.

He leans against the stone wall, lets the vibration ease the tension in his back, and watches as the data streams fold into silence.

He will wait as long as she needs.

She does not hear his approach, but she feels it—a shift in the air, a subtle realignment of presence, the way a tide turns without warning. Apochi is there, just outside the reach of the fire's old light, more silhouette than substance in the growing dark. His feet know every root, every soft hollow, and he moves as if he has always belonged to this land.

Eliza stands at the inlet's rim, the world behind her already less real. Her hands are quiet now, and her breath moves with the rhythm of the marsh, unhurried and unconstrained. She senses the Array before she sees its light; there is a gold shimmer at the edges of things, a glimmer in the surface of the water that echoes the bands of energy now active in some future stone chamber.

He waits until she turns to face him.

They stand for a while, saying nothing. The hush is as complete as anything she has known, more real than the drone of insects or the slow creak of water shifting debris from bank to bank. He regards her, head cocked, eyes reflecting the little bit of sky still left.

"You are changed," he says at last, his words as soft as the river's surface.

She nods, but cannot speak yet. There is a pressure behind her eyes, like a tide building, but not the panic of containment—more like the anticipation of a season's first flood.

He walks closer, steps so deliberate that each one could be a line drawn across a map of the world.

"You must go back to your people," he says. The words carry no accusation, no plea—only certainty.

"I wanted—" she begins, but the thought slips sideways, impossible to trap in words.

He lifts his hand, palm open, and shakes his head. "Not for them," he says. "For you."

The marsh behind him shifts: the movement of a heron, or maybe just the world refusing to stand still.

Eliza tastes salt on her lips.

"I never meant—" she tries again, and fails again.

He steps closer, so close she can feel the radiating heat of his skin, the bright electric field that has always separated her from the world around her, now made tangible and living.

"No one owns the tide," he says. "Not even you."

The pressure inside her resolves—not into relief, or grief, or surrender, but into clarity. She sees how it will happen: the gathering gold at her periphery, the light that is not light but the presence of a physics that does not care about human longing. She knows that in another world, a man is watching a monitor, hands off the override, letting her become whatever story she is willing to finish.

She wants to say something. To make a promise or an apology. But all the words dissolve before they reach her tongue.

Apochi does not move to hold her, but he does not step back either. Instead, he lifts his chin, meeting her gaze fully, and says, "You belong to both shores."

She feels it as a benediction.

He presses his hand—warm, strong, real—against her wrist, grounding her one last time. The gesture is so achingly familiar that she nearly forgets how to breathe.

"You will remember," he says, and it is not a question.

The light at her edges grows more insistent. She can see the quantum field coalescing: flecks of gold, streaks of indigo, the signature of her own molecular disassembly written in color on the dusk. The pressure does not hurt. It pulls, but only as much as she allows.

Apochi leans forward, forehead resting briefly against hers. She closes her eyes, and in that darkness, she holds the heat of his skin, the exact texture of his hair, the smell of river water and fire, and a hundred untranslatable things. She wants to clutch at him, to hold on past what the world allows, but she knows better.

She opens her eyes. The world is doubling, fracturing; the marsh, the water, the dark figure before her all begin to recede into light.

She lets go.

The field intensifies. Her body is dissolving, but her memory does not blur. Every nerve sings with the clarity of the present moment.

"You are remembered," he says, voice fading into the gold.

She smiles, or thinks she does.

In the last instant before she is gone, she sees him standing at the edge of the water, unbowed, the tide lapping his feet.

The transition is not a tearing. It is a folding—space over space, time over time, a brief reunion of all that has been split.

She is gone.

The marsh quiets. The tide claims what is left. Apochi stands alone, watching the place where she vanished, and does not look for her in the sky.

He closes his eyes and listens to the water resume its rhythm, unchanged and yet transformed.

Somewhere beyond centuries, the lantern rises.

Chapter 23: Return

Gabe POV / Eliza POV — 2026, Control chamber

The Lantern Array's afterburn sang itself into extinction.

One moment, the chamber beneath the Castillo de San Marcos vibrated with the live-wire hum of a temporal bridge extended across five hundred years; the next, the noise folded inward, leaving a negative echo in the stone. The overhead lights adjusted for the sudden absence, dimming and then recalibrating, as if unsure whether to illuminate the present or the ghost of the past.

Gabe stood at the control panel with his shoulders hunched and his knuckles splayed white against the steel edge. The touch screen bled ambient gold, its surface crawling with the final metrics of Eliza's phase realignment: heart rate, temperature, neuro-electrical storm. All ascending, all dangerous, then—all at once—resolved.

The numbers crashed down like a fever breaking.

He exhaled once, hard, and let his hands go slack. The rest of his body stayed locked in the hunched posture of a man waiting to receive impact. His eyes found the Array's center, and he counted silently.

The Array was not a thing of beauty in rest. A ring of industrial composite set with twelve finger-thick rods, it resembled a modernist crown dropped onto the tiled floor by someone who had no interest in royalty. But when activated—when calibrated precisely to the right coordinates—the rods crackled with an inward-spiraling light, and the air above the Array liquefied, as if preparing to birth something not entirely belonging to this century.

It began with a point. A distortion, no larger than a spark, then a widening, then a quick convulsion in the electromagnetic field, like the punchline to a joke about God and creation. Gabe saw it before he heard it: a shimmer, blue-white, then the rapid build of silhouette, then the clotted gold halo of coquina stone trying to remember its own formation.

The Array did not produce her whole. It pulled Eliza Rowan into the present the way tidewater hauls debris from the storm: uneven, urgent, and slick with the residue of all previous journeys.

She reappeared at the center of the ring, knees buckling as if the room had stolen her gravity. Her lab coat—white, but already ringed at the cuffs and collar with an unfamiliar brown—hung askew, and her boots left brackish prints on the Array's ceramic lip.

The first thing that struck him was not her expression, but the sound she made: a sharp, involuntary inhalation, as if surfacing after a very long dive.

"Eliza," he said, voice flat but charged.

She did not answer at first. Her arms dangled loosely at her sides, fingers curled as if she were still gripping the hilt of something long vanished. The line of her jaw trembled; her eyes were wild with the white static of sensory overload. A strand of hair—dark auburn in the harsh lab light, but salted through with actual salt—plastered itself against her cheek. Even from a few feet away, Gabe could see the grit of old-world earth under her nails.

She took another breath, this one shallower. The room registered the sound.

Gabe let protocol win out for a moment: he flicked his gaze to the monitor, checked the stabilization, confirmed that her bio-signature was within acceptable range. Then he stepped off the platform, closing the gap in two strides, and caught her by the shoulders just as her knees finished giving way.

She was heavier than he remembered, or maybe just more present.

"Sit," he said, guiding her toward the polymer chair positioned a safe distance from the Array. She stumbled, but his grip held, and he managed to lower her into place without letting her skull rebound off the edge of the table.

The room settled around them, a new gravity.

Eliza pressed her palms into her thighs, as if unsure whether the muscle would obey. She blinked rapidly, then focused on the surface of her own hands. There were welts along the back of her wrist—mosquito bites, angry and raw, the kind that would not be seen in this century outside of the Everglades. She flexed her fingers, then closed both hands into fists.

Gabe crouched in front of her, his knees popping audibly. He placed one hand on her shin, careful not to startle.

"Say something," he murmured. Not a request. A need.

She tilted her face toward him, and the look in her eyes was not relief or confusion. It was rage.

He recognized it instantly. The same look she had worn in the conference hall in Boston, when the room had threatened to erase her with politeness.

She tried to speak, but the first attempt was a dry rasp. She coughed, spat, then managed: "Did it work?"

He nodded once.

"How long—" She stopped, recalibrated, "—how long gone?"

He checked the monitor, but she was already reading the answer in his posture.

"Seventeen minutes, real time," he said. "Three days, subjective?"

She nodded. Her eyes drifted to the ceiling, then to the seam where wall met floor.

"I thought it would feel different," she muttered. "The return."

He waited.

She flexed her jaw, working grit loose from the back teeth. "I thought there'd be... resolution." The words were frayed at the ends, but deliberate.

He watched her. Waited for more.

Instead, she looked down at her hands again. She brought them up to her face, sniffed. A grimace: "I smell like a dead thing."

"You smell like the Atlantic in a heat wave," he said,

meaning it as comfort.

A single, joyless laugh. "That's worse."

He shrugged. "Still you."

The Array behind them powered down completely, a low whine descending into absolute silence. The only illumination was the desk lamp overhead and the glow of the screen, which now looped her biometric data on infinite replay.

Eliza found her breath. The rhythm was not steady, but it was hers. She closed her eyes, then opened them with effort, staring directly at Gabe.

"I didn't touch anything," she said.

He wanted to believe her. But he had seen the metrics: the spike, the phase instability, the sudden flare of emotion that nearly collapsed the window. "You almost did," he said.

She bit the inside of her cheek, then nodded. "Yes."

His hand remained on her shin, grounding her.

"What stopped you?" he asked.

Her mouth worked around the answer for a long moment. "I don't know," she said, finally. "Maybe the same thing that started me."

He nodded, though he did not understand.

She reached up with one hand, and only then did she realize it was shaking. She brushed something from her cheek—a fleck of silt, or maybe dried blood.

The silence stretched.

Gabe stood, slowly. His knees ached from the crouch, but he

ignored it.

"You're bleeding," he observed, voice gentler now.

She stared at the cut on her wrist. "Marsh grass. It bites."

He crossed to the supply drawer, fished out an alcohol wipe, and returned to her. She let him take her hand without resistance. He dabbed at the cut, careful to avoid the worst of the welts.

Eliza watched him work, her gaze growing steadier. "You always do that," she said.

He glanced up. "Do what?"

"Fix things," she said. "Patch them up. Even when they're supposed to scar."

He absorbed that. Returned to cleaning her wrist.

The lights in the Array chamber flickered once—power cycling—then settled to their lowest setting. The coquina walls absorbed the new silence with the patience of sediment. In the faint, underwater glow, the only movement was Gabe's hands, careful and sure, pressing a bandage into place.

Eliza flexed her wrist, testing the tension.

He did not release her hand.

For the first time since her re-entry, she did not pull away.

Instead, she said, "I remember everything."

"I know," he said.

"Not just the facts."

He met her eyes, and the pause contained five hundred years.

"It's still happening," she said. "In here." She tapped her chest.

He nodded. "That's why you came back."

She tried to smile, but the effort failed. "Maybe," she said. "Or maybe I just needed someone to hold me together on the way out."

He did not flinch at the honesty.

For a long time, they sat in the nearly dark, coquina stone holding its breath around them.

On the monitor, her data settled into perfect regularity.

In the physical space, neither one moved. The residue of the past clung to her skin, salt and blood and history.

He let her keep his hand.

When she finally spoke again, it was soft, uncertain: "I was afraid the first time. I wasn't this time."

"What were you afraid of?" he asked.

"That I wouldn't come back," she said. "Or that I would come back and not belong anywhere."

He held that, a weight neither numbers nor science could balance.

"You belong," he said, and this time he did not qualify it.

The Array's memory faded, but the room held the afterimage of crossing.

She drew a slow breath.

He watched her. Waited for the next storm.

But the tide had slackened, and for a moment, neither past nor future demanded to be first.

In the silent chamber, under a dying halo of artificial light, a historian and a physicist sat, wrists bandaged and hands entwined, unanchored from every narrative but the one they were writing now.

The monitor's pale light flattened every color in the chamber to blue and bone. It painted the two of them as artifacts under glass—specimens captured in the instant before comprehension.

Eliza sat forward, elbows on knees, her fingers running a slow path along the mud-stiffened crease of her sleeve. She stared at her own hands, as if expecting them to explain something that language could not. She didn't shake anymore. Instead, her whole body was drawn inward, every muscle complicit in the crime of having returned.

Gabe waited. He always did. For all his engineering, for all his calibrations and thresholds, his most honed instinct was knowing when to let silence do the work.

She kept tracing the line: mud, salt, a thin thread of dried blood under her thumbnail. The past was a sediment that could not be scrubbed out with wipes or with time.

Finally, she looked up. Her eyes were dry, but not unbroken. There was a clarity there that had not existed when she stepped into the Array.

"I loved him, Gabe," she said.

The words were a whisper, but they detonated in the quiet.

He did not flinch.

"I loved Apochi," she said, this time louder, the syllables

fitted with the shape of commitment. "And I almost stayed."

He absorbed it. Waited.

"I know that doesn’t make sense," she went on, voice uneven now. "I know you built this thing to bring me home. I know you trusted me to observe, not to—" Her voice cracked. She shook her head once, sharply. "But I did. I loved him, and I wanted to stay there."

Gabe's hands were folded in his lap, but his shoulders had relaxed. He let the confession settle, its gravity shifting the center of the room. When he spoke, it was not with the detachment of a scientist, but the raw honesty of someone who had stayed awake for seventeen minutes of eternity.

"You’re allowed," he said quietly.

She blinked.

He clarified. "To love him. To want to stay. That doesn’t make you less here."

She made a noise—half laugh, half wounded animal. "You always do that," she said. "Say the thing that doesn’t make sense and then make it feel like it’s the only sense there is."

He smiled, but not the way he smiled in photographs or at faculty meetings. It was a small, half-made gesture, as if he wasn’t sure how to fit it on his face.

"I felt it," he said.

She tilted her head, not understanding.

He nodded toward the inert Array. "Through the resonance. Your signature. I told the oversight committee it was just for phase calibration, but… I saw when you weren’t afraid anymore. I saw when you started fighting to anchor there, not here."

She looked down again, ashamed.

"It didn't scare me," he said. "It… clarified things."

She snorted, but the sound was mostly gratitude.

He shifted his weight, then reached for the nearest tablet. His hand hovered over the glass, then scrolled quickly through a sequence of dashboards—bio-metric logs, timeline overlays, event windows. He opened a secure archive file, then turned the screen to face her.

There, in the stark, cataloged font of institutional memory, was a name. Not hers.

Apochi.

There was a date: 1565. And under it, a small annotation in gold highlight.

Eliza's breath left her in a gasp.

"You—"

He held up a hand. "I only flagged it. You made the mark."

She read the entry again. This was not a footnote. It was a record. A line that would not be erased by time or by the men who built walls to last centuries.

Her eyes shimmered, just for a moment. "You risked it," she said, unable to hide the awe. "You risked the stability, just to make sure he was in the record."

He shrugged, but the gesture was too humble to be real. "Some risks are worth taking."

She exhaled, then leaned forward, her fingertips hovering over the name on the glass. "He told me once that no one owns the tide. That the land and the memory move through you, not the other way around."

Gabe nodded. "He sounds like someone who understands the long game."

She smiled again, truer this time.

"I tried to forget him, before I even left," she confessed. "I tried to hold only the facts, not the feeling. But it's not possible. Not for me."

"You don't have to," Gabe said. "The Array—" He stopped, searching for the right word. "It's not just a machine for observation. It's a witness. It's a memory engine. If we were documenting numbers, we'd be no better than the rooms that tried to erase you in Boston."

She let her palm fall flat on the table, pressing the glass so hard her skin blanched white at the edge.

"He loved me, too," she said. "But he didn't try to keep me. He didn't even ask me to stay."

Gabe's eyes softened. "That's why you're here now."

"Is it?" She looked up, naked in her uncertainty.

He nodded. "You wanted to know if the past could survive being observed. Suppose love could outlast the witnessing. I think you got your answer."

She gave a slow, deliberate nod. The tears had vanished, replaced by something denser. Not joy, exactly. Not closure, either. Continuity, maybe. The sense that her two lives did not have to cannibalize each other.

She reached for Gabe's hand again. This time, he took it without hesitation. His grip was rough, the skin dry and marked by a thousand minor lab accidents. She closed her fingers over his.

"You know this doesn't make me love you less," she said.

"I know," he replied.

The moment stretched. The Array behind them was silent, but the golden text on the screen glowed as if carrying the torch for every name that had been left out of history.

She took another breath, steadier than the last. "You could have erased him," she said.

He squeezed her hand. "I could have. But then you wouldn't have come back as you."

She smiled, a wet glimmer in her eyes. "Maybe," she said.

He shifted forward, close enough now that their knees touched.

"I love you, Eliza Rowan," he said, as if reading it into the official record.

She leaned her forehead against his. The touch was an echo—marsh wind and salt, yes, but also present, anchored in the hum of living memory.

She opened her eyes, let them rest on the line of text one more time.

"We build with memory," she said.

He repeated it, the syllables slow and certain: "We build with memory."

This time, neither of them pulled away.

And in the darkened control chamber, surrounded by the stone that had outlasted empire and ambition alike, they sat together—witness and engineer, chronicler and accomplice—watching as a name that should have drowned five centuries ago floated up, bright and impossible, refusing to be lost to the tide.

Eliza stands.

It takes her a moment to find her balance, but when she does, the tremor in her hands is gone. Her body remembers the marsh, the years of damp and hunger and wary patience; now, it adjusts to this world's gravity, the invisible magnet of Gabe's presence drawing her to him.

He stands as well, slower, the exhaustion of seventeen sleepless minutes stretched across his features. The shadows beneath his eyes are bruised by worry and calculation, and yet the lines at the corners—etched from laughter, or pain, or some negotiation between the two—soften when he meets her gaze.

She crosses to him, closing the space between them with the easy certainty of a woman who has traversed worse distances.

Their hands meet over the still-warm edge of the console. Hers, stained with salt and remnants of old mud; his, ink-smudged and marked by the faint blue glow of the touchscreen. She runs a thumb along the heel of his palm, surprised at the roughness. She wonders—absurdly—what her own hands must look like to him now.

"You risked the timeline for me," she says. There's no accusation, only awe.

He shrugs, the movement small and slow. "Some risks are worth taking." The smile that plays at his mouth is neither bashful nor arrogant; it is the resigned joy of a man who has finally said the thing he meant, even if it costs him everything.

She wants to laugh, but the feeling catches in her chest. Instead, she presses his hand harder, anchoring herself to the present.

The Array is completely dark now, the ring of rods silent and inert. For the first time, the hum is replaced by a clean, unremarkable silence. The coquina walls, older than almost anything else in the city, hold that silence with the patience of sediment. If there are ghosts here, they are quiet tonight.

Eliza leans forward and rests her forehead against his. For a long moment, neither of them moves.

"You saved him," she says, voice so low he feels it on his lips before he hears it.

"You saved both of us," Gabe replies.

She draws back just enough to look at him fully, as if making a new record in her mind. Then she releases his hand, turns, and wipes her own across her thigh, brushing away flakes of salt and dirt. The gesture is matter-of-fact. Practical. But it is also a ritual, a way of letting go of what cannot be carried.

He powers down the console, each click of the interface an exhale, a benediction. Eliza stands beside him, reading the data scrolling past—Apochi's name, his mark, her own metrics, all now layered in the official record.

For a moment, she feels the urge to say something grand: a summation, an epilogue, a closure for what they had done. But nothing comes. She realizes she doesn't want an ending, not anymore. She wants the continuity, the sediment.

Together, they move to the door.

Gabe pauses, hand on the release, and looks back at the empty ring of the Array.

"You know," he says, "the first time we ran the system, I wondered if it would ever really work. Or if it was just another machine built to prove we mattered."

Eliza watches the Array with him. "Maybe it's both," she says.

"Maybe it has to be."

He opens the door. The harsh fluorescent hallway outside is jarring, but it makes her smile. The world above waits for them, oblivious. She imagines, for a moment, the festival crowds already staking out space on the seawall, children chasing each other with glow bracelets, the distant vendors shouting over the din. The fireworks would start soon.

Gabe lets her go ahead.

In the hallway, she walks deliberately slowly, letting her body relearn its old routines. Her hands are already clean by the time they reach the elevator.

They step inside. The doors slide shut, and for a moment, they are alone again, but with the gentle hum of modern electricity.

She looks at Gabe, studies the place where her thumb pressed too hard on his wrist, leaving a faint mark.

"You're not afraid anymore?" she asks.

He considers this, then shakes his head. "I'm terrified," he says, with the ghost of a grin. "But I'm not afraid of the future. Just not living it with you."

She nods, as if she always knew this would be the answer.

The elevator ascends, humming through the layers of sediment, concrete, and history. When the doors open, the night above is alive with anticipation. The city glows. The air, humid and bright with the coming celebration, feels less like a homecoming and more like a debut.

They walk out together. The heat outside is a different kind of pressure, but it is bearable.

From the top of the ramp, Eliza can already see the waterfront, the first bright flowers of fire beginning to reflect on the water. The crowd roars approval. The city, with all its ugly and beautiful memories, is visible at once. She reaches for Gabe's hand, squeezes it. His fingers close around hers, and this time, she knows he will not let go.

Behind them, the Castillo stands, layered in centuries, an old wound made new each day by the tide. Before them, the sky unfolds.

She inhales the future—smoke, salt, the faint tang of possibility—and feels, for the first time, that she belongs to it.

Their hands swing between them, a pendulum of history and hope. The old stories haven't changed. But their telling has.

They move toward the seawall, where the fireworks promise to outshine the stars, and where, tonight, every name—remembered and forgotten—rides the wind across Matanzas Bay.

Some risks, she thinks, are worth everything.

Chapter 24: The Fireworks

Eliza & Gabe POV — July 4, 2026, Matanzas Bay

By noon, the Plaza de la Constitución is already thick with the physics of human celebration: noise ricocheting off historic facades, the pulse of distant bass from rented speakers, heat radiating upward from ancient coquina. There are more flags than people, it seems—every official interval occupied by a red, white, and blue, or the strident gold-and-crimson of the Spanish monarchy, or the blunt, geometric sunrays of the St. Augustine city banner. Vendors have colonized the perimeter, selling boiled peanuts, churros, empanadas, and an unholy number of logoed T-shirts. Children high-step through fountains intended for aesthetics, not for the reckless joy of feet in water. There is no breeze, but flags snap anyway; it's the tension in the air, and the stage at the plaza's north end.

At the center, an aluminum riser disguised as dignity. Local officials mill backstage in crisp linen and campaign-grade smiles. News vans bob in the crosscurrent, their antennas raised like insect feelers above the crowd. The schedule for the city's Semiquincentennial runs on a timeline more rigid than the coastline: opening remarks, musical tribute, "Heritage Honoring," then the evening's main event at the bay.

A minor riot of folding chairs forms a perimeter around the statue of Frederick Douglass. Eliza stands just to its left, where the new bronze plaque is bolted, at hip height, to a granite pedestal that did not exist until last week. The plaque's face is unblemished, the etched letters sharp as if the world might cut itself on what they spell out:

IN REMEMBRANCE OF THE PEOPLE WHO WERE HERE FIRST. TIMUCUA. BUILT WITH MEMORY, ENDURED WITH MEMORY. DEDICATED JULY 4, 2026.

The name "Timucua" is twice the size of the rest. She insisted.

Gabe finds her there, just as the city band starts their prelude, the brassy punctuation of "This Land is Your Land" threading through the crowd. His hand grazes her lower back—a territorial gesture, but so brief and feather-light it might as well be a recalibration of her center of gravity.

"You did it," he murmurs.

She doesn't answer. Her focus is on the stage, on the program in the mayor's hands, on the nervous energy vibrating through the MC's jaw.

A toddler in a sequined U.S.A. tank top stares openly at Eliza's hair, which, for lack of better styling, she has let half-loose in the humidity. The mother tugs the child away, but not before the kid's sticky hands leave prints along the edge of the plaque.

Eliza inhales and smells sunscreen, kettle corn, and, faintly, the suggestion of ozone from the pyrotechnic platforms assembled by the seawall. The city's entire budget for the year seems to have been funneled into this, and for the next six hours, nobody here will remember anything else.

The mayor strides onstage to the applause of at least half the crowd; the rest are tourists, too sun-stunned to differentiate city government from street performance.

"We gather today," the mayor intones, "not just to mark an anniversary, but to honor the accumulation of centuries of persistence, of culture, of sacrifice." The speech is practiced, each phrase weighted for sound bite and re-broadcast. "Four hundred and sixty-one years since our founding, two hundred and fifty years since the first experiment in self-government that would become this great nation."

Eliza notes the phrase "experiment in self-government." She suspects it was cribbed from the PR packet she annotated and returned, with notes in the margin about Jamestown being a bankruptcy scam and Plymouth an accidental theocracy.

Next to her, Gabe's fingers flex in a slow, nervous pattern—thumb across knuckle, repeat. She knows he's not worried about the technical stability of the Lantern Array; that's done, sealed, as safe as anything in physics. He's worried for her. For what it cost.

The opening speaker yields to a rotating sequence of "heritage representatives." First, the Daughters of the American Revolution, led by a woman who pronounces St. Augustine with a long a, as in "August." She delivers a few lines about the indomitable spirit of our founders, then cedes the microphone to a bishop in ceremonial white, who invokes God, Spanish Florida, and the "peaceful conversion of native souls."

Eliza hears, not for the first time, the word "peaceful" recited like an anti-curse.

Next up is the Timucua commemoration. A local university student, neither Timucua by descent nor even Floridian, reads the plaque aloud in halting but careful cadence. The crowd rustles. The phrase "people who were here first" draws a measurable shift in posture—some in the audience nod, a few scowl, most simply look bored, as if time before their own arrival cannot possibly count.

Gabe leans in. "You said you wanted it in the record. That's the record now."

She shakes her head. "It's only the margin."

He says nothing further. The silence between them is charged—an old argument, never concluded, about what survives and what doesn't.

The next speaker is a woman in a T-shirt reading "Civil Rights are Human Rights," who tells the story of 1964 in the city, the attempt to desegregate the beaches, and the mass arrests at the Monson Motor Lodge—the plaza quiets for this. Even the children pause, sensing the seriousness that adults transmit in low voices and held breath. Eliza sees an older man in a wheelchair wipe his eyes. Behind him, a group of high schoolers record the entire event for social media, the phone cameras at chest height, the filter already applied.

The final speaker is a reenactor in Revolutionary drag, complete with tricorn hat and faux-military frock. He reads the original declaration from the city's archives, mangling every Spanish loanword but delivering the English lines with a clipped, North Atlantic vigor. The performance is so at odds with the rest of the program that Eliza almost laughs, but catches herself. She thinks of Apochi, of his voice when he said, "You look at the place as if it has already ended." She wonders, even now, how this city would sound to his ears.

The speeches end. The band plays a medley of "America the Beautiful," "Guantanamera," and, for some reason, "Lean on Me." The crowd, already fracturing, begins its slow migration toward the waterfront, drawn by the promise of fireworks and the Instagram-perfect sunset over Matanzas Bay.

Eliza stays behind. The bronze of the plaque glimmers as the sun tilts lower, the etched letters filling with shadow.

She runs her fingers over the word "Timucua." The surface is cool, almost greasy with the residue of earlier hands, but the grooves are clean, deep enough to endure at least until the next hurricane.

Gabe stands a step away, giving her the moment.

A memory slips in: marsh grass at dusk, a thumb pressed to her pulse, the words "you will remember."

She closes her eyes and breathes.

The plaza empties, leaving only pigeons and the ghost of old speeches echoing in the coquina arcade.

She does not move until she is ready.

Then she follows the crowd, her fingerprint left behind in the record.

Twilight flattens Matanzas Bay into a vast sheet of mercury, the seawall crowded but not yet impassable. The heavy summer air sweats condensation from every stone; the Castillo de San Marcos floats on a tide of tourist flashlight beams and low conversation. The city's 250th celebration has achieved critical density. Every surface is occupied—by feet, by elbows, by the slow grind of anticipation for the night's promised spectacle.

Gabe leads Eliza to the far end of the seawall, where the

tourists thin out and the old fort's shadow reaches longest. They find space on a bench that is more suggestion than reality, its concrete flanks stained with decades of salt, initials, and bird droppings.

The bay smells of brackish water, rotting kelp, and the faintest hint of diesel from the fireworks barges anchored in the channel. Fireworks crews move with disciplined boredom, arranging mortars, checking lines. On shore, the crowd's hum is high, nervous, eager for the scheduled release.

Eliza sits, letting the fatigue of the day leech into stone. Gabe unscrews a bottle of water and offers it without saying a word. Their fingers touch for the length of a pulse.

The fireworks start with the predictable drama of modern pyrotechnics: red, white, and blue volleys, the boom and aftershock rolling across the bay, echoes trapped by the old city walls and sent careening down St. George Street. The first few bursts are met with applause, but soon the rhythm becomes background, punctuation for the real event—which is here, in the space between two people trying to measure the distance between now and everything before it.

Gabe watches the sky, not the show. He looks for patterns in the bursts, in the way each shell splits into many, then drifts down in golden tendrils. His hand rests between them, knuckles white against the bench. Eliza drinks the water and passes it back, her arm brushing his for a moment longer than necessary.

The next barrage is a series of cascading chrysanthemums, the city briefly awash in artificial daylight. In that moment, Eliza turns fully to him, her profile lit in stark relief.

"I loved him," she says. Her voice is low, almost lost in the rumble of the next volley. "Apochi. I truly did."

Gabe's jaw tightens. He blinks once, twice, calibrating his response.

She waits. Her stillness is not coldness, but a willingness to let him catch up.

He tries to smile. "I know," he says, and means it. "He was the past. I get that."

Eliza shakes her head. "It wasn't that he was the past. He was...complete. He belonged to his world without apology. I never knew anyone like that."

The sky splits again, this time in a bloom of silver that rains down over the Castillo. The fort's walls glow, the coquina ignited for one impossible instant before returning to its usual, unyielding opacity.

Gabe looks down at his hands. "And me?" he asks quietly.

She turns to face him fully, studying the planes of his face in the erratic light. "You belong here," she says, and the words are neither consolation nor compromise.

He laughs once, not unkindly. "You mean I'm what's left after the sediment settles."

"No," she says, "I mean, you're the future I chose. That's not the same thing."

They fall into silence, watching the next sequence of rockets erupt. Eliza leans forward, elbows on her knees, and watches the surface of the bay. Each firework is duplicated there, distorted and inverted by the motion of the tide.

She finally speaks. "It doesn't have to be a choice between then and now. You can love more than one place. More than one person. It's not zero-sum."

He nods, slowly. "You think about him. Even here."

"I do," she admits. "But it doesn't change what I want now."

Gabe's hand finds hers, tentative but persistent. She lets him take it. His thumb traces over her knuckles, an unconscious scan for certainty.

Another battery of shells launches, the noise so immediate it feels as if it were inside the chest—the crowd at the far end of the seawall cheers as one.

In the glow, Eliza studies his profile. The old burn scar on his forearm, the slight curve of his glasses, the way he blinks whenever the light is too bright. None of it matches Apochi, or anyone before him. None of it needs to.

"I used to think memory was about keeping things unchanged," she says. "But that's not it. It's about holding on to what matters while letting the rest drift away."

Gabe squeezes her hand once. "You're not going to let me go, are you?"

She smiles, genuine this time. "Not unless you want me to."

He looks at her, really looks, and for once doesn't analyze the moment to death.

Above them, the fireworks reach their crescendo—a volley of gold, then a brief and stunning silence, as if the world itself is suspended in the aftermath. In that pause, Eliza and Gabe remain, hands linked, neither pulling away.

When the noise resumes, it is less overwhelming. The connection, once exposed, settles into something durable.

She leans her head on his shoulder, just for a minute. He shifts to fit her there, as if this is a position practiced over years rather than weeks.

The fireworks continue, but neither of them watches the sky

now. They watch the water, the traces of light that linger there, the way each ripple distorts and carries the color just a little farther.

The show will end, but the memory will not.

It will layer, sediment on sediment, lasting long after the echo fades.

The fireworks end as they always do: too soon, too loud, the sky above Matanzas Bay left bruised and smoky, the crowd at the seawall stretching upward as if their longing could snag one last burst from the empty air. The city, briefly united in awe, exhales as a single organism.

Then, quietly, a new light rises.

It is not a programmed effect. It is not the white-hot dazzle of magnesium or the calculated powder of a digital simulation. It is a simple amber, the glow of flame rather than filament. It hovers above the water, untethered and slow, holding its shape as if conscious of its own singularity.

Gabe sees it first, and his body tenses—not in fear, but in curiosity. "That's not part of the show," he says, his voice low and almost reverent.

Eliza's attention snaps to it. She knows, immediately and in every part of her, what the lantern is and what it means. The color is exactly the shade of marsh reeds at sunset, the shape exactly the one she remembers from another world—handmade, deliberate, impossible.

The lantern floats higher, the light steady and sure. For a moment, it seems to pause directly above the water, aligning itself with the Castillo's oldest bastion. Then, as if guided by memory, it drifts toward the south, toward the inlet where history bled into the sand, and the tides refused to wash it away.

No one else sees it, or if they do, they dismiss it as an afterimage, as an echo of the grander show. The crowd is already dispersing, their attention fractured by the demands of hunger and thirst, and by the glow of a thousand phone screens replaying the just-finished spectacle.

Only Eliza and Gabe remain, fixed on the amber point as it recedes. She feels her fingers tighten around his, not in panic but in confirmation. This is not haunting. This is the opposite. The lantern is not a ghost; it is what endures.

Gabe's eyes never leave the light. "You see it, too?" he whispers.

She nods. "I do."

He leans closer, his voice breaking just enough to betray what this costs him to admit. "Do you think—"

"It's memory," she says. "It's what's left."

He is silent, accepting. They watch together as the lantern shrinks to a pinprick, then vanishes into the night air above the inlet.

Around them, the city recovers its ordinary self. Children whine about going home. Food trucks blare pop music. The Castillo, unperturbed, returns to shadow.

Eliza keeps her gaze on the horizon, even after the light is gone.

For a moment, she feels the impossible: the pressure of a thumb on her wrist, the certainty that nothing is ever truly erased. Not names, not loves, not the brief shimmer of a man who walked between tides and left a trace in the water for anyone willing to remember.

She leans into Gabe, letting the warmth of his body pull her back into the present.

The city celebrates, layer upon layer, unbothered by what it nearly forgot.

The walls of the Castillo will stand another hundred years. The plaques will tarnish, but the names are there, in record and in memory, outlasting even the stone.

Eliza closes her eyes, just once.

She sees the lantern rising.

And for the first time, it does not fade.

Chapter 25: The Final Lantern

Eliza & Gabe POV — later that night

The waterfront empties as if on cue. The crowd unspools down Avenida Menendez—fathers hauling tired children, high schoolers kicking at plastic cups, a pair of old men squabbling over whether the finale was better last year or the year before. Only the residue of the celebration lingers: blue confetti strips clinging to the seawall, sugar grit underfoot, the afterimage of fireworks pulsing in the bay's dark mirror. Overhead, the sky is bruised with the smoke of spent ordnance, which the onshore wind presses down to mingle with the brine.

Eliza stands with both hands on the railing, elbows locked, shoulders rigid as the battlements behind her. The Castillo glows in the city's upward spill of sodium light, stone turned butter-soft by distance and hour. Gabe leans beside her, closer than manners but not quite touching, as if he fears that even a graze could fracture this hard-won silence.

For a while, neither speaks.

They watch a single police launch cruise the perimeter of Matanzas Bay, its siren soundless but blue strobes flaring every thirty seconds. The water reflects each pulse, rendering the city as pure color and line, stripped of depth.

Eliza inhales, lets the salt sear her sinuses. Her hair, still wind-stiff from earlier, tickles the edge of her jaw.

"I keep waiting for it to feel different," she says.

Gabe does not look over. "Tonight?"

"In general." Her right hand lifts unconsciously, thumb rubbing the bridge of her nose in a gesture that once belonged to her father. "You spend your life imagining the moment you'll see proof—actual, hard, unarguable proof. I thought I would feel... triumphant, maybe."

She snorts, a short, dry sound. "Instead, I feel like a kid holding a sparkler when the whole sky is on fire."

Gabe's mouth opens, but the words snag. He nods, barely perceptible.

She keeps her gaze forward. "He was nothing like you," she says. The admission is a sandbag to the gut, but she forces it through. "He didn't need to be right. Or first. He didn't need to leave a mark on anything except the water."

"You loved him?" Gabe's voice is soft—softer than she expects, almost gentle. He does not edge away, though she can feel the tension hitch in his chest.

"Yes." The word is a drop into still water. "But it's not the same as—" Her hand flattens against the stone, palm splaying wide. "It was never a competition. He belonged to his time; in a way, I've never belonged anywhere."

She glances at him, eyes flicking sideways through the fringe of her hair. "You asked what I learned from all this," she says. "That's what I learned. How it looks when a person lives without apology to their own time and place."

Gabe's fingers tap out a stuttering rhythm on the rail. "And me?"

She turns fully now, shoulder brushing his sleeve, the bay at her back. "You're the reason I survived it."

His eyebrows lift, skepticism knitted with longing.

"I mean it," she says. "You're the reason I ever dared to go."

He studies her face, scanning for irony or evasion, but finds neither. The waterfront is so quiet they can hear the clink of flags against the tourist boats moored upriver, the hiss of street sweepers clearing away the night's debris.

She reaches out, lightly, her hand hovering just above his. "I could have stayed. In that time, I mean. I could have let it take me."

"Why didn't you?"

She thinks about the taste of marsh water, the ache of holding memory in unrelenting humidity, the way Apochi's presence sharpened every hour rather than blurring it. She thinks about the moment she watched the Spanish wall rise, stone by stone, and realized that survival is never the same as victory.

"Because I already belonged to someone else's future," she says.

The words hang there, exposed.

Gabe turns his hand over, palm up, inviting. She slips her fingers into his, lets him squeeze once, tight.

"You know," he says, "I almost didn't come down here tonight."

"I know," she says.

"I figured you'd want to be alone. Or with your thoughts. Or with him."

A laugh, this time not bitter. "He's five centuries dead, Gabe. I don't think he'd have made much small talk."

"Stranger things have happened," he says, and she hears the echo of their old banter, pre-Boston, pre-Lantern Array, back when everything was hypothesis.

They stand that way, joint hands braced against stone, facing the ripple of tide and the awkward, hopeful tangle of what remains.

"I'm not threatened," Gabe says finally. "By what you felt for him."

"You should be," she says. "It was... complete. There was nothing left for regret."

He considers this. "Then teach me how."

She's startled. "How to what?"

"How to love you without apology to my own time and place."

Eliza closes her eyes, lets the request soak into the fine cracks of her resolve. "Start by not trying to erase him," she says. "Or your own failures."

Gabe's head dips, the old wound surfacing just above the

collar. “I was a coward in Boston.”

“You were human,” she replies.

“That’s the worst part.” The admission lands heavier than the humid air, but he lets it settle.

She shifts so they are shoulder to shoulder again, both arms now on the rail. The Castillo looms behind them, mute but watchful.

She speaks to the dark water. “Do you know what I envied most? About him?”

“Tell me.”

“He didn’t carry centuries of expectation. Or shame. Or ambition.” She exhales. “He was the only person I’ve ever met who knew how to just... exist. To belong.”

“And you think I can’t learn that?” Gabe asks.

“I think you want to.”

He is quiet for a long time. “I do,” he says.

She lets her fingers trail along the stone, searching for a line of continuity in the centuries-old surface. “That’s enough,” she says.

A small boat drifts by, engine off, two kids dangling their feet over the gunwale, voices muted to a private orbit.

Above, the smoke of fireworks thins to nothing. The air grows clear.

Eliza turns to Gabe, their faces close now, city lights painting each in unfamiliar angles.

She says, “I don’t want to be remembered for what I didn’t do.”

"Neither do I," Gabe replies.

She leans into him—not desperate, but deliberate.

He accepts her weight, and they hold the moment without speaking.

In the distance, the chime of church bells marks the top of the hour. Midnight. A new day, layered invisibly over the old.

They remain at the waterfront, side by side, watching the tide move forward, as if the next beginning is always possible.

Gabe's confession takes shape only after the night has settled, the last echoes of the crowd fully dissolved into background hum. The bay is quieter now, moonlight turning the top of every ripple silver and making silhouettes of the palms that line the walk. A neon sign from a closed bar throws a weak pink arc across the water, just enough to outline two figures at the railing, heads bowed in a private sphere.

For several minutes, he says nothing. His hand remains folded around hers, knuckles whitening in small pulses, the only clue to his interior struggle.

Eliza is the one to break it. "You were right," she says softly. "About the Array. It was always going to hurt."

Gabe lets out a breath that's almost a laugh, but lands more like a sigh. "You always want the pain catalogued," he says. "You never wanted it wasted."

She tilts her head, searching his face. "What are you afraid of wasting now?"

Gabe flinches, but not from her. He looks out over the bay, where a tourist schooner has gone dark, its outlines swallowed by the night. “I could have stood up for you,” he says at last. “That day in Boston. I should have.”

“You didn’t have to.”

“I did,” he insists, louder than before. His free hand comes up, gesturing as if trying to grasp the right words from the air. “You don’t get it. I calculated everything—the risk, the optics, the outcome. I thought if I just kept my head down, it would blow over. That Cartwright would get bored and move on. That your data would speak for itself.”

She tries to interrupt, but he shakes his head. “That’s the thing. I never said it out loud. I thought support was something you could give invisibly, like a force field. But when it mattered, I stayed silent.”

His voice thickens. “And you walked away, and I watched, and every second since I have replayed it.”

Eliza touches his cheek. The gesture is not staged for comfort; it’s practical, as if checking for fever. “Gabe, you don’t need to make a speech—”

“Let me finish,” he says, softer this time. “I want to finish.”

She drops her hand and waits.

He looks at the water again, as if searching for a place to deposit the pain. “I watched you defend the coastline of an idea. And I stayed seated. That’s the truth.”

A silence follows, heavy but uncharged.

Eliza rotates toward him, so their bodies are nearly parallel, shoulders aligned. “Do you think that’s why I love you?”

He blinks. “What?”

She searches his eyes, careful and patient, as if calibrating a new instrument. "Do you think I love you because you're safe? Or because you know how to disappear in a room, and let someone else take the risk?"

He tries to answer, but the words fragment.

"I love you because you are terrified, and you do it anyway," she says. "I love you because when the Array was spiking, and every protocol said to pull the plug, you trusted me to come back. You trusted me to survive it."

He shakes his head. "That's not courage. That's—"

"Devotion," she says, finishing for him. "It's what makes a life possible. Not the one I could have had in another time, or with another man, but the life I can have now. With you."

Her words settle, each one precise, as if she has rehearsed the argument for years.

Gabe's eyes are wet. He doesn't try to hide it. "I thought I had to win you back," he whispers.

"You never lost me," she replies. "You just lost sight of where I was going."

He laughs, a wet, embarrassed sound, and wipes his cheek with the back of his hand.

"I'll always carry him," she says. "Apochi. He's part of what I know now. But you—"

She grips his forearm, anchoring him. "You are the future I choose. Not because you're a default, or what's left over. Because you are the only person who can see the entire arc, and still want to write more."

He is silent, eyes wide.

She steps closer. "I don't want to erase the past," she says. "I want it layered. I want it messy and full of sediment."

He leans his forehead against hers, breathing her in. The touch is intimate, but not possessive—just confirmation, proof of presence.

"You terrify me," he says.

She smiles. "You terrify yourself."

They stay pressed together like that, eyes closed, the wind lifting her hair and wrapping it around his jaw.

"I'm not brave," he says after a while. "Not really."

"No," she agrees. "But you know what's worth being afraid for."

Their hands find each other again, this time not tentative. Fingers interlace, grip unyielding.

She says, "I want to show you something."

He straightens. "What?"

She taps her phone awake, thumbprint rapid-fire, and pulls up the photo she took earlier—of the new plaque, set in the seawall beside the older commemorations. The bronze gleams against the stone, a permanent record: Timucua remembered, Spanish founding, the chain of continuity visible for anyone who looks closely.

She holds it up for him to see.

"It worked," he says.

She nods. "Not because I changed the past. Because I carried it forward."

He exhales, tension leaving his frame in a visible slump.

Their conversation drifts, now, into quieter waters. They talk about the future: whether the Array will run again, whether she wants to publish, and what to do with the data. They talk about travel, food, and the little things that root a person to a particular century.

At one point, Gabe says, "I used to think if I just waited long enough, everything would make sense."

Eliza looks at the water, the city lights, the worn faces of the coquina wall. "That's not how sediment works," she says. "It doesn't clarify. It accumulates."

He pulls her close, arm around her waist, as if to test the principle in real time.

And when they walk away from the railing, together, it is not as two people leaving history behind. It is as if the two have learned to carry it.

Their hands remain joined, steady against the shifting tide.

The bay resumes its ancient breathing.

Eliza and Gabe wander from the seawall, moving in a slow parallel to the water. Above, the city's lights reflect in faint blurs across the surface, disrupted only by the wake of a late-night tour boat.

Then, without warning, a light appears on the water—not a sodium flare or a leftover firework, but a true lantern: golden, persistent, silent. It floats just beyond the reach of the current, untethered to any visible line, a solitary ember refusing to sink.

Gabe stops walking. "Do you see that?"

She nods, heart ratcheting in her chest. "It's not on the program," she says.

“It’s not anything,” he replies. “But it’s still here.”

They watch together as the lantern drifts, immune to the wind, as if it moves by a memory of someone’s hand rather than by the law of tide. The light catches the edges of the new historical plaque embedded in the seawall—Apochi’s name shining with every flicker. The inscription is simple, but it endures: the record of a life, neither erased nor footnoted away.

Eliza presses closer into Gabe’s side, and he responds by folding his arm around her waist, drawing her fully against him. The sensation is grounding, anchoring.

The lantern holds steady for an impossible moment, defiant against the pull of the inlet. Then, gently, it gutters. The gold dome thins, dims, and finally disappears—leaving only a faint afterglow, like a secret kept between water and sky.

Gabe whispers, “You didn’t change history.”

Eliza smiles. “I changed the remembering.”

They stand silent, letting the new layer of memory settle.

When she rests her head on his shoulder, it is not surrender but certainty—a knowing that the world can be more than loss, that love and memory are not zero-sum.

They stay that way, side by side, until the last ripple has smoothed itself out on the water.

Then, as the city’s chimes ring the half-hour, they turn and walk together up the empty street, footprints audible in the soft salt-crust on the stones. The Castillo glows behind them, and in the periphery, the bay resumes its ancient, unbroken tide.

Above, the lantern’s reflection lingers—layered over the dark, refusing, for one more moment, to vanish.

Epilogue: The Layer Beneath

The new channel at Matanzas Inlet opens itself in increments—sand out, memory in. Six months since the fireworks, and the coastline is unrecognizable: a ragged break in the spit where water forced through after the last king tide. Every local has a theory, but none can explain the artifact scatter except the old explanation—the sea, when bored, will always excavate.

On this day, the wind is up, and the first true cold front of the season bites through every seam. The archaeological team marks out grid squares in the sand, their boots stirring up a foam of shell and dead microplastic. The team lead—a woman with a clipped British accent and the posture of a martial artist—presides with a patience that is equal parts scientific method and that of an elementary school teacher.

Field jackets are zipped to the chin; everyone wears gloves, not for cold, but for the precision of touch. A junior member unpacks the mesh sieves and sets them in place above the tidal watermark, as the oldest grad student, for the fifth time, explains the need for careful stratigraphy even when the layers are this scrambled.

It is a day of almosts—almost rain, almost sunlight, almost the kind of breakthrough that funds a grant renewal. The work proceeds in increments: brush, brush, photograph, log, bag, repeat. The current task is to isolate all post-contact artifacts—no mean feat on a shore that is itself a palimpsest of centuries.

Midmorning, they uncover a first fragment: an oyster shell, smooth and pierced at the margin. The grad student picks it up, thumb stroking the incised groove. "Definitely indigenous," she calls, voice muffled by her scarf. The team lead glances over, nods, and motions for a tray. The bead goes into a numbered cell, nothing more than another point on the infinite scatterplot of the past.

By noon, the wind drops. The sun lifts a little, painting every pooled depression with a false heat. The team is three square meters into the new site when the lead's trowel hits something that does not yield—neither shell nor stone, but not plastic, either. She calls for brushes. Four hands work down, slow and deliberate, until a pale curve emerges: a length of wood, not drift, but artifact. Someone produces a ruler, another a soft toothbrush, and the shape resolves into a segment of a tool handle, ancient or just colonial.

"Document as you go," the team lead says. "Photogrammetry, please." The grad student fumbles with the rig, almost drops it, and steadies. The pictures tick away, each a digital ghost. Someone radios to headquarters: new find, possible context, no contamination.

The news spreads up the line, and by midafternoon, two more field techs are on site, shoring up the grid, sealing off the perimeter with flagging tape. A couple of local news drones hover at the boundary, lensing the excavation as a pointillist drama.

Late in the day, a car pulls up at the access road. The driver is a woman in field pants, boots spattered, jacket zipped up to the throat. She wears her hair in a bun so tight it looks like an admonition. A badge is visible beneath the layers: Dr. Eliza Rowan, Historical Consultant.

She walks the last hundred meters to the site, each step measured, as if she is counting out time. She takes in the whole grid before approaching: team leads and grad student over the tray, another tech bagging soil samples, a photographer with knees in the sand, snapping from the lowest possible angle.

The team lead spots her, offers a brisk wave. "Dr. Rowan. You came early."

Eliza nods. "I was in town for the campus interview." She glances at the artifact table. "Heard you had something."

The team lead gestures her in. "You'll want to see this."

They step aside, making a space at the table. Three objects, each labeled and bagged, sit in a line of increasing improbability.

First, the shell bead: iridescent, marked by the tools of a vanished hand.

Second, a twist of woven fiber, so fine it could be modern, but for the tang of estuary and the presence of a single blue jay feather, woven through the core.

Third, and most arresting, the length of wood. It is weathered, splintered at the end, but one side is planed flat, and on that flat a faint inscription is visible, letters still black against the grain.

The grad student holds a magnifier and slides it to Eliza. "It's not ink," she says. "Could be iron gall. Early Spanish."

Eliza bends over it, eyes narrowing. The letters are rough, as if carved with a hurried knife, but unmistakable: three syllables, the third trailing as if the writer was unsure whether to make it a c or an h. The handwriting is an ancient nemesis—her own dissertation was on colonial scripts—but this is legible, as clear as a scream.

Apochi.

The rest of the team falls silent, as if the artifact itself is making an announcement.

The team lead says, "We thought it was a marker, maybe a staff." She points to the break. "The pattern matches Spanish-era markers, the ones they used in surveying new territory."

Eliza does not answer. She rotates the wood, careful not to disturb the fragile letters.

The team lead continues, "We cross-referenced your notes from the parish ledgers. I think this lines up with the marginalia you highlighted—about the Timucua intermediary who survived the 1565 siege."

The grad student, who has followed every conference spat between Eliza and her critics, cannot restrain herself: "If this is what I think it is, it would mean he survived at least to the Spanish census in 1570."

Eliza closes her eyes. For a moment, she does not breathe. When she opens them, she lifts the artifact, cradling it with both hands.

The team lead says softly, "You want the first analysis?"

Eliza shakes her head, the motion precise. "You log it. I'm just here to witness."

But her hands shake as she sets the artifact back in the tray.

She steadies herself, runs one finger lightly along the groove where the letters cut deepest.

She has seen this name before. Once in a ledger, then on the air, then in the impossible present tense of memory. The ink is centuries old, but the name is not a ghost.

She steps back. The wind has shifted again, carrying the faintest tang of tide. She tastes salt, and—absurdly—catches the memory of a mosquito in her mouth, the echo of a hundred biting hours.

The grad student speaks quietly, reverent: "It's not every day we recover a person."

The team lead nods. "Especially not one of the records said was erased."

Eliza looks out at the sea, which is tearing away the shore with the same indifference it has shown for every century.

"I always thought history was a straight line," the team lead says. "But it's more like this coast. It doubles back, eats itself, leaves random pieces for whoever comes next."

Eliza nods. "Sediment," she says.

The word lands, and the grad student grins, recognizing the reference.

They return the artifact to its padded case. The work will go on: analysis, cross-check, digital rendering, a lifetime of papers to be written.

But for now, the site is quiet except for the scrape of brushes and the hush of retreating water.

Eliza stands with her hands deep in her pockets, eyes fixed on the new horizon line. The name still reverberates in her chest, not as an ache but as a pulse.

Behind her, the team bags the day's last sample. The light is nearly gone, and the tide is rising.

She watches until the inlet darkens, until the only thing visible is the faint shine of shell scattered along the wet sand—proof that nothing is ever lost, only layered.

Then she turns and walks back up the beach, leaving a single line of prints for the water to erase or keep.

The sea, when bored, will always excavate.

But tonight, it yields up a name that will not sink.

The campus at night is a matrix of sodium light and humidity so dense it could be mistaken for the afterimage of a summer storm. In her second-floor office, Dr. Rowan sits in a nest of books and unwashed mugs, the only movement the slow orbit of her fingers over the trackpad.

She has the wood fragment on her screen; three angles uploaded from the field site and a fourth rendered by the lab's 3D scanner. Every splinter, every groove, every faint brush of carbon is magnified and framed in a halo of false color. She flips between layers: raw photo, infrared, spectral analysis, then the overlay of her own annotation— "possible post-contact, Timucua intermediary, see: ledger discrepancy 1565."

On the table beside her, a battered field notebook is open to a page she has nearly worn through from rereading. The ink is faded, but the notations—her own, years ago—run in columns along the margin. She compares her scrawl to the artifact on the screen, noting the kinship in angles and spacing. For the first time since the dig, she allows herself a private, silent laugh. She's not looking for proof anymore. She's just savoring the resonance.

Her phone buzzes, screen flickering with a notification: message from Gabe.

She hesitates, then opens it.

The message reads.

She lets the phone drop onto the desk; the impact is lost in the clutter.

The room is cold. She rubs her arms, then moves her hand to the edge of the laptop, hovering over the image. She expands it until the name fills the monitor—Apochi, rough and perfect, each letter a scar on the grain.

For a moment, she presses her palm to the glass. The warmth does not transfer, but the gesture grounds her. In the artifact, the person. In the person, the story. In the story, the refusal to be lost.

The burden she has carried—of needing to rewrite, to defend, to be right—eases. Instead, she feels the lighter, stranger weight of preservation. A name is not immortal, but it is sometimes enough.

She opens her inbox. Three dozen emails from reporters, five from the provost's office, one from an undergraduate whose question is mostly emojis. She responds to none, instead opening a new file.

She titles it: "Persistence: Notes Toward a Sedimented History."

She starts to type, then stops.

Instead, she stands, walks to the window, and cracks it open. The air is sharp, flecked with salt and the far-off sound of a foghorn. Down below, the old stone of the Castillo is barely visible, but she traces its outline by memory.

She imagines the inlet—sand shifting, shell drifting, and beneath it all, the fossil imprint of a man's hand holding a marker, making a name for someone who had no guarantee of surviving the page.

She does not cry. She breathes, slow and deep, letting the air clear her lungs.

The phone buzzes again.

This time, the message is shorter:

She smiles, the expression unfamiliar on her face, but not unwelcome.

She closes the window, returns to the desk, and reopens the digital image.

This time, she does not analyze or cross-reference.

She looks.

The artifact sits quietly in its tray, history layered over present, name preserved, not as a monument, but as a memory chosen.

Later, when she powers down and steps into the night, the air is colder, but the path to the shore is clear. She walks it, boots crunching on the loose shell of the university's walkway, then across the lot, and onto the beach.

The tide is out. Wet sand gleams in the light from the Castillo, the water smooth as hammered silver.

She takes off her boots, steps into the cold, and lets the Atlantic wash over her feet.

She watches as the water advances, then recedes, leaving a perfect negative of her toes in the sand. For a moment, she thinks of how easily the next wave will erase it.

But the sand is not empty; it is layered with the record of every footstep, every storm, every accidental survival. Nothing is ever truly lost, not while someone still remembers it.

She stays until the tide returns, fills her footprints, and moves on.

At the shoreline, the wind is up. She closes her eyes, lets the salt sting her skin, and listens to the water, carrying forward names that will not drown.

Tomorrow, the work will begin again—more artifacts, more stories, more questions.

But tonight, Dr. Rowan is satisfied.

She walks home barefoot, leaving a trail for anyone who cares to notice.

Above the bay, the Castillo stands unchanged. In the archives, a new entry waits. In the memory of the shore, nothing is erased. Everything persists.

Even the name, battered and fragmentary, endures.

Apochi.

She does not look back. She does not have to.

The sea, when bored, excavates.

Memory, when chosen, survives.

ABOUT THE AUTHOR

Terri Propst is a storyteller inspired by Florida's wild places, coastal waters, and the history hidden within them. Her books blend imagination, adventure, and a love for the natural world. With a background connected to parks and outdoor recreation, she enjoys creating stories that encourage readers to appreciate nature, explore new ideas, and see the world with curiosity.

When she's not writing, Terri can often be found near the water, exploring nature trails, photographing wildlife, or at home with her five cats—who believe they are the real authors behind the scenes.

www.ingramcontent.com/pod-product-compliance
Lightning Source LLC
LaVergne TN
LVHW100512110826
845146LV00002B/608

* 9 7 9 8 9 9 3 6 5 7 2 3 3 *